MW00647596

# PYRAMIDS
## OF
# GLASS

# PYRAMIDS
## OF
## GLASS

Short Fiction from Modern Mexico

*Edited by*
David Bowen and Juan A. Ascencio

*With an Introduction by* Ilan Stavans

Corona Publishing Company
San Antonio
1994

The translation of "Jesus, May my Joy be Everlasting" was originally published in *TriQuarterly 85*, and is reprinted here with permission.

"The Mandarin" from *Burnt Water* by Carlos Fuentes, translated by Margaret Sayers Peden, is reprinted by permission of Farrar, Straus & Giroux, Inc. Copyright ©1979, 1980 by Farrar, Straus & Giroux, Inc.

The translation of "The Trip" was originally published in *The Faber Book of Contemporary Latin American Short Stories* (1989) and is reprinted here with permission. Copyright ©1989 by Nick Caistor.

The translation of "Doctor's Prescription" appeared originally in *Tamaqua* (Spring 1993) in a slightly different version, titled "Social Security."

The translation of "Permission Granted" appeared in *The Texas Observer* (Jan. 14, 1994).

Cover design by Lightbourne Images.
Type by Extra Mile Type of Richardson, Texas.

Library of Congress Catalog Number 94-71404

ISBN 0-931722-83-7 (pbk)
ISBN 0-931722-99-3 (cloth)

# ACKNOWLEDGMENTS

The publisher wishes first of all to thank the writers who so promptly and generously granted permission for translation and use of their stories in this volume. Pedro López Cortezo of Mexico City and Amalia Mondríguez of San Antonio gave valuable assistance early in the process of selecting potential authors and stories. Thanks also are due to Wilbur L. Matthews for his generous contribution in support of the translation process, and to Dr. Miguel Bedolla González for advice on some fine points of Spanish usage in northern Mexico.

# A NOTE ON STYLE

When the early drafts of these translations began to arrive, our copy editor for many years, Alice Evett, emitted a burst of colorful Post-it notes questioning the unruly usage of punctuation, capitalization, paragraphing, and related matters. The revered *Chicago Manual of Style* was being flouted on every page. How to deal with this?

A stimulating correspondence with our translators led to a broadening of our view: In Spanish, at least, these matters can be part of a writer's personal style. Each of the writers in this anthology has a distinctive voice; right translation is difficult enough without denying ourselves the help of such subtle idiosyncrasies. We decided to strive for a reasonable consistency within each story, but not to impose our stylebook indiscriminately on all 27 authors. The result, we think, is refreshing.

Then we went a step further . . . Readers of Spanish are alerted to an impending question or exclamation by an inverted punctuation mark preceding the relevant phrase. ¿Could it be that we were missing out on a useful device? After some debate, we decided to experiment with this usage *in the English translations*. This produced a less unanimous response among translators and staff. ¡Brilliant innovation! some exclaimed. Too distracting, said others. In the end, we utilized this device in three of the stories (which we leave you to find). Free trade needs to flow in both directions.

*D. B.*

# CONTENTS

# INTRODUCTION
## Ilan Stavans

⌐⌐⌐ At the center of the Mexican flag is an eagle abiding
on a cactus, devouring a serpent, an emblem recalling the nation's Aztec ancestry. In foreign eyes, Mexico is, has always been,
that scowling eagle: a large, solitary bird inhabiting an exotic
stage where passion, magic, and instinctual violence intertwine;
a predatory bird with a beak nearly as long as its head, eating
a poisonous reptile. Open any tourist guide. In the popular *Mexico: Places and Pleasure*, for instance, Kate Simon writes, "In
a world which is becoming homogenized with fearsome rapidity,
Mexico is still a wonderful confusion and melding of disparate
facts, eras, art, sociology, and mental climates." Confusion of
course implies anarchy; thus, Mexico is known to be ruled by
the kind of order that prevails in the misnamed Third World:
a jumbled orchestration of earthly things, a fractured legal
system, the eagle and the snake: voraciousness and wrath.

But chaos, we are beginning to learn, is an alternative
form of order, at once sophisticated and enigmatic. In Mexico
a different order, intricate, unconventional by western standards,
prevails. Add to it the fact that beyond its borders, the country
emanates another image: that of innocence and primitiveness.
Look at the fiction about Mexico by writers in Europe and the
United States. Katherine Anne Porter, the author of *Flowering
Judas and Other Stories*, who lived in Mexico for long periods
of time in the early decades of our century, once commented,
"Mexico seems a simple place . . . a region not far from Eden."
Truth is, the neighbor south of the Rio Grande is anything but
simple; few Mexicans would perceive themselves as innocent,
primitive, and naïve. Things are much more complex: the
crossroad where hope, purity, and blood meet the green, white,
and red of the flag is always painful. In Mexico reality and fiction, history and fantasy, braid in a mysterious, labyrinthine way
and nothing is simple.

Torn between these extremes, Mexico's traumatic birth, its chaotic origin in 1523, has not yet healed. The suffering that resulted when Hernán Cortés and his army of Spanish conquistadors viciously subdued the imperial Aztec metropolis of Tenochtitlán, refuses to fade away. Two empires with distinctive world views and disparate understandings of chronological time, totally incapable of accepting each other's essences, collided in apocalyptic battle. Loss and destruction gave place to the *mestizo* people: what José Vasconcelos, an early twentieth-century scholar and education minister, called *la raza de bronce*, the bronze race neither Spanish nor Aztec. Bronze is an amalgam of copper, phosphorous, tin, zinc, and other elements—a hybrid, a mongrel, a sum of heterogeneous parts. Similarly, Mexico, in a relentless struggle to understand its collective identity, oscillates between loyalties to Spain, France, the United States, and the autochthonous self that refuses to die, one that flourishes in the elevated plateau where Tenochtitlán was built—a region characterized by broad, shallow lakes and transparent air, where the itinerant Aztec people, so the legend claims, found the eagle devouring a snake, an irrefutable sign that the land was theirs and they were the land's.

History in Mexico is asymmetrical, non-progressive. No matter how much people hope for a redemptive future, the past always returns to haunt the living and no clear lesson is ever learned. This cyclical rhythm is evident in the Calendar Stone, sculptured in a huge round flat rock segmented into multiple cubicles, each with Aztec symbols of time and the natural elements, inspired by the myth of eternal return. Indeed, the Aztecs prophesied that a white, bearded man, a messianic figure, would come from distant oceans to begin history anew: Hernán Cortés's annunciation. Consequently, since early days diplomats, artists, and intellectuals are occupied in understanding the many sacrifices Mexico ought to make to become modern; the road is uncertain, the answer unclear.

The United States and Mexico: progressive time and cyclical time, democracy and ideological uncertainty, tomorrow and yesterday. Nowhere in the whole globe do more dissimilar neighbors share a common border. The Spanish soldiers were bachelors inspired by renaissance chivalry values, enamored with Machiavelli's philosophy as expressed in *The Prince*, knights equipped with copies of Leon Ebreo's *Dialogues of Love*, who raped maidens and subdued entire armies. The pilgrims that arrived in the Mayflower and eventually configured the British Colonies had very different goals in mind. Their sense of destiny was unequivocal. While copulating with Indian women and thus gestating a new progeny, the Spanish soldiers never dreamed of building up a new society; under a missionary banner, they forced Catholicism on the native population, attempting to erase idolatry. And they gave way to syncretism: Mexico, still today a land where witchcraft will not perish, where Jesus Christ and Quetzalcóatl cohabit, where fantasy is to be found in the colorful way people eat and make love, and in daily newspapers, where the government-sponsored news never quite matches with reality. On the other hand, the Anglo-Saxon puritans, self-proclaimed "the New People of Israel," arrived at Plymouth silently wishing to distance themselves from Great Britain to find the Promised Land, an utopian geography where they might construct an improved version of the mother land: the Old World in the New World, England in America. Unlike Mexico's, time in the United States is lineal, teleological; its population is obsessed with its collective mission: to be the best among the best. Mexico is stuck in its traumatic past, committed to untangling its baroque national identity.

Ironically, the most resourceful way for us Mexicans to untangle ourselves, to decipher our collective identity, seems to be through fiction. One senses a deep desire to exorcise ancient ghosts through novels and stories. As Carlos Fuentes once asked: Why is it that our writers are so imaginative and our politicians so unimaginative? Fiction is a fiesta of possibilities, an improvised gathering of assorted guests wearing masks to hide a true identity. Not surprisingly, the mask is Mexico's most ubiquitous symbol. Octavio Paz, winner of the 1990 Nobel Prize for Literature, writes in his 1950 masterpiece, *The Labyrinth of Solitude*: "The Mexican, whether young or old, *criollo*\* or *mestizo*, general or laborer or lawyer, seems to me to be a person who shuts himself away to protect himself: his face is a mask

---

\* A person of pure Spanish blood living in the Americas.

and so is his smile." Indeed, we hide ourselves from the world; we pretend to be somebody else; we assume different roles. Isn't that what fiction is about? Fiction is at the core of the relationship between man and history in Mexico: the hero, the assassin, the lover never die: eternal masks, they inhabit a time outside time, a dimension beyond history.

Most readers in the United States have been misguided to believe that the novel is Mexico's favorite literary genre, the best theatrical stage for the never-ending fiesta of the collective mind. Actually, fiction seems to find an incomparable vehicle in the short story. Its evanescent brevity, the challenge to find just the perfect amount of words to convey its message, the chance to use it as a mirror to the collective soul, make it a beloved genre. Mexico has produced outstanding stories: Alfonso Reyes' "The Dinner," Juan José Arreola's "The Switchman," Salvador Elizondo's "History According to Pao Cheng," and Juan Rulfo's "Luvina," to name just a few outstanding examples. Fables, legends, rumors, folktales, and whispers, present at the birth of the nation and never eclipsed, are the recurring substance of short fiction.

An incredibly popular genre since the turn of the century, the story has been practiced by almost every writer of note. Its genealogical tree can be easily traced. During colonial times, the written confession often evidenced the enviable structure of an autobiographical tale. Before and during independence and the 1910 Revolution, *corridos,* folksongs about legendary events and heroes, had the structure and shape of brief tales. Then come the border legends celebrating the adventurous life of bandits like Tiburcio Vásquez and Gregorio Cortez. Mariano Azuela and Martín Luis Guzmán, among many other early-twentieth century literati, practiced a naturalist type of short story, conveying the customs and beliefs of the lower class and the rebel armies. Many subsequent practitioners, from Arreola to Rulfo, from Rosario Castellanos to Ángeles Mastretta, have renewed the genre focusing on alternative topics: urban dwelling and rural life, unhappiness among rebellious student and blue-color workers, as well as the plight of women in Mexican society.

Unfortunately, very few outside the nation's borders are acquainted with the vitality and heterogeneity of the story. Allow me to speculate why this is so. The most obvious reason is that literature north and south of the border are the result of opposing traditions; fantasy and history talk to each other differently. In Mexico it tends to be lavish, politically conscious, self-absorbed, ornamented, with a surrealist edge, directly linked to the source of sources: Miguel de Cervantes. In the United States, on the other hand, the writer of fiction is primarily perceived as an entertainer.

This anthology serves a threefold purpose: to introduce Mexican fiction writers to a broad audience in the United States; by doing so, to present a convincing mosaic of contemporary Mexico; and to demonstrate the incredible stamina of the short story in an environment where writers are perceived as discoverers of hidden facets of reality. A few issues should be kept in mind while traveling through the forthcoming pages. First and foremost, the reader ought to understand the complex role literary figures play in Mexico, and for that matter in Latin America as a whole. As in Eastern Europe, art and politics are entangled: they are often understood as faces of the same coin. In a society where a large segment of impoverished citizens have no voice in the national debate, the writer is asked to become a speaker, a mediator, an interpreter between suffering and the ruling powers. As a result, literature carries enormous weight: it opens up new venues, it facilitates dialogue between opposing groups, and more than anything, it gives fantasy a place in daily life. It goes without saying that not all writers take seriously this social responsibility. Practitioners of Latin American letters could easily be divided into two groups: those like the argentine Jorge Luis Borges, dreaming perfect intellectual worlds for us, isolated in what the Nicaraguan modernist poet Rubén Darío used to call *torres de dios,* a celestial ivory tower; and those like Eduardo Galeano, using literature to advance political causes. The separation between the two groups is sometimes foggy.

Another important aspect to pay attention to is the heterogeneity of styles displayed in *Pyramids of Glass.* Since the end of World War II, as a result of the immediate availability of translations, literary influences have been crossing linguistic and cultural borders. Today writers everywhere respond to stimuli in their milieu that come from all corners of the planet and Mexico is no exception. As the reader of this volume will soon discover, the short story in Mexico is a monster with multiple tentacles capable of digesting foreign trends and creating new styles. From the impoverished region of Yucatán to the wealthy northern states, an infinite number of linguistic nuances are recorded by short-story writers, and the focus frequently shifts from the rich impresario to the militant peasant, from the Europeanized bourgeoisie in the nation's capital to the forgotten Indian population. Indeed, the genre tells us more about the ancient land of Moctezuma and Pancho Villa than much of the scholarly and journalistic reportage that is regularly put before us. As such, this volume is an invaluable door to the collective soul of what *The New York Times* journalist Alan Riding has called "our very distant neighbor" a key to the enigmas of Mexico's conflicted identity.

Assorted collections of Mexican short stories (in Spanish) have been in the market for at least seventy years, since 1924 when Bernardo Ortiz de Montellano published a collection of tales, mostly written in the nineteenth century. Joaquín Ramírez Cabañas prepared another one in 1943, followed by an outstanding volume edited by the renowned scholar Luis Leal in 1957: *Antología del cuento mexicano,* incorporating stories from precolonial times to Rulfo. Maria del Carmen Millán is responsible for a widely-known selection first published in 1976 and frequently reprinted. This is to show that in Mexico the genre is carefully cultivated; it has been endlessly analyzed and promoted even though no broad popular market for the short story exists as it has, via mass magazines, in the U.S. As a genre, its historical development takes a sharp turn in 1953, the year Rulfo's *The Burning Plain* first appeared. Almost immediately, the Mexican short story came of age; it acquired new stamina and a concise style still evident today.

Among the contemporary cornerstones are Fuentes, Inés Arredondo, Jorge Ibargüengoitia, and Sergio Pitol. (The first three were born in 1928; the fourth in 1933.) Fuentes is a seasoned post-modern ventriloquist. He navigates under the banner of multiculturalism, shaping his persona as a pluri-national hybrid (he was born in Panama City, the son of a Mexican diplomat, and raised in the River Plate and Washington, D.C.) He writes in Spanish and English and remains the most successful fiction writer from Mexico outside the nation's borders. "The Mandarin" is vintage Fuentes: self-referential and carefully stylized, it evidences a cosmopolitan appetite and an unequivocal desire to bring Mexican fiction to the international literary banquet.

A native of Sinaloa, Arredondo, author of the classic collection *La señal* who died in 1989, is known for her intimate portraits of domestic life, often echoing biblical and Greek myths. "Puzzles" is about the suffering that Teresa, the protagonist, undergoes, as she understands her place in her parents' hearts must now be shared with a new family member. Her themes and usage of language make me think of her as Mexico's Alice Munro. Ibargüengoitia, who died in the same 1983 plane crash in Madrid that took the lives of the Uruguayan literary critic Angel Rama and his wife Marta Traba, is a first-rate humorist best known for his novel *The Dead Girls*, about a group of adolescent prostitutes assassinated by their selfish matron and her lover. Ibargüengoitia is unequaled in Mexican letters in his sarcastic comedy: in a country where the pantheon of historical heroes cannot be touched, he has made fun of the Mexican Revolution of 1910, as well as of crucial players in the war of independence against Spain in the early years of the nineteenth century.

Finally, Pitol, originally from Puebla, is one of the most original and personal writers in the country's literature. As an ambassador and cultural attaché in Eastern Europe, he has been exposed to aesthetic trends that left a mark in his art. His constellation of characters dance to a nostalgic music; they reveal themselves to us without ever explaining what possesses them and limits their freedom. The oeuvres of Fuentes, Arredondo, Ibargüengoitia, and Pitol summarize the consuming conflict of opposites that runs through all of Mexico's short stories: the personal enthralled in the collective, the intimate absorbed in the political, the individual immersed in the historical.

The year 1968 marks a crucial rite of passage for the country. As the nation was preparing to celebrate the Olympic Games, unhappy students, with the support of housewives and blue-collar workers, marched in the streets of Mexico City accusing the government of intolerance and abuse. The whole world was watching and the government, impatient at the complaints, massacred scores of students gathered in a Tlatelolco plaza, in the capital. The exact number of victims was concealed by the dogmatic regime of President Gustavo Dias Ordáz. Almost immediately, intellectuals and artists set forth to record the tragedy in writing: to use literature to reveal what the government had rushed to conceal. A handful of writers included in this treasury of modern Mexican stories, including Elena Poniatowska and José Agustín, belong to a literary generation marked by Tlatelolco, committed to political democratization.

Born in Paris, France, in 1933, Poniatowska, alongside the multifaceted man of letters Carlos Monsiváis, personifies the so-called new journalism. She combines in her craft historical data, an engaging prose style, and firsthand reportage. An evidence of her very personal writing is *La noche de Tlatelolco*, a record of the crucial date when modernity pushed the country to tragic consequences. Similarly, Agustín is part of a movement known under the rubric of *La Onda*, heavily influenced by the French *nouveau roman* and U.S. beatniks, which produced short stories about adolescent rites of passage in urban centers where drugs, alcohol, and rock prevailed. After Fuentes's novel *Where the Air is Clear*, they shifted the attention from the rural settings frequented by Rulfo to urban scenes, almost exclusively in Mexico City. Seen in context, Poniatowska and Agustín are transitional figures, preparing the atmosphere for newer voices emerging in the late seventies.

The social and aesthetic consequences of 1968 are countless. A concrete result was the emergence of women writers and their long-repressed point of view. Women, it should be said, have been active in Mexican literature since the late seventeenth century: the poet and playwright Sor Juana Inés de La Cruz might well be the most accomplished and admirable pen to emerge in the Hispanic American world during colonial times. But a quick glance at any biographical dictionary of national fiction writers announces the undeniable: for every twenty-some male writers, there is one woman active as prose writer. This unbalance can be felt in the overall power-oriented quality of Mexican fiction; a more gentle, introverted, and intimate facet is missing, a ghost frequently invoked but until recently absent. As *Pyramids of Glass* shows, things have changed: Ángeles Mastretta, the celebrated author of *Arráncame la vida,* is represented here alongside Marta Cerda, Silvia Molina, Maria Luisa Puga, Guadalupe Dueñas, as well as Poniatowska and Arredondo which points to another invaluable asset of the present volume: its desire to make available a voice often excluded from the old-boy network.

Another result of 1968 was the promotion and increasing seriousness of alternative literary subgenera: spy and detective fiction, romance, *novela rosa* (known in France and elsewhere as *feuilleton),* and science fiction. The best, most refreshing example in this respect is Paco Ignacio Taibo II, whose story "Apaches in 'La Granja' " displays the writer's ongoing concern for *realpolitik,* syndicalism, and left-wing ideology. PITII, as Taibo is known, is largely responsible for the surprisingly large readership detective fiction from Latin America has acquired in recent years. A prolific historian, journalist, fiction writer born in Spain in 1949, PITII is the Mexican counterpart of Raymond Chandler and Dashiell Hammett. His legendary private-eye, Héctor Belascoarán Shayne, gets involved in the underworld of drugs and crime in the chaotic Mexico City, denouncing political corruption and using literature as a way to simultaneously entertain and create social consciousness. *Some Clouds* and *No Happy Ending,* his best-known books, have a light, hard-boiled style, that never hides the writer's commitment to his overpopulated and pollution-saturated environment and always leaves a refreshing flavor in the reader's mouth.

Perhaps the story that best exemplifies the newest trends in the Mexican short story is "Rear–View Mirror" by Juan Villoro, born in the nation's capital in 1956 and a pupil of the famous Guatemalan fabulist Augusto Monterroso. Villoro belongs to a generation, including David Martin del Campo and Daniel Sada, often concerned with stylistic formalities, that one of his own characters describes as "very modern"; a product of consumerism, his concern is to examine an urban middle class bombarded by international products, always in vogue, drinking Maalox, eating sushi, looking for evanescent love affairs. Samuel Ramos, a sociologist influenced by Freudian thought, once wrote a book, *Profile of Men and Culture in Mexico*, in which he analyzed Mexico's inferiority complex, a result, he claimed, of a traumatic collective past. Villoro's eternally adolescent characters are quite removed from what Ramos had in mind when writing about *el pelado*, a city dweller personified in the movies of the forties by Cantinflas: they are Americanized in their style and mentality, concerned with their sexuality, the product of a cosmopolitan society looking for external influences.

The authors of these stories chart paths which twist and turn each day, and sometimes come to a halt in the pain of impasse. The eagle sitting on a cactus while devouring a serpent, Mexico's all-time symbol, cannot be eclipsed. The cycles of history, the cycles of fiction, will always return. Tomorrow's reader might be acquainted with a totally different Mexico and thus might use the fiction in this book as a helpful testament of changing times. Born out of historical rape and with no democratic tradition, Mexico is still trying to move from *becoming* to *being*: like the *axólotl*, a native type of salamander, Mexico is in constant metamorphosis, always in the process of becoming. Our morality is not only ambiguous but malleable. Since colonial times, federal, state, and local institutions have been intrusive, tyrannical, dogmatic, and intransigent. Corruption and fraud, the law of the land, are impossible to eradicate. In power since 1929, the ruling party has perfected a dictatorial system where dissent is welcomed only to be quickly erased from public debate. Democracy is still a fragile, uninvited guest; and the imagination never ceases to hope for a redemptive tomorrow.

History and fiction: Today we might be (or have been) witnessing what the Jewish historian Gershom Scholem once called "a plastic moment," one in which new possibilities are taking shape. From a poor and isolated nation looking south, to Central and South America, for sympathy and support, Mexico, industrialized and focusing on a free-market economy, has shifted its sight toward the north. Rather than aligning itself with dictatorial regimes in the Caribbean and the southern cone, the last few presidential cabinets, led by technocrats trained in the United States, have promoted a more open, less self-absorbed image of Mexico. They have done it by attracting foreign investors and have tried to rapidly push the whole country into the twenty-first century. Such transformation has left many out in the air. While increasing the middle class and protecting the rich, the Mexican government also left the lower class far behind, particularly the Indian populations in southern states like Chiapas, Yucatán, and Oaxaca that Eraclio Zepeda pays homage in "The Truth," a story where the idiosyncratic oral tradition of poor peasants is strikingly recorded. As a result, bloody struggle and political instability have flourished.

As this volume is published in fall 1994, a crucial election year, Mexico appears to have suddenly become a time bomb—the Aztec myth of cyclical return again haunting the nation's history. Once again, the country is struggling to understand its non-western form of order. Curiously, the central image in Pitol's story, "The Panther," about the need to grasp an evasive message delivered through a dream, condenses powerfully Mexico's present historical challenge: the continuous search for a unifying vision to better understand the chaos.

Ilan Stavans, a Mexican novelist and critic, is the author of *The Hispanic Condition* (HarperCollins), *Imagining Columbus* (Twayne-Macmillan), and editor of two anthologies: *Growing Up Latino* (with Harold Augenbraum, Houghton Mifflin); and *Tropical Synagogues* (Holmes & Meier). The recipient of many awards, including the 1992 Latino Literature prize, he teaches at Amherst College in Massachusetts.

# PYRAMIDS

### OF

# GLASS

# THE DICE BOX
## Emilio Carballido

Since the cupboard door creaked
loudly when it was opened, Mario's wife knew exactly what he
was doing.

"Mario! That's my money for the market."

"You'll have it back by noon."

"But how will we eat today? That's everything I have."

He held the bill between his first two fingers, waggled it,
and kept looking at her.

"But I don't have a centavo. And there's always something
I need a little money for."

"Then *how are we going to eat today?*"

"Won't that friend of yours lend you something?"

"I already owe her thirty-five pesos."

She wielded her cooking spoon like a weapon; she stood

1

tensely, as if about to attack. They stared at each other several seconds. Then a current of indifference seemed to flood through her veins. Slowly, she walked over and sat on the edge of the unmade bed and gazed at the wall with a shrug that erased Mario and his actions from the room, from the world. I'm too tired, that shrug seemed to say. Do whatever you want. Mario had won, once again.

He hesitated a second, then shoved the money into his pocket. He smiled broadly, with the infectious warmth he had never lost.

"Don't be mad, *mi ,vieja*. We'll eat at a restaurant, how about that? See if you can be ready when I get home."

His wife regarded him with skepticism. He might come home and he might not; he might have money and he might not; he might not come home until evening, or even the next day. That was how he had been since he got mixed up in politics. I'll ask Mama to lend me a little, she thought, and a wave of dark anger made her clench her teeth.

"We'll be dressed and waiting," she lied. "Without a bite to eat till you get home. We'll see whether we go hungry."

He kissed her, happy because the quarrel was behind them. He checked his appearance in the mirror: well-groomed, almost elegant, in a carefully pressed linen suit. He practiced a smile, tried out two or three expressions. He approved; the reflection exuded prosperity and self-confidence. He kissed his wife a second time and started toward the door. Not fast enough, however, to escape her shout: "You heard me. Sitting in the living room, dressed to go out. And not one bite till you come home."

"I heard you the first time, woman."

Then the final lament: "I curse the day you went into politics."

He closed the door gently, and leaped onto a passing streetcar.

When he descended in the Plaza de Armas the sun was already blazing. It's going to be a scorcher, he thought. The sound of whirring fans issued from every archway and the sea unleashed an occasional breeze that had little effect against the oven-like vapors beginning to rise from the asphalt. And it was barely ten o'clock.

All the regulars were already installed in the archway of the *Diligencias*. Calling on his repertoire of expressions, Mario greeted the men one by one.

"How's it going, Deputy?"

"Hey, old pal. What's up?"

"General, what a pleasure to see you."

There were two or three people he had never seen, but he would soon learn who they were. *Don* Leonardo was due to arrive before long, and they filled the waiting with off-color stories, predictions about a major shift toward the right in the cabinet and the imminent fall of a local boss, and descriptions of the new girl, a real winner, who had brought to their customary brothel a bagful of technical novelties.

Conversation lagged. *Don* Leonardo was late.

Mario questioned Ciro, *sotto voce:* "Who are those guys?"

Ciro explained that the two older men were seeking important forest concessions. The cadaverous one had interests in something he didn't know much about, the fishing industry.

"Which one will you let me handle?"

"Well, whatever Argüelles says."

"Right."

"Maybe the one who's here about the fishing."

Eleven-thirty. Everyone was languishing. Then, without preamble, *don* Leonardo was there, excessively well-groomed, with the inevitable carnation in his buttonhole and his thin hair smoothed back to perfection. He never stood on formalities. He greeted everyone familiarly; they replied in chorus. He sat down; there was a scraping of chairs. Imperceptibly, each of them corrected his posture, sat up a little straighter, almost as when a particularly frightening, although superficially affable, teacher enters a classroom.

A waiter hurriedly picked up the beer bottles, even those only partially empty, because, from this moment, cognac would be the only drink. The long democratic round-table had begun, famous among the port inhabitants, some of whom paused a second to greet *don* Leonardo, with the hope of afterward seeming more important—because everyone knew that he devoted the same pleasantries and backslappings to every passerby, friend or stranger, the same extremely photogenic smile, and the same long-held handshake.

"I'd like to buy the first round," Ciro offered respectfully.

Mario was unsure whether or not to feel relieved. All he had in his pocket was the money he'd taken from the cupboard, only fifty pesos. If each of them paid in turn, he couldn't imagine what he would do when his turn came. He was sitting near the head of the table, too close for his failure to stand a round to go unnoticed. And anyone with empty pockets lost all respect. Who was going to entrust a deal of thousands to a man who couldn't even pay for a round of cognacs?

"No, no ..." Ciro's offer to pay was refused. "Bring us the dicebox."

Mario breathed a little more lightly, he would bank on chance. He tried to evaluate the cadaverous man but could draw no impression. Perhaps, almost surely, he was an intermediary between the person setting up the deal and the nearly omnipotent power of *don* Leonardo, who was the one who would grant, or not grant, the solicited favor.

If it's a hundred thousand, that's ten thousand for Ciro, and one or two thousand for me. The forest concessions were bigger ventures; a couple of months ago one had come along for nearly two million, but it had gone to Sáenz. Argüelles likes him, he'll give him the fishing deal. That's how the chain worked: men like Sáenz, or Mario, agreed to be responsible for the arrangements. Ciro took charge, but quietly let *don* Leonardo make the decisions, and obtained in the space of a chat or in a couple of telephone calls the verbal promise that the deal would go through. Ciro, never mentioning *don* Leonardo, collected the signatures. The newer men, like Sáenz or Mario, did the groundwork, the trotting from office to office—nothing too time-consuming or difficult—because everyone knew the name behind the negotiations.

Damp from sweat, the dicebox passed from hand to hand; the dice rattled like fragments of bone inside the padded leather, rolled onto the table, and each called out his points in a loud voice.

"Two pairs."

"Three of a kind."

"*Nada.*"

Mario noticed that everyone was losing ground; it was going to come down to him and Argüelles. For an instant his pulse stuttered and he felt a sudden dryness in his throat. He took the dicebox, shook it, and rolled the dice, not even thinking. Two kings. He picked up three dice. He shook. He was performing a difficult mental maneuver that consisted of thinking about something else, something very vague, while in the darkest and deepest part of his mind commanding the dice to give him another king. They acceded.

"Three kings," he said, quite normally, and downed his cognac in one swallow. Now it was up to Argüelles.

The dicebox rattled in the other man's hand; the dice rolled.

"Son of a bitch!" Argüelles said quietly. He had rolled snake eyes. He pulled money from his pocket and held it out to the waiter. "The same all around." Orders were paid for at the time they were made, following the code of the round table.

Now Mario heard the cautious comment that Argüelles was going to be put up for Federal Deputy. If that happened, the place at *don* Leonardo's right hand would be available for someone else. Ciro, undoubtedly. There was among them an arbitrary seniority system, one that depended on gifts, or like interests, or complicities of the brothel and cantina, or a repertory of jokes, or gravity, or generosity ... so many mysteries and minutia of personal relations.

For a long time, Mario felt he was master of his dice. In that dark corner of his mind he gave them orders but pretended not to, obstinately thinking of something else, while there, in a place where things are not formulated in words, he directed: a pair of fives, a king, an ace. Then suddenly, something went wrong. The compliance of the dice had shifted to a different, a stronger, master down the table.

"Nothing here," said Mario. He kept one die, an ace. He threw again: a pair.

His power was failing, he knew it. One more round and he would finally lose. (Almost everyone had lost, almost everyone had paid a round, even *don* Leonardo). "Borrow it." The two words came floating up like loose boards from a sunken ship. He clung to them with panic. He saw faces: Sáenz, Ciro, Argüelles . . . all his friends. He released his grip on the two boards and kept swimming, exhausted. That fan . . . not enough air. . . .

Just as the order for the new round was being taken, he saw the anxious face, the timid gesture. A man, beside a column, was making frantic but discreet signs to him. Hector Cervera! A creature from a different universe. Someone who had been an office mate and a friend, one of the many he never saw once he had obtained the post in the union and, through that, entered the world of politics. He gave no indication he had seen him. (Always play it cool, you never know, was another of the nebulous laws in the intuited code of the roundtable.) He rose from the table, as if leaving to urinate, and went inside. There, out of view of the others, he signalled Hector. They embraced in greeting and walked to a quiet corner.

Hector had suffered a string of misfortunes: a son had died and he had had to mortgage his small and only half-finished house. And now his mother was ill in Baja California, and where was he going to get enough money to travel the enormous width of the country and reach her bedside in time?

Mario listened sympathetically (if slightly distractedly) to his friend's misfortunes. All this was leading up to a loan. Yes he would have helped him had he been in different circumstances. But more important at the moment was the matter of the imminent round of cognacs (and how the shit he was going to pay for it), and he could not truly absorb all that his unfortunate friend was telling him.

"Polio. Poor kid. He was your most . . ." He searched for the word. (Only yesterday, *don* Leonardo had told Mario a joke, told it specifically to him, Mario, and that meant. . . .) "Your brightest. Poor kid."

He didn't know what else to say. He squeezed Hector's arm. And your mother . . . so ill . . . her heart. What was the complication? He couldn't remember whether the lungs were the boy or the mother, or who had the bad kidneys, or the liver. Too many viscera, and he was taking too long away from the table. Poor old Hector, he really did feel sorry for him. Mario was so impatient—no, so moved—that he thought of making a magnificent gesture (and could see himself doing it) by giving him his only bill, the fifty pesos, which actually wasn't doing him any good, anyway. But then, like a lightning flash, an extraordinary plan unfolded in his mind. He stood staring at his friend, critically, cataloguing him: tear-filled, humble eyes; two days' growth of beard; clothing disheveled but decent and clean. The very image of a man on speaking terms with death.

"Hector, listen. You find me without a centavo. But I want you to repeat everything at the table, exactly as you told me."

Hector didn't understand; Mario quickly explained.

Mario returned to his seat; nearly everyone had thrown the dice and, artfully, he had avoided a turn. No one had noticed the length of his absence. The dice were coming round still again when Hector approached the table. Mario pretended not to see him, and so it was Ortega who told Ciro, and Ciro who told Mario, that someone was looking for him. He looked up.

"Hector!"

His old friend! He left his place at the table and embraced him. Such a long time! Now he could think about Hector as a human being, without the fear of the dicebox hanging over him, without the uneasiness at being away from the table. Sentiments flowed with such sincerity that even Hector forgot he had seen Mario only a few minutes before. The scene played itself out again, this time to perfection. Now they truly were two old friends. Almost without realizing, Mario raised his voice, underlining key parts of the conversation, making it dimly intelligible for the listeners.

"Your youngest son. . . ."

"Your mama. . . ."

"In Baja California. So far away. . . ."

"And of course your wife will be left alone. And your other children?"

Ah, now he understood. The lungs were the son; the heart, the mother; the liver, the wife, who would be all alone if Hector made his trip.

End of story. Mario sat there, sober, pensive, suffering along with Hector, thinking hard. How can I help? He thrust his hand into his pocket, glanced at the others. He made what seemed to be the spontaneous decision of a generous heart. He said, "I want you all to know an old friend of mine, Hector Cervera. He just lost a son; his mother is ill in Baja California. . . ."

He nearly surprised himself when he heard his voice, hoarse with authentic emotion. He was able to describe the situation with discreet and convincing pathos. He finished with a gesture that nearly passed as impulsive: he seized Sáenz's hat and threw into it the single bill in his possession, concealing the denomination.

"That's all I can do. But I'm sure that my friends. . . ." He gestured. "We all know what it is to have a sick mother, or to leave our wife on her own. Hector is a hard worker, like the rest of us."

He added a few details. Although all the men could hold

their liquor, at this point the cognac enhanced the sentiments Mario was evoking. The hat passed from hand to hand. Sáenz watched it filling with bills. When it passed through his own (my God, they're so sweaty!), he tossed in a hundred pesos, ill-humoredly, thinking all the time that his new hat was going to get filthy.

*Don* Leonardo tossed in a bill Mario couldn't identify but made the cadaverous man gulp, for since he was next it was impossible to do less. And the other two men seeking favors also contributed.

The hat was nearly back to where it had begun, and it seemed appropriate for *don* Leonardo to say a few words. He looked at Hector and, with that sympathy that radiates from important men, said gravely, his eyes shining with idealism, "We have only one mother in this life."

Every face was charged with emotion, and Ciro murmured, "Only one."

The hat was overflowing with bills, and Hector couldn't decide whether he felt like a clown or like a man struck with good fortune. Mario embraced him, but by now Hector's embarrassment was overwhelming. He mumbled his thanks and fled inside, holding the hat.

Mario sat down again. An emotional silence floated above the table. The deed was done, and now Mario had only to follow Hector and split the pot. Suddenly, his heart lurched. And what if Hector took off with it all? Copious sweat began to stream down his forehead; the heat was a blessing because even others were sweating, although his sweat was ice cold. What if Hector *did* take everything? The dicebox rattled in *don* Leonardo's hands. The throw of the dice was beginning again, and he would have to wait, stuck there, before going to look for Hector.

Sáenz didn't know how to say it, but this was his only hat. Finally he ventured, "Your friend. . . . Your friend was so stunned. . . ," he tried to sound casual, and amused, ". . . that he carried off my hat."

The burst of laughter was so loud that curious

pedestrians stopped to peer in. *Don* Leonardo laughed so hard he wept. The skin-and-bones stranger turned red. Emotion they had struggled to contain found an affirmative release. They howled, they beat the table.

"Sáenz! That's terrible!" Mario, too, was doubled over with laughter. "I'll go find him."

"No, it's not important. . . . Forget it." Poor Sáenz tried to laugh as hard as anyone, but he felt that somehow the throw of the dice had worked against him.

Mario hurried from the table, playing a slightly farcical part. He pretended to look in the street, questioned a waiter, and then went straight to the place they had agreed to meet, by the urinal.

Hector was there waiting for him, hat clutched to his chest, still not daring to appraise the results of the collection. They counted it together, and Hector felt dizzy; he leaned against the wall and began to sob. Nine thousand, eight hundred and fifty pesos.

"You've always been like a brother to me."

He couldn't go on. As he threw his arms around Mario in a convulsive embrace, he dropped the hat in a puddle of urine. He picked it up.

". . . brother."

He blew his nose, and began to feel more calm.

Mario, too, was shaken. His eyes filled with tears; he felt good—capable, important, generous. "Just give me four thousand."

Hector hiccuped. "No, Mario, no, no, no. I can't take more than half . . . or less . . . ?"

Mario poked the money into his pocket. He left Hector weeping beside the urinal.

The delivery of the hat provoked new belly laughs. Ciro whispered in Mario's ear that the fishing deal would fall to him. Someone was talking about a vacancy for a minor post, a replacement for a local deputyship (but it was a rung on a ladder, and it could be a sturdy rung). In that dark region of his mind, Mario promised himself it would be his.

He threw the dice. Three of a kind. He picked them up and knew he would roll a full house. He shook the dicebox, made the dice rattle like seeds rolling in the belly of a ripe gourd, and with the sharp and hollow sound he felt he was moving mountains and coastlines, planted fields and fishing grounds, mines and cattle, the entire nation he'd learned about in his civics and geography lessons. He rolled the dice and announced, calmly: "Full house."

*—Translated by Margaret Sayers Peden*

# WHITE LIES
## Ángeles Mastretta

She had unquiet shoulders and a neck of porcelain. Her hair was chestnut brown and unruly, and her quick, merciless tongue could tell all regarding the life and miracles of whoever was under discussion.

Everyone liked talking to her because her voice was like a beacon, and her eyes could turn the most insignificant gestures and obscure stories into clear words.

It wasn't that she made up lies about other people or knew more gossip than anyone else. It was her ability to get to the core of any intrigue, to discover the divine oversight behind a person's ugliness, or to latch onto the verbal miscue that would betray the candid soul.

Aunt Charo enjoyed being involved with the world, checking it out with her eyes, honing it with her anxious voice. She was not one to waste time. As she spoke, she would sew, embroider her husband's initials on his handkerchiefs, knit vests for anyone who was cold in the winter, play handball with her sister, make the most delicious cornbread cakes, shape *buñuelos* on her knees, and help the children with their homework.

She would never have been ashamed of her passion for words had she not accepted an invitation one afternoon in June to one of those spiritual meetings where the priest spoke on the topic, "Thou shalt not bear false witness." At one point, discussing big lies, he noticed that his drowsy listeners remained totally unmoved. So he began to blast away at those tiny venal sins that pop up when talking about other people and which, put together, add up to one big mortal sin.

Aunt Charo left church with a deep sense of remorse in the pit of her stomach. Could it be she was guilty of a mortal sin, the sum of all those times she had talked about this lady's nose and that one's legs, this man's jacket and the hump on so-and-so's back, the guy who struck it rich, and the wandering eyes of such and such a married woman? Could it be that her heart was rotten with sin as a result of knowing everything that went on beneath all the skirts and pants in town, knowing all the folly that stood in the way of other people's happiness and all the happiness that was nothing more than folly? These thoughts only increased her fears. Before going home, she stopped for confession with the recently arrived Spanish priest. He was a small gentle man who wandered about the parish in search of faithful souls willing to place their confidence in him.

Now, people in Puebla can love with an intensity that is much greater than in other places, only it takes them time. They don't just latch onto the first stranger who comes along and open up to him as if they had known him all their lives. But in this respect the aunt was not like everyone else in town. She was one of the Spanish priest's first clients. The old priest who had presided over her first communion died leaving her with no one in whom to confide her innermost thoughts, the thoughts that she and her conscience reserved to themselves, the ones dealing with her wayward moments, with her doubts regarding her most private garments, the gurglings of her body, and the dark facets of her heart.

"Hail Mary, full of grace," said the Spanish priest with the terse accent that seemed better suited to a gypsy balladeer than a priest educated in Madrid.

"Who conceived without sin," said the aunt, smiling in the darkness of the confessional, as she did every time she repeated that phrase.

"Are you smiling?" the Spanish priest asked her, guessing that she was, as if he were some kind of wizard.

"No, Father," said Aunt Charo, fearing the unpleasant aftertaste of the Inquisition.

"*I* am," said the little man. "And you may too, with my permission. I can't imagine a more ridiculous greeting. But tell me, how are you? What is it that's troubling you so late in the day?"

"I've been asking myself, Father," said Aunt Charo, "if it's a sin to talk about other people. You know, talk about what's happening to them, find out what they're thinking, disagree with what they say, call the cross-eyed man cross-eyed, the lame woman lame, the skinny guy a slob, and the woman who blabs about her husband's millions snooty. Knowing where the husband got his millions and who else he spends them on. Is that a sin, Father?" asked the aunt.

"No, my dear," said the Spanish priest. "That's called having a thirst for life. What are people around here supposed to do? Just work and say their prayers? That leaves a lot of time in the day. Seeing is no sin, and neither is talking. Go in peace. You have nothing to worry about."

"Thank you, Father," said Aunt Charo, and she ran home quickly to tell it all to her sister.

Free of guilt from that point on, she continued to rejoice in the soap opera the city laid in her lap. Her head was filled with everyone else's comings and goings; it was guaranteed entertainment. That's why she was invited to knit at all the charity bazaars. A dozen women fought to have her at their canasta tables. Those who couldn't see her there invited her over to their houses or stopped by to visit. No one was ever intentionally misled by listening to her, nor was there any new gossip that did not originate with her.

And so life flowed along its course until one evening at the bazaar of Guadalupe. Aunt Charo had spent the afternoon struggling with the beads on a belt, and since she had nothing new to offer she decided to listen.

"Charo, you know the Spanish priest at the church of San Javier, don't you?" a lady asked her as she was finishing the hem on a napkin.

"Why?" asked Aunt Charo, who did not part easily with information pertaining to herself.

"Because they say he's no priest but a lying Republican who came over with the other exiles that the Cárdenas government took in. And since he couldn't find work as a poet, he made up the story that he was a priest and that his papers were burned by the communists along with the church in his village."

"Some people talk too much," said Aunt Charo, then added in her most authoritative manner, "The Spanish priest is devout, a true Catholic. He is incapable of telling a lie. I saw the letter issued by the Vatican that sent him to see the parish priest at San Javier. That the poor old priest was dying just as he arrived wasn't his fault. He didn't have time to give it to him. But as for whether they sent him, of course they sent him. I wouldn't have a faker for a confessor."

"He's your confessor?" asked one of the curious.

"I'm proud to say he is," said Aunt Charo, keeping her eyes fixed on the beaded flower she was embroidering and putting an end to the conversation right there.

The next morning she went to the Spanish priest's confessional.

"Father, I've told lies," said the aunt.

"Were they white lies?" asked the priest.

"They were necessary lies," answered the aunt.

"Necessary to protect someone?" the priest asked again.

"To protect someone's honor," said the aunt.

"Is the party in question innocent?"

"I don't know, Father," confessed the aunt.

"Then it was a double good deed that you did," said the Spaniard. "May God grant you a clear head and good milk. Go with Him."

"Thank you, Father," said the aunt.

"Thank *you*," answered the strange priest, which made her tremble.

*—Translated by John Incledon*

Carlos Fuentes (Panama, Embassy of Mexico 1928)
has made an international reputation not only as a
writer of fiction but as an essayist, political commentator, and lecturer. His penetrating historical essay on
Latin America, El espejo enterrado ("The Buried Mirror" 1992) has been seen by millions on public television. Many of his works are familiar to readers of
English, notably Where the Air is Clear (La región
mas transparente) 1958, The Death of Artemio Cruz
(1962), Distant Relations (Una familia lejana) 1980,
and Old Gringo (1985). Fuentes' latest novel is Diana,
o la cazadora solitaria (1994). He has been a visiting
professor at Cambridge, Columbia, Harvard, Pennsylvania, and Princeton, and has received the Villaurrutia Prize (1976), the Cervantes Prize (1987), and
the Prince of Asturias award (1994).

# THE MANDARIN
## Carlos Fuentes

### I

Once Mexico City had been a city
whose nights held the promise of the morning to come. Before
going to bed, Federico Silva would walk out on the balcony of
his house on Cordoba Street at two o'clock in the morning, when
one could still smell the dampness of the earth of the coming
day, breathe the perfume of the jacarandas, and feel the nearness
of the volcanos.

Dawn brought everything near, mountains and forests.
Federico Silva closed his eyes in order to smell even better that
unique odor of dawn in Mexico City: the sapid, green trace of
the long-forgotten mud of the lake bed. To smell that odor was
to smell the first morning. Only those who can perceive the
nocturnal scent of the lost lake really know this city, Federico

17

told himself.

That was a long time ago. Now his house stood only a block away from the huge sunken plaza of the Insurgentes metro station. An architect friend had compared that anarchical intersection of streets and avenues—Insurgentes, Chapultepec, Genova, Amberes, and Jalapa—to the Place de l'Etoile in Paris, and Federico Silva had had a good laugh. Actually, the Insurgentes intersection was more like a giant-sized stack of tortillas: a busy thoroughfare, at times elevated above the flat rooftops of the bordering houses, then streets blocked with cement posts and chains, then the stairways and tunnels communicating with an interior plaza jammed with seafood restaurants and taco stands, itinerant vendors, beggars, vagrant troubadours ... and the students, shocking numbers of youths lolling around while shoeshine boys polished their shoes, eating sandwiches, watching the slowly drifting smog, whistling and calling veiled obscenities at passing round-breasted, round-bottomed, skinny-legged girls in miniskirts; the hip world, girls with feathers and blue eyelids and silver-smeared mouths, boys wearing leather vests over bare skin and yards of chains and necklaces. And finally, the entrance to the metro: the mouth of hell.

They had destroyed his morning-scented nights. The air in his neighborhood became unbreathable, the streets impassable. Under Federico Silva's nose—between the wretched luxury of the Zona Rosa, a gigantic village's pitiable cosmopolitan stage set, and the desperate, though useless, attempt at residential grace in the Colonia Roma—they had dug an infernal, unsalvageable trench, a river Styx of gasoline vapors circulating above the human whirlpool of the plaza, hundreds of young men whistling and watching the smog drift by, sweating, loafing, sitting in the filthy saucer of the sunken cement plaza. The saucer of a cup of cold, greasy, spilled chocolate.

"Infamous!" he exclaimed impotently. "To think that this was once a pretty, pastel-colored small town; you could walk from the Zócalo to Chapultepec Park and have everything you needed, government and entertainment, friendship and love."

This was one of the standard tunes of this elderly bachelor clinging to forgotten things that no longer interested anyone but him. His friends Perico and the Marqués told him not to be so pigheaded. It was one thing, as long as his mother had been alive (and God knows she took her time in going), to respect the family tradition and keep the house on Cordoba Street. But what was to be gained now? He'd had stupendous offers to sell; the market would top out; he ought to take advantage of the moment. He should know that better than anyone; he was a landlord himself, that was his living: real estate.

Then they'd tried to force his hand by constructing tall buildings on either side of his property; modern, they called them, although Federico Silva insisted that one can call modern only that which is built to last, not what's slapped together to begin to disintegrate in two years' time and fall down in ten. He felt ashamed that a country of churches and pyramids built for eternity should end up contenting itself with a city of shanties, shoddiness, and shit.

They boxed him in, they stifled him, they blocked out his sun and air, his view and his odors. And, in exchange, they gave him a double helping of noise. His house, innocently imprisoned between two cement-and-glass towers, began to tilt and crack under the excessive pressure. One afternoon, while he was getting dressed to go out, he watched a dropped coin roll until it came to rest against a wall. Once in this same bedroom he'd played with his toy soldiers, marshaled historic battles, Austerlitz, Waterloo, even a Trafalgar in his bathtub. Now he couldn't fill the tub because the water spilled over one edge.

"It's like living in the Leaning Tower of Pisa, but without the prestige. Just yesterday plaster fell on my head as I was shaving, and the whole bathroom wall is cracked. When will they learn that the spongy soil of our ancient lake bed cannot support the insult of skyscrapers!"

It wasn't a truly old house, but the kind of mansion

of supposed French inspiration that was popular at the beginning of the century, and no longer built after the twenties.
Actually, it more closely resembled a Spanish or Italian villa,
with its flat roof, capricious stone designs on pale stucco, and
grand entrance stairway leading to a foyer elevated above the
dampness of the subsoil.

And the garden, a shady, moist garden, solace against
the burning mornings of the high plateau; during the night
a natural collector of the perfumes of the morning to come.
What luxury: two large palm trees, a small gravel path, a sun-
dial, an iron bench painted green, burbling water channeled
toward beds of violets. With what animosity he regarded the
ridiculous thick green glass with which the new buildings tried
to defend themselves against the age-old Mexican sun. How
much wiser the Spanish conquistadors, who had understood
the importance of convent shadow and cool patios. Of course
he would defend all this against the aggression of a city that
first had been his friend and now had become his most
ferocious enemy! The enemy of Federico Silva, known to his
friends as the Mandarin.

His features were so markedly Oriental that they
obscured the Indian mask underlying them. It happens with
a lot of Mexican faces. The stigmas and accidents of known
history recede to reveal the primal face, the face that goes
back to Mongolian tundra and mountains. In this way Federico Silva was like the lost perfume of the ancient lake of Mexico: a sensitive memory, practically a ghost.

The hair of the man who wore this immutable mask
was still so black it looked dyed. But because of the changes
in the national diet he lacked the strong, white, enduring teeth
of his ancestors. Black hair, in spite of the changes. But the
essential benefits of chili peppers, beans, and tortillas, which
contain sufficient calcium and vitamins to make up for a
limited diet, were no longer present in the bodies of those
generations that had forsaken them. Now in that wretched
cup-shaped plaza he watched the young people eating junk—
carbonated drinks and synthetic caramels and potato chips

in cellophane bags, the garbage food of the North added to the leper food of the South: the trichina, the amoeba, the omnipotent microbe in every slice of pork, tamarind-flavored soft drink, and wilting radish.

In the midst of so much ugliness it was only natural that he maintain his little oasis of beauty, his personal Eden which nobody envied him anyway. Voluntarily, consciously, he had remained on the edge of the mainstream. He'd watched the caravans of fashion pass him by. He preserved a few fashions, it was true. But what he chose he preserved. When something went out of style he continued to wear it, he cultivated it and saved it from the vagaries of taste. So his style was never out of style, his suits, his hats and canes and Chinese dressing gowns, the elegant ankle-high boots for his tiny Oriental feet, the suave kid gloves for his tiny Mandarin hands.

He had been this way for years, since the forties, all the time he was waiting for his mother to die and leave him her fortune, and now, in turn, he would die, at peace, in any way he wished, alone in his house, freed finally from the burden of his mother, so extravagant and at the same time so stingy, so vain, so painted, powdered, and bewigged till her dying day. The attendants at the funeral parlor had outdone themselves. Feeling an obligation to bestow in death a more colorful and lavish appearance than life, they presented Federico Silva, with great pride, a raving caricature, an enameled mummy. The moment he saw her he'd ordered the casket sealed.

Family and friends had gathered during the days of the wake for Doña Felicitas Fernández de Silva, and her burial. Discreet, distinguished people everyone else referred to as aristocrats, as if, Federico Silva mused, an aristocracy were possible in a colony settled by fugitives, petty clerks, millers, and swineherds.

"Let us content ourselves," he used to tell his old friend María de los Ángeles Negrete, "with being what we are, an upper middle class that in spite of the whirlwinds of history has managed through time to preserve its very comfortable personal income."

The oldest name in this assemblage had acquired its fortune in the seventeenth century, the most recent before 1910. An unwritten law excluded from the group the noveaux riches of the Revolution, but admitted those damaged by the civil strife who'd then used the Revolution to recover their standing. But the customary, the honorable, thing was to have been rich during the colonial period, through the empire and the republican dictatorships. The ancestral home of the Marqués de Casa Cobos dated from the times of the Viceroy O'Donoju, and his grandmother had been a lady-in-waiting to the Empress Carlota; Perico Arauz's ancestors had been ministers to Santa Anna and Porfirio Diaz; and Federico, on the Fernández side, was descended from an aide-de-camp to Maximilian, and through the Silvas from a magistrate to Lerdo de Tejeda. Proof of breeding, proof of class maintained in spite of the political upheavals of a country known for its surprises, somnolent one day, in tumult the next.

Every Saturday Federico joined his friends to play Mah-Jongg, and the Marqués always told him, "Don't worry, Federico. No matter how it shocks us, we must admit that the Revolution tamed Mexico forever."

He hadn't seen the resentful eyes, the caged tigers lurking in the nervous bodies of the youths sitting watching the smog drift by.

## II

The day he buried his mother he really began to remember. Moreover, he realized that it was because of her disappearance that detailed memories were returning which had been buried beneath Doña Felicitas's formidable weight. That was when he remembered that once mornings could be perceived at midnight, and that he'd gone out on his balcony to breathe them, to collect the anticipated gift of the day.

But that was only one memory among many, the one

most closely resembling a revival instinct. The fact is, he told himself, that the memory of old people is stimulated by the deaths of other old people. So he found that he was waiting for the death of some uncle or aunt or friend to be announced, secure in the knowledge that new memories would attend the rendezvous. In the same way, some day, they would remember him.

How would he be remembered? Meticulously grooming himself every morning before the mirror, he knew that he had changed very little over the last twenty years. Like Orientals, who, once they begin to age, never change until the day they die. But also because all that time he'd kept the same style of dress. No denying it, in hot weather he was the only person he knew who still wore a boater like the one made famous by Maurice Chevalier. With delight, savoring the syllables, he enunciated several foreign names for that hat: *straw hat, canotier, paglietta*. And in winter, a black homburg with the obligatory silk ribbon imposed by Anthony Eden, the most elegant man of his epoch.

Federico Silva always rose late. He had no reason to pretend that he was anything other than a wealthy rent collector. His friends' sons had fallen prey to a misplaced social consciousness, which meant they must be seen up and in some restaurant by eight o'clock in the morning, eating hotcakes and discussing politics. Happily, Federico Silva had no children to be embarrassed by being wealthy, or to shame him for lying in bed till noon, waiting for his valet and cook, Donde, to bring him his breakfast so he could drink his coffee and read the newspapers with tranquillity, shave and dress with calm.

Through the years he'd saved the clothes he'd worn as a young man, and when Doña Felicitas died he gathered up her extraordinary wardrobe and arranged it in several closets, one corresponding to the styles that predated the First World War, another for the twenties, and a third for the hodgepodge style she'd dreamed up in the thirties and then affected until her death: colored stockings, silver shoes, boas of shrieking scarlet, long skirts of mauve silk, decollete blouses, thousands of necklaces, garden-party hats, and pearl chokers.

Every day he walked to the Bellinghausen on Londres Street, where the same corner table had been reserved for him since the era of the hand-tailored suits he wore. There he ate alone, dignified, reserved, nodding to passing acquaintances, picking up the checks of unaccompanied ladies known to him or his mother, none of this backslapping for him, no vulgarity, shouting, What's new! What-a-sight-for-sore-eyes! or You've-made-my-day! He detested familiarity. An almost tangible aura of privacy surrounded his small, dark, scrupulous person. Let no one attempt to penetrate it.

His familiarity was reserved for the contents of his house. Every evening he took delight in looking at, admiring, touching, stroking, sometimes even caressing his possessions, the Tiffany lamps and ashtrays, the Lalique figurines and frames. These things gave him particular satisfaction, but he enjoyed equally a whole room of Art Deco furniture, round mirrors on silvered boudoir tables, tall tamps of tubular aluminum, a bed with a headboard of pale burnished metal, an entirely white bedroom: satin and silk, a white telephone, a polar-bear skin, walls lacquered a pale ivory.

Two events had marked his life as a young man. A trip to Hollywood, when the Mexican consul in Los Angeles had arranged a visit to the set of *Dinner at Eight,* where he'd been shown Jean Harlow's white bedroom and even seen the actress from a distance: a platinum dream. And in Eden Roc he'd met Cole Porter, who'd just composed "Just One of Those Things," and Zelda and Scott Fitzgerald, who was writing *Tender Is the Night.* He'd had his picture taken with Porter that summer on the Riviera, but not with the Fitzgeralds. A photograph with a box camera that didn't need a flash. And in his room in the Hotel Negresco he'd had an adventure with a naked woman in the darkness. Neither knew who the other was. Suddenly the woman had been illuminated by moonlight as bright as day, as if the moon were the sun, a prurient, blinding spotlight stripped of the fig-leaf effect of the silver screen.

The visit to the Côte d'Azur was a constant topic of nostalgic reminiscences during the Saturday afternoon reunions. Federico was a skilled Mah-Jongg player, and three of the habitual players, María de los Angeles, Perico, and the Marqués, had been with him that summer. It had all been memorable but that one event, the incident of the blonde girl who resembled Jean Harlow. If one of the friends felt that another was about to venture into the forbidden territory, he warned him with a heavily charged look. Then everybody changed the subject, avoided talking about the past, and turned to their usual discussions of family and money.

"The two cannot be separated," Federico said as they played. "And as I have no immediate family, when I'm gone my money will be dispersed among distant branches of the family. Amusing, isn't it?" He apologized for talking about death. But not about money. Each of them had had the good fortune to appropriate a parcel of the wealth of Mexico at an opportune time—mines, forests, land, cattle, farms—and the luck to convert it quickly, before it had passed out of their hands, into the one secure investment: Mexico City real estate.

Half daydreaming, Federico Silva thought about the houses that so punctually produced his rents, the old colonial palaces on Tacuba, Guatemala, and La Moneda streets. He'd never visited them. He was totally ignorant about the people who lived there. Perhaps one day he would ask one of his rent collectors to tell him who lived in the old palaces. What were the people like? Did they realize they were living in the noblest mansions of Mexico?

He would never invest in a new building like those that had blocked out his sun and made his house list to one side. That much he'd sworn to himself. Smiling, he repeated his oath as they walked to the dining table that Mah-Jongg Saturday in his home. Everyone knew that to be received by Federico Silva was a very special honor. Only he entertained with such detail, the seating plan in a red leather holder, the places set in accord to the strictest protocol—rank, age, former posts—and the card with the name of each guest at its precise place, the menu written out in the host's own hand, Donde's impeccable service at the table.

That night as he glanced around the table, counting the absent, the friends who had preceded him in death, there was scarcely a flicker of expression on Federico Silva's Oriental mask. He rubbed his tiny porcelain Mandarin hands together: ah, there was no protocol as implacable as death, no priority more strict than that of the tomb. High overhead, the Lalique chandelier shed a vertical beam, perversely illuminating the Goyaesque faces of his table companions, the flesh of curdled custard, the deep fissures at the corners of the mouths, the hollow eyes of his friends.

Whatever became of the nude blonde girl of that night in my room in the Hotel Negresco?

A Mayan profile thrust between Federico Silva and the lady seated at his right, his friend María de los Angeles Negrete, as Donde began to serve the soup. The bridge of Donde's nose began in the middle of his forehead and his tiny eyes were crossed.

"Isn't it extraordinary," Federico Silva commented in French. "Do you realize that this type of profile and crossed eyes was a mark of physical beauty among the Mayas? To achieve it they bound the infants' heads when they were born and forced them to follow the pendulum motion of a marble suspended on a thread. How is it possible that centuries later those artificially imposed characteristics continue to be transmitted?"

"It's like inheriting a wig and false teeth." María de los Angeles whinnied like a mare.

Donde's profile between the host and his guest, his arm holding the soup tureen, the brimming soup ladle, the unexpected offense of Donde's sweat, he'd warned him for the last time, bathe after you finish in the kitchen and before you begin to serve, sometimes it isn't possible, señor, there isn't enough time, señor.

"Yours, or my mother's, María de los Angeles?"

"What, Federico?"

"The wig. The teeth."

Someone jarred the ladle, Federico Silva, Donde, or María de los Ángeles, who knows, but steaming chickpea soup disappeared into the woman's bodice, screams, how could that have happened, Donde, I'm sorry, señor. I swear, I didn't do it, ay! the curds-and-whey breasts of María de los Ángeles, ay! the scalded tits, go take a bath, Donde, you offend me, Donde, my mother's wig and false teeth, the naked blonde, Nice . . .

He awakened with a fearful start, the anguish of a desperate effort to remember what he'd just dreamed, the certainty he would never recapture it, another dream lost forever. Drunk with sadness, he put on his Chinese dressing gown and walked out on the balcony.

He breathed deeply. He sniffed in vain for odors of the morning to come. The mud of the Aztec lake, the foam of the Indian night. Impossible. Like his dreams, the lost perfumes refused to return.

"Is anything the matter, señor?"

"No, Donde."

"I heard the señor call out."

"It was nothing. Go back to sleep, Donde."

"Whatever you say, señor."

"Good night, Donde."

"Good night, señor."

### III

"As long as I've known you, you've been a real stickler about what you wear, Federico."

He'd never forgiven his old friend María de los Ángeles, who had once made fun of him by addressing him as Monsieur Verdoux. Maybe there *was* something Chaplinesque in antiquated elegance, but only when it disguised a diminishing fortune. And Federico Silva, as everyone knew, was not down on his luck. It was just that, like every person of true taste, he had the good sense to choose things that lasted. A pair of shoes, or a house.

"Save electricity. Go to bed early."

He would never, for example, wear spats and carry a cane at the same time. In his daily stroll down Cordoba Street to the Bellinghausen restaurant, he was careful to offset the showy effect of a brick-colored jacket with a Buster Brown belt he'd had made in 1933 by draping a nondescript rain-coat over his arm with studied insouciance. And only on the infrequent days when it was really cold did he wear the der-by, the black overcoat and white muffler. He was well aware that behind his back his friends whispered that the way he hung on to his clothes was really the most humiliating proof of dependence. With what Doña Felicitas had put him through, he had to make things last twenty or thirty years.

"Save electricity. Go to bed early."

But why after Doña Felicitas's death did he continue to wear the same old outfits? That was something they'd never asked him, now that he'd inherited the fortune. You could say that Doña Felicitas had deformed him, and he had turned necessity into a virtue. No, that wasn't it. His mother only pretended to be stingy. It all began with that sacred sentence —save electricity, go to bed early—said as if it were a sar-castic joke one night when she wanted to conceal her real intent, to save face, to pretend she didn't know her son was grown up, that he went out at night without asking her per-mission, that he dared leave her by herself.

"If I support you, the least I can expect is that you won't leave me here all alone, Feddie. I could die at any moment, Feddie. I know Donde's here, but I am not thrilled at the idea of dying in the arms of a servant. Very well, Feddie. I sup-pose it must be, as you say, a very, very important engage-ment to cause you to abandon your own mother. Abandon, yes, that's the word. I pray to God you make up for the hurt you've caused me, Feddie. You know how. You promised me this year you'd follow Father Tellez's spiritual exercises. Please do that little favor for me, Feddie. I'm going to hang up now. I'm feeling very tired."

She replaced the white receiver. Sitting in the bed with the burnished metal headboard, surrounded with white cushions, covered with white furs, a great ancient doll, a milk-white Punchinella, lavishing powder on a floury face in which her blazing eyes, orange mouth, and red cheeks were obscene scars, flourishing with panache the white puff, enveloping herself in a choking, perfumed cloud of rice powder and aromatic talcum, her bare skull protected by a white silk cap. At night the wig of tight, shiny black curls reposed on a cotton-stuffed head on the silver boudoir table, like the wigs of ancient queens.

Sometimes Federico Silva liked to interject a touch of the fantastic into the Saturday conversations. Nothing more satisfying than an appreciative audience, and inevitably it was easy to frighten María de los Ángeles. Federico Silva found this flattering. María de los Ángeles was older than he, and he'd been in love with her as a boy; he'd wept when the precious little sixteen-year-old had chosen to go to the Country Club ball with older boys, not with him, the devoted little friend, the humble admirer of her blond perfection, her rose-colored skin, the filmy tulle and silken ribbons that veiled and encircled her desirable flesh. Oh, beautiful María de los Ángeles. Now she looked like Goya's Queen María Luisa. He realized that in frightening her Federico Silva was still paying homage, just as he had at fifteen. But was the only possible homage gooseflesh?

"Supposedly, the guillotine was invented to spare the victim pain, you see. But the result was precisely the opposite. The speed of the execution actually prolongs the victim's agony. Neither the head nor the body has time to adjust. They feel they are still joined together, and the awareness that they are not takes several seconds to be comprehended. For the victim those seconds are centuries."

Did she understand? this long-toothed woman with the horse laugh and curds-and-whey breasts; the cruel overhead light from the Lalique chandelier could favor only a Marlene Dietrich, exaggerated shadows, funereal hollows, hallucinatory mystery. Beheaded by light.

"Without a head the body continues to move, the nervous system continues to function, the arms jerk and the hands implore. And the severed head, stimulated by a rush of blood to the brain, experiences extreme lucidity. The bulging eyes stare at the executioner. The accelerated tongue curses, remembers, denies. And the teeth clamp ferociously on the basket. Every basket at the foot of the guillotine looks as if it had been gnawed by an army of rats."

María de los Angeles exhaled a swooning sigh; the Marqués de Casa Cobos felt her pulse, Perico Arauz offered her a handkerchief dampened in cologne water. At two in the morning, after everyone had left, Federico Silva walked out onto his bedroom balcony wondering whose would be the next corpse, whose the next death, that would allow him to reclaim a bit more of his memories. One could also be a landlord of memory, but the only way to collect that rent was through another's death. What memories would his own death unleash? Who would remember him? He closed the French windows of his balcony and lay down on the white bed that had been his mother's. He tried to go to sleep by counting the people who would remember him. They might be the "best" people, but they were very few.

After the death of Doña Felicitas, Federico Silva began to worry about his own death. He instructed Donde: "When you discover my body, before you notify anybody, put this record on the record player."

"Yes, señor."

"Look at it carefully. No mistakes, I'm putting it right on top."

"Don't worry, señor."

"And open this book on the table beside my bed."

"As you wish, señor."

He wanted to be found to the strains of Schubert's "Unfinished" Symphony, with Dickens' *The Mystery of Edwin Drood* open beside him. This was the least elaborate of his fantasies about his death. He decided to write four letters.

In one he would describe himself as a suicide; in another, as a man condemned to death; in the third, as incurably ill; and in the fourth, as a victim of a human or natural disaster. This was the letter that presented the greatest difficulties. How could he synchronize the necessary three factors: his death, mailing the letter, and the disaster, an earthquake in Sicily, a hurricane in Key West, a volcanic eruption in Martinique, an air crash in ... ? He could send the other three letters to people in places scattered around the world asking them please to mail the letters written and signed by him and addressed to his friends as soon as they learned of his death; the suicide letter to María de los Angeles, the condemned-man letter to Perico Arauz, and the incurable-illness missive to the Marqués de Casa Cobos. Confusion. Uncertainty. Eternal doubt. The man about whose body we've gathered, the man we are burying, was he actually our friend Federico Silva?

Nevertheless, the predictable confusion and uncertainty of his friends were as nothing compared to his own. As he reread the three letters, Federico realized that he knew whom to send them to, but no one who would do him the favor of mailing them. He had never again traveled abroad following that trip to the Côte d'Azur. Cole Porter had died smiling, the Fitzgeralds and Jean Harlow, weeping. To whom would he send the letters? In his mind's eye he saw his bathing-suited young friends, Perico, the Marqués, and María de los Angeles, in Eden Roc forty years ago. Where was the girl now who looked like Jean Harlow? She was his only secret ally. In death she could atone for the pain and humiliation she had caused him in life.

"And who the hell are you?"

"I myself don't know as I look at you."

"Sorry! I'm in the wrong room."

"No. Don't go. I don't know who you are."

"Let me go. Let me go or I'll scream."

"Please ..."

"Let me go. Not even if you were the last man on earth.

Filthy Chink!"

The last man. Carefully, he folded the letters before replacing them in their envelopes. A heavy hand fell on his fragile shoulder: a clatter of bracelets and chains, metal striking against metal.

"What's in the envelopes, old man? Your dough?"

"Is it him?"

"Sure it's him. He goes by the snack bar every day."

"I didn't recognize him in his darling Fu Manchu bathrobe."

"You'd know him with his cane."

"Or the cute little bibs over his shoes. Shit!"

"Hey, old man, don't get nervous. These are my buddies, the Barber, and Pocahontas. They call me Artist, at your service. We won't hurt you, I promise."

"What do you people want?"

"Only a lot of stuff you don't need."

"How did you get in here?:"

"Ask the little fruit when he wakes up."

"What 'little fruit'?"

"The one who runs your errands."

"We put him out for a while. Like a light."

"I'm sorry to disappoint you. I don't keep any money in the house."

"I told you, we didn't come for your fucking money. Screw the money, old man."

"Come on, Artist. You're wasting time. Let's get going."

"Right on!"

"Barber, you entertain the walking dead here while Poca and I start collecting stuff."

"My party, Artie."

"Are the others downstairs?"

"The others? How many are there of you?"

"Christ, don't make me laugh, you old shit. Hey, he says how many are there? Christ!"

"Cuddle up to him, Pocahontas, and see how he likes that beautiful puss of yours. Give him a big smile, now; wiggle that cute little nose. That's the way, baby. Now tell him how many, what the fuck."

"Haven't you ever noticed us when you walk by the snack bar, old man?"

"No. Never. I don't lower myself to .. ."

"That's just it, baby. You should pay more attention to us. We pay attention to *you*. We've been paying attention to you for months. Right, Barber?"

"You said it. Day after fun-filled day. But let me tell you, Pocahontas, if I was you I'd feel pretty bad that the old shit didn't pick up on me, all decked out like that, all that pretty skin showing. Tongolele, you are *with* it!"

"Yeah, Fu Manchu, you sure put me down. You never once noticed me. But I bet you don't forget me now."

"All right, stop fooling around. Go see what you find in the closets, Poca. Then get the boys up here to carry out the furniture and lamps."

"On my way, Artist."

"And you, Barber, I want you to entertain his lordship here."

"Well, now, look here. I never had the pleasure of shaving such a distinguished gentleman, like they say."

"Artist! Would you look at all the old asshole's hats and shoes. He couldn't wear all these if he had a thousand legs."

"He's loaded, all right."

"What is it you want from me?"

"I want you to shut up so I can lather you nice and pretty."

"Keep your hands off my face."

"My, my. First you never noticed us, and now it's Keep you hands off my face. You sure are touchy, Fu."

"Get a load of this, but don't let it blow your mind."

"Knockout, Poca! Where'd you find the feather boas?"

"In the department store in the next room. He's got three closets stuffed full of old clothes. On my mother's grave, we hit the jackpot. Necklaces, hats, colored stockings. Anything, my lords, your heart desires!"

"You wouldn't dare. Keep your filthy hands off my mother's belongings."

"Cool it, Fu. I told you, we're not going to hurt you. What the hell's it to you? It's just a lot of junk that doesn't mean anything to you, your lamps and ashtrays and doodads. Now what the fuck good do they do you?"

"You savages would never understand."

"Hey, you hear the bad word he called us?"

"Hell, that's not bad. It's a compliment. I wear a leather vest with nothing under it and you stick a few feathers in your hair, Poca baby, but tell me, does that make us look like dumb Indians? We're the Aztecs' revenge! Well, take a good look, you old turd, because you can kiss your furniture good-bye. And I'm taking your fancy clothes and Poca's taking your mommy's. That's what we came for."

"To steal my clothes?"

"Shit, yes. All of it, your clothes, your furniture, your silver, every-*thing!*"

"But why, what value can ... ?"

"Now you put your finger on it. All this old stuff's back in style."

"And you're going to sell my possessions?"

"*Are* we! In Lagunilla market this stuff sells better than Acapulco Gold. What we are going to clear on all your pretties, old man!"

"But first, my beauty, you keep what you like best, the best necklace, the hippest feather boa, whatever grabs you, my little sweet-ass bitch."

"Don't start messing around with me, Artist. I've got my eye on that big white bed and if you get me all hot I might want to keep it for some extra slick dick tricks."

"How about a little right now?"

"Cut it out. Just take off. *You're* always hot."

"You, Barber, you entertain *him.*"

"Does he look pretty? With his face all lathered up he looks like Santa Claus."

"Do not touch me again, sir."

"Whaaaat? Here, turn this way a little so I can give you a good shave."

"I told you, don't touch me."

"Tip your head a little to the left, be a good boy."

"Keep your hands off me, you're messing my hair!"

"Be good now, little fellow."

"You miserable beggars."

"What did you call us, fathead?"

"Us, beggars?"

"Beggars beg, old man. We take."

"You're a plague. Filth. Running sores."

"We're what? Hey, Artist, you think the old man's stoned?"

"No, it just burns him to be done in while we're riding so high."

"I'm the one who'll do the riding. I'll ride the whoring mothers of every one of you cockroaches. Pigs! Worms!"

"Whoa, there, Fu Manchu. You shut your mouth when it comes to my *mamacita*. I don't stand for that."

"Cool it, Barber."

"You, the one they call Barber, you ..."

"Yes, you old bastard?"

"You are the most filthy son of a bitch I ever saw in my life. I forbid you to touch me again. If you want to touch something, make it your fucking mother's cunt!"

"Shit ... Yeah, I think we've blown it ..."

## IV

Among Federico Silva's papers was a letter addressed to Doña María de los Angeles Valle, widow of Negrete. The executor delivered it to her, and before reading it the elderly lady reflected a moment about her friend, and her eyes filled with tears. Dead barely a week, and now this letter, written when?

She opened the envelope and removed the letter. It was undated, though it bore a place of origin: Palermo, Sicily. Federico wrote of a series of slight earthquakes that had taken place recently. The experts were forecasting a major earthquake, the worst in the island since the devastating quake of 1964. He, Federico, had a premonition that his life would end here. He had ignored the evacuation orders. His situation was unique: a desire for suicide annulled by a natural catastrophe. He was closed in his hotel room, watching the Sicilian sea, the "foamy" Sicilian sea, Góngora had called it, and how fine, how appropriate, to die in such a beautiful place, so removed from ugliness, lack of respect, and mutilation of the past ... everything he most despised in life.

Dear Friend. Do you remember the blond girl who caused the commotion in the Negresco? You may believe, and with some justification, that I am so simpleminded, that my life has been so monotonous, that I have lived that life under the spell of a beautiful woman who did not wish to be mine. I am aware of the way that you, Perico, the Marqués, and all my other friends avoid the subject. Poor Federico. His one adventure ended in frustration. He grew old alongside a tyrant of a mother. And now he's dead.

You will be correct insofar as the heart of the matter is concerned, but the outward appearances were not what they seemed. I have never told anyone this. When I begged that girl to stay, to spend the night with me in my room, she refused. She said, "No, not if you were the last man on earth." Those excruciating words—can you believe it?—saved me. I told myself that no one is the last man in love, only in death. Only death can say to us, "You are the last." Nothing, no one else, María de los Angeles.

That sentence might have humiliated me but it did not intimidate me. I admit that I was afraid to marry. I felt a horror that I might prolong in my children what my mother had imposed upon me. You should know what I mean; our upbringing was very similar. I could not educate badly children I never had. You did. Forgive my frankness. The situation, I believe, authorizes it. Never mind; call my reluctance what you will—religious fear, ordinary avarice, sterile upbringing.

Naturally, you pay for this cowardice when your parents have died and as is my case, you have no offspring. You have lost forever the opportunity to give your children something better, or at least something different from what your parents gave you. I don't know. What I do know is that you run the risk of dissatisfaction and error, whatever you do. At times, if you're a Catholic, as I am, and you find yourself forced to take a young girl to the doctor for an operation, or, even worse, you send by your servant the money for her abortion, you feel you have sinned. Those children one never had: did you spare them from coming into an ugly, cruel world? Or, quite the opposite, would they throw in your face that you never offered them the risks of life? Would they call you a murderer? A coward? I do not know.

I fear that this less than forceful image of myself is the one each of you will remember. That is why I'm writing to you now, before I die. I had one love in my life, only one. You. The love I felt for you at fifteen lasted to the time of my death. I can tell you now. In you I centered the excuse for my bachelorhood and the needs of my love. I am not sure that you will understand. You were the only person I could love without betraying all the other aspects of my life and its demands. Being what I was, I had to love you as I did: faithfully, silently, nostalgically. But I was as I was because I loved you: solitary, distant, barely humanized, perhaps, by a certain sense of humor.

I don't know whether I've made myself clear, or even whether I myself truly understood myself. We all think we know ourselves. Nothing is further from the truth. Think of me, remember me. And tell me whether you can explain to me what I am about to tell you. It may be the only puzzle of my life, and I will die without solving it. Every night before I go to bed I walk out on my bedroom balcony to take the air. I try to breathe the presages of the following morning. I had learned to identify the odors of the lost lake of a city equally lost. With the years it has become increasingly difficult.

But that was not the real motive for my moments on the balcony. Sometimes, standing there, I begin to tremble, and I fear that once again the hour, the temperature, the eternal threat of storm—if only a dust storm—that hovers over Mexico City have made me react viscerally, like an animal, tamed in this clime, free in another, savage in some distant latitude. I fear, too, that with the darkness or the lightning, the rain or the dust storm, the ghost of the animal I might have been will return—or the son I never had. I carried a beast in my guts, Maria de los Angeles. Can you believe it?

The elderly woman wept as she returned the letter to its envelope. She paused for an instant, horrified, remembering the story about the guillotine that Federico liked to tell on Saturdays to frighten her. No. She'd refused to view the body with its neck slit from ear to ear by a straight-edge razor. Her morbid friends Perico and the Marqués had not been so fastidious.

*—Translated by Margaret Sayers Peden*

*Guadalupe Dueñas (Guadalajara, Jal. 1920) has dis-
tinguished herself as an essayist and writer of short
fiction, since the appearance of* Las ratas y otros cuen-
tos *in 1954. She was the recipient of a fellowship
from the Centro Mexicano de Escritores, 1961–62.*

# MARIQUITA AND ME
## Guadalupe Dueñas

I never knew why we used to move so
often. Our greatest concern was always where to put Mariquita.
Having her in her bedroom disturbed my mother; putting her
in the dining room wouldn't do, either; leaving her down in the
basement offended my father's sensibilities; and displaying her
in the living room was impossible. Visitors would have driven
us crazy with their questions. And so, invariably, after considering all the possibilities, they would install her in our room. I
say "our" because it belonged to all of us. There, counting Mariquita, seven of us slept.

My dad was always a practical man; he had travelled widely and was familiar with ships' cabins. That's where he got the
idea for the double-deck bunks, which saved space and allowed
each girl to sleep in her own bed.

39

As I explained, what mattered was finding the right place for Mariquita. Sometimes it was under a bed, other times in a strategic corner; but mostly we placed her on top of the wardrobe.

This situation only interested us two oldest girls; the rest, who were still little, weren't concerned.

To me, enjoying her company seemed like great fun; but my sister Carmelita lived oppressed by the horror of this arrangement. She would never go into the room by herself, and I'm sure it was Mariquita who was responsible for her yellow complexion; although she only saw her once, she swears that Mariquita used to follow her around the house.

Mariquita was the first-born; she was our eldest sister. I first met her when she had been in water for ten years, and I had a hard time uncovering her story.

Her past is brief and very sad: She arrived one morning with an uneven heartbeat, premature. Since no one expected her, the cradle was cold and had to be warmed with hot water bottles; they brought blankets and were careful to keep all the windows closed. Isabel, who was going to be her godmother at the baptism, thought she looked like a discolored almond, lying there on the tulle pillows. The infant looked so helpless in that canyon of glass that she was moved by tenderness to bury it in her arms. Isabel predicted that she would have blonde curls and eyes bluer than heliotrope blossoms. But the baby girl was so sensitive and delicate that she started to die.

They say that my father rushed to baptize her, and that he sat for hours on end before her little cradle, unwilling to accept her death. No one could convince him that she should be buried. He carried his foolish determination so far as to hide her in that chile jar which I found one day in the wardrobe, protected by such an odd-shaped crimson container that anyone would feel obliged to ask what it was.

I remember that, at least once a year, Papa would replace the liquid in the jar with a new chemical substance of his own design—I imagine it must have been homemade rum with caustic soda. He carried out this task with great feeling, perhaps thinking to himself that his other daughters would also be better off in silent crystal flasks, beyond all the dangers that he expected us to encounter in the world.

Naturally, we kept the secret in the family. Very few people managed to find out about it, and none of them continued being our friends. At first they were filled with astonishment, then they would move about fearfully, and finally they would hold forth with disagreeable comments about our customs. Total ostracism resulted when one of my aunts told someone that my father kept the umbilical cord of one of his daughters in a silk case. That was true. Now I preserve it; it's little, like a seahorse, and I won't throw it away because it might be mine.

Time went by, we all grew up. My parents were no longer with us; but we kept moving from house to house, and Mariquita's situation kept getting more problematic.

We rented a stately old mansion in ruins. The cracks foreshadowed its demolition. In order to shut the mouths grimacing on the walls of the rooms, we hung paintings and pictures without regard for aesthetic effect. When the crack was long, like a tunnel, we covered it with some Gobelin tapestry where cranes, swimming in indigo blue cross-stitching, could have dived into the deep hole. If the crack was cave-like, we covered it with a fine plate, a ribbon, or floral sketches. There was a problem with the cave-like hole in the lower living room; we couldn't decide whether to cover it with a Ming vase or decorate it as a suitable niche or set a Japanese engraving over it.

A musty corridor leading into the rooms framed the fountain of our palace. With righteous delusions of grandeur, we patched with marble dust the fountain's hopeless cement, which turned out to be made not of porphyry or jasper but base earthenware masquerading as stone. Behind the house, where other people would have kept chickens, we put in an American-style garden, with a lawn, a green pergola, and all sorts of vines, roses, and whatever would let us express our manorial complex.

The house looked very cheerful; but even so, there were ghosts. On the rare occasion when there was silence, there were inexplicable falls, sudden cavorting of chandeliers and walls, or unexplained shattering of pots and windows. The first few times, we minutely inspected the rooms; then we started to get used to it, and when the nonsense recurred we paid it no mind.

The servants falsely claimed that the one responsible was the little girl that we kept hidden in the wardrobe; they said that at night her ghost roamed the neighborhood. Word got around, and we were obliged to explain; since all of us were single, with impeccable reputations, the situation became very complicated. There was so much gossip that it seemed like the only decent sister was the baby in the bottle; she, at least, managed to escape the slander.

In order to bury her, we needed a death certificate, which no doctor was willing to issue. Meanwhile the baby, who had gone three years without a change of water, had sat down on the bottom of the jar, definitely bored. The yellowish liquid clouded her view.

We decided to bury her in the garden. We marked her grave with a watercress halo and a little cross, as if we were burying a canary.

Now we've moved again, and I can't get out of my mind the patch of grass that imprisons her little body. I worry whether there's someone to tend the green Limbo she inhabits, and whether the doves still coo her to sleep in the evening.

When I contemplate the beloved container which held her for twenty years, my heart clouds over with nostalgia, like the heart of one who keeps an empty cage; I feel the rush of sadness that I used to experience as I watched her sleep; I reconstruct my solitude, and discover that this little girl anchored my childhood to her mute companionship.

*—Translated by Cynthia Steele*

*Juan Villoro (Mexico D.F. 1956) is a journalist, translator, and rock music critic, as well as an accomplished writer of fiction. Following five collections of short stories, his most recent work is a novel, El disparo de argón, and he has produced two books for children.*

# REAR–VIEW MIRROR
## Juan Villoro

Felipe sat next to Roxana all through their junior year of high school. In fact, he passed biology thanks to her serious application to the study of phanerogamous plants.

Roxana dreamed of becoming a designer, and of marrying a movie actor who at the time was dedicating his energies chiefly to wrestling crocodiles and breaking the necks of jungle cats. The first project seemed to be as impracticable as the second. Roxana's clothes were a disaster. She wore earrings shaped like tiny airplanes, pointed downwards as though headed for a major accident. The fact that these earrings were a gift of the airline for which her father flew, three weeks on and one off, only partly excused her bad taste. And she was not satisfied with mooning over pictures of the muscular prince of the jungle; she had decided to take advantage of the neighborhood version,

43

in the shape of one Adolfo, whose only obvious talent was an ability to crack bricks with a karate chop (pretty modest in comparison with subduing pumas). Anyhow, Felipe spent a year alongside Roxana, admiring everything about her. Except her bad taste.

There were those who said that actually Roxana was stuck on Felipe, but decided not to go steady with him because his voice hadn't yet changed. In his third year of high school, Felipe had the mellifluous voice of an airline stewardess giving instructions about what to do in the unlikely event of a loss of compression in the cabin. He tried to roughen it by using aerosol sprays intended to combat laryngitis. Actually, for him a cold was a blessing. For a whole week he talked like Adolfo. But then he returned to being the only boy in 3-C not yet endowed with those longed-for baritone warbles that were impelling his classmates to fly off to more exotic lands, far from the flat coastal plain where he wintered alone, periodically examining the hairless armpits that kept him from taking flight.

It was certainly possible to believe that Roxana was not, could not be, in love with Adolfo. They were never seen to converse (though someone had seen them kiss, at a party). Adolfo spent recess shooting baskets, while she gossiped with her girlfriends, laughing and giggling, until she realized that Felipe was eavesdropping, straining to hear fall from her lips "Check that little piece, what a whore" and similar locutions, boldly misused but to Felipe's ears as delicious as rum-flavored caramels to the tongue.

In every class room there seemed to be at least one kid who was ridiculously rich. Tonio Bustillos Clark was the loathsome and enviable name of 3-C's millionaire. Once, when he invited the whole class to go swimming, Felipe was knocked between the eyes by the package Adolfo was showing in his swimming trunks. At first he figured it was one of Adolfo's little jokes—like when he wore big plastic ears, or hands that looked like they had been charred in the oven. In the dressing room, however, he could see that this was no prosthesis; the vision provoked a glassy stare of the kind he did not wear again until many years later when he first tried cocaine.

Felipe dog-paddled to the corner of the pool where Roxana was twitching her nose because she had gotten water in it.

"You're always crowding me," she said, squirting a stream of water in his face.

"No, what it is I've got this great story for you," and he proceeded to invent a piece of gossip that he well knew would send her into fits of laughter, as long as it took a good swipe at someone else.

At fifteen, Roxana had a body somewhat less powerful than the rest of the girls in the class. She didn't quite seem up to the 1000-meter trials. (In contrast, Pat had breasts that could always be relied upon to buoy her up, and which focussed nearly all glances in the pool.) Roxana was thin. Felipe would not have dared to say that she was thin. But she was thin. She had chestnut hair down to her waist and a constellation of moles on her neck that Felipe studied like a crazed astronomer. There was a space between her front teeth and she amused herself in the pool by squirting water through it. Her bathing suit was as ugly as the rest of her attire: bright pink anchors emblazoned on her frail waist, under her tentative breasts, in the curve that led to the place where Felipe's gaze had so often come to rest. He would have been willing to have his back teeth removed without anesthetic, in exchange for the chance to caress the hills and valleys of Roxana's beauty. Not so: he was even more captivated by her eyes, her nose, her lips—so delicate that a caress might seem an assault. Impossible to imagine that Adolfo might touch her without causing damage. Felipe had seen him crush soft-drink cans as though they were Kleenex, and hold a basketball with one hand (downward, of course, a trick not everyone can manage).

One afternoon when there was nothing good on television, Felipe decided to do a little body-building. He did so many push-ups that, on the last one, his arms turned to jelly and his mouth fell shut so that he bit his tongue. He spent two weeks talking like a three-year-old.

Hardly had he recovered from this punishment when some nervy lady on a bus approached him and asked if he were a boy or a girl. This was early in the 70s, a time when even soccer players wore their hair long (and were the last to give it up), and Felipe had slight curls over his ears. When he got home, he spent three hours in front of the mirror, trying to force into his features some sign of virility.

At that time, the movie *Death in Venice* was showing. Felipe would not have gone to see it except for the comments about the "angelic child" (that was how his mama described him, while his stupid sister said "Mmmmmmm") who appeared in it. He walked out of the theatre convinced that compared to this creature he was Pedro Armendáriz. But the sensation lingered until the next day. He spoke to Roxana about the film.

"Oh yes, the boy is so beautiful!" The words hit him like a shot of novocaine. It made no sense when everybody (public opinion in this crowd was frightfully authoritarian: "one" was the same as "everyone") had seen Roxana kissing Adolfo, who had all the refinement of a Basque jai alai player, and at the same time she could admire this boy who, truth to tell, seemed almost a Nordic version of Roxana.

The time came when Felipe gave up hope: his voice would never change nor would his testicles grow. Two doctors reassured him that if all else failed they could inject hormones. In fact it wasn't necessary. His voice changed . . . two months after he and Roxana went their separate ways.

The school they attended didn't have its own college preparatory level. Felipe's father reminded him that the family's financial condition was shaky, spoke of private prep schools as though they were inaccessible chalets in Switzerland, and encouraged his decision to enroll in a cheap college nearby. Roxana, in contrast, pointed her airplanes toward a private school that would help her to realize her dream of being an interior designer.

Felipe knew that he would see her for the last time at their graduation party. Actually, she asked him to be her formal partner for the waltz. Later on, he would reproach himself for not responding with more enthusiasm. He had occupied the next desk to Roxana for a whole year, had passed biology thanks to her help, danced the Viennese waltz with her at the junior ball ... What more could he want?

Adolfo danced with Paz and together they were the most agile and the most photographed couple. Felipe skimmed over the parquet of the ballroom floor, feeling for a brief moment a kind of aristocratic glamour. Afterwards, he wondered if perhaps Roxana had asked him to dance because they were about the same height.

When the dance was over, they all went to the home of Tonio Bustillos Clark, with the thrilling assurance that this time their parents would let them party until dawn. The girls got drunk for the first time in public, there were pillow fights and other commotions. Adolfo broke a Chinese vase and Felipe enjoyed more than ever the scolding he got.

A few minutes before three in the morning, Felipe was wandering the hallways, his necktie on his forehead and a glass of mineral water in his hand. For no particular reason, he entered a room that was completely in darkness. His eyes had barely begun to adjust when he heard the voice of Roxana.

"Here I am, stupid."

He approached, without knowing for sure that he was moving in the right direction, until he felt Roxana's arms around his neck. She kissed him, her impetuous tongue surprising his. The glass of mineral water fell to the floor, the bubbles burping themselves out on the carpet. Roxana's hand moved to Felipe's chest and continued downward to the same place that was the frequent object of Felipe's own preoccupation. She broke away suddenly and turned on the light. Even so, she continued to behave as though he were the one she had been waiting for in the bedroom.

"Not here. I'll wait for you in the garden in half an hour."

Of course, who did Felipe encounter in the hallway but Adolfo, strolling with his hands in his pants pockets and his shirt half unbuttoned, with that I-don't-give-a-damn look. Just a few yards away was his dream of dreams, that fleeting image that Felipe had tried to capture in his solitary nights, and Adolfo proceeded in complete calm, even stopping to tell Felipe a nasty joke about a Russian, an American, and a Mexican Indian.

At three-thirty Felipe was in the garden, sure that she would not show up. True to form, Roxana had worn to graduation a terrible outfit: an intense strawberry pink, much too tight, as if she had been wrapped forcibly in the fabric. She had glowed like a flame among her classmates, in their gowns the color of champagne or of butter pecan ice cream. If she did appear in the garden, it would be something like a chromatic explosion. Felipe awaited the bright flash with the urgency of an accident victim waiting for an ambulance.

The surprise of seeing her on the terrace that adjoined the garden was cancelled out by another even greater: the tight dress forced Roxana to walk with tiny Japanese steps, so that she decided to hop on one foot in order to reach Felipe. He stood firm as a goalie about to defend a penalty kick. About three yards away from the spot where he stood with arms and legs tensed—as if in fact the ball were hurtling toward him—Roxana gave a quick half-turn and ran in the opposite direction. Felipe followed. The home of Bustillos Clark was in the Pedregal district, so his pursuit involved leaping among chunks of volcanic rock, maguey plants, and spiny yuccas. She was barefoot and it was impossible to imagine that she could run on those stones without crying out in pain.

After three circuits, Roxana headed straight for the house. Felipe saw her running directly toward a glass wall. he shouted, but she ran on, hearing nothing but her own laughter and sure that what she saw ahead of her was the entrance to the terrace.

He saw her fall amid a shower of glass. He ran to find someone. The maid and the gardener accompanied him to the spot where Roxana was crying in a pool of blood.

The ambulance arrived with the dawn. Felipe, in tears, stood on the sidewalk. Adolfo, too, was wet-eyed. He placed a large hand on Felipe's shoulder and confessed that he had screwed her. But Felipe could not bring himself to confess that the accident was his fault. There they remained for almost two hours, linked by their mutual suffering, until Felipe decided to leave behind what remained of the party.

At least he thought he was leaving it behind. For months he could think of nothing else but Roxana's features disfigured by the accident: a face even redder than that awful graduation dress, her teeth bloodied.

After two years Felipe met the first girlfriend who agreed to be his lover. In a moment of automotive intimacy (the windows covered, their bodies in the back seat), he told her the story of Roxana. His highschool love was a flirt, she said. Felipe defended Roxana with such passion that his girlfriend decided to call it quits.

He kept thinking he saw Roxana in movie theatres, restaurants, airplanes. It was always some other girl with irregular features.

Felipe's own features changed so much that at one point he feared that his face was going to turn out exactly the opposite of what it had been in adolescence. But some mysterious genetic design halted this rough transformation.

On graduating from the university, he had not-married. His belated success with women encouraged him to put off any commitment. At least that was his interpretation of the matter. But there was something more. And this something wore ankle sox. Ruben Saavedra, his best friend in recent years, pointed out that at twenty-five Felipe had a girlfriend of twenty-two, at twenty-eight one of nineteen, and the current one was seventeen.

"Forget Roxana, my friend. You're never going to find her again."

"I guess I just like the young ones."

"Hmmmm. Humbert Humbert," said Ruben.

Felipe didn't get the allusion, but he did understand the admonitory gesture: the wagging index finger that dubbed him a satyr, a nostalgic fool trying to copulate with the past, a hopeless pervert.

Eventually Ruben changed his tune and advised Felipe to seize any opportunity to track her down. But they seemed to be on separate paths that would never cross. Felipe never knew her address or her telephone number. They had no friends in common. When he inquired at Aeromex, they informed him that Captain Meléndez and his crew had died in a plane crash. He found no Roxana Meléndez in the telephone book.

When he reached his thirty-fifth birthday, his friends gave up introducing him to women and started to recommend gay bars.

Ruben was in the habit of giving little dinner parties on Fridays. He sought out exotic Indian recipes to ignite his friends' palates with three-alarm curries. He prepared Arab pastries (that presumably could be digested with the help of a two-hour ride on camelback) and many other emphatic dishes. The diners varied as much as the menus; there were not many of Ruben's acquaintances who were wiling, on a weekly basis, to let their stomachs be a landing-field for UFOs. Certainly Ruben could not harbor any doubt about Felipe's friendship: every Friday, Felipe violated his bland diet and his Maalox therapy with his friend's bizarre cuisine.

The supper on this particular Friday was vegetarian. The air reeked of ginger. Ruben introduced one married couple to Felipe and assured him that the rest of the guests would be along at any moment.

"Just stay in that chair. I don't want you falling to the floor when you see the surprise I've invited for you." The couple laughed heartily. Both of them, Ruben said, were "very modern."

The next guest to arrive was a good-natured Hercules who worked in film doing special effects. The first effect was

his face: he had a tic that came near to hypnotizing Felipe.
In half an hour, he consumed three Cuba Libres, his features
seemed to soften even more, and the tic got worse. If this
was Ruben's surprise, Felipe figured he might as well go right
ahead and eat his tofu sandwich. The couple kept on laughing at everything, casting some doubt on Ruben's notion
of modern.

At this point the bell rang. Ruben was busily engaged
washing the cauliflower. Felipe answered the door. If he had
been drunk, the vision he saw in the hall would have sobered
him up.

He couldn't believe that she recognized him immediately—despite the inroads in his hairline, and his long,
almost mutton-chop sideburns. Ruben must have given her
a few hints.

"You haven't changed a bit," he exclaimed.

"Liar!" she said.

Of the two, she told the truth, It wasn't that Roxana
had aged, but the features that had seemed almost charm-
ing in a skinny little girl now appeared to be character flaws.
She had put on a little weight, losing the slightly sunken
cheeks that had made her the most photogenic girl in the
class album, and gained a definite sensuality in the legs that
now were crossed before Felipe's gaze.

Roxana had met Ruben in the most casual manner.
Ruben had started a conversation with her in a bakery.

"Right away he started to talk as if I were a lost sister."
Roxana laughed and Felipe suddenly recalled what the sudden shock of seeing her had momentarily erased from his
mind. The Roxana who was talking to him now had nothing
in common with those spectral visions, sprung from crypts
or hospitals, that had invaded his nightmares. When they
spoke of the long-ago accident, Felipe told her that not a sign
of it remained.

"Don't bet on it," she said. "Look. There's a little chunk
of lip missing." Roxana lifted her upper lip and Felipe could
see a whitish scar, hardly bigger than a mole.

Later, the special effects monster took over Roxana. By the seventh Cuba Libre his words were eruptions and his face volcanic lava. Felipe used the time to inventory the changes that had taken place in Roxana: the generous curve of her bosom that had come (so to speak) with the fullness of time; the hands, thicker and more capable; a bruise on her heel, showing almost black through her stocking. She was the kind of woman one called "attractive", to distinguish her from those who were truly beautiful. Although he no longer felt any guilt, he recalled uneasily the graduation party at which Roxana had played a double deception: she was not a virgin, nor did she really want him.

A little while later they were chatting again. Roxana filled him in on the events of her life since they had parted. To Felipe it seemed providential that she had recently been divorced. Roxana had two children and, she said, she certainly didn't want to wake them; wouldn't it be better, she asked, if they went to his apartment?

He helped her to put on her raincoat, a garment he had neglected to notice earlier. It was an awful plastic number, red and wrinkled. Her tastes had not entirely changed.

Outside it was drizzling. Felipe had parked his car several blocks away and had to negotiate the puddles that trembled with the drops of rain and the shimmer of the mercury lamps.

"Look at the moon." Roxana paused while the light rain touched her face. In the sky there was indeed a tenuous blur, something that behind many layers of cloud must have been a full moon.

They kissed. The wind wrapped a sheet of newspaper around their legs.

He opened one button of her raincoat. She stopped him. "Not here. Let's go to your place."

Arriving at the corner, Roxana broke away from him, gave him a quick glance, then started to run. Felipe started after her and slipped. The red raincoat shimmered in his gaze. Then he saw the car turn treacherously into the street. Rox-

ana crossed directly in front of the annihilating speed of the
vehicle. Felipe heard the horn and closed his eyes. The quiet
of the night was shattered by the burst of sound. There was
a light skidding sound, strangled by the water.

When Felipe opened his eyes the car was fishtailing
out of sight. On the other side of the street was Roxana. Smiling. Waiting for him.

*—Translated by David Bowen*

*Rafael Pérez Gay (Mexico D.F. 1957) is a widely read journalist, presently editor of the magazine Nexos. His most recent collection of short fiction is Llamadas nocturnas (1990).*

# BIG TEARS
Rafael Pérez Gay

The sun was beginning to warm the morning when Javier Espitia approached the front door of the house and gave two urgent knocks.

"Good day, ¿what can I do for you?" said the fat man who opened the door.

"I'm here to cry," Espitia said, his eyes already full of tears.

"You don't say. ¿And you expect me to believe such a big lie?" The fat man pushed out his chest as if to drink in the air of that warm April morning whose mildness was unexpected and uncertain.

"Really," Espitia repeated, "I'm here to cry."

"If someone's died, forget it."

"No one close to me's died."

"If your woman's left you, tough."

"No woman's ever left me."

"If you've lost your job then, better move on along."

"I've never been run off a job."

"I'll tell you something: people come here to cry, to cry buckets. But frauds have it tough. We don't accept little crocodile tears."

"I'm not going to be a slacker, I promise."

"We'll have to make some tests," Fatso told him with the look of someone about to uncover an imposter. Espitia had two swollen eyes and a red nose.

He now had to follow the fat man through a corridor of colonial arches. At the back was the fountain of a central patio onto which the upper storey rooms opened with their high ceilings and opaque glass doors. In the inner corridors some men were walking, looking down at the toes of their shoes, moving along the way sad people do. There were women sitting on the benches of a side garden where geraniums were growing and chestnut trees gave a cool, peaceful shade.

Espitia entered the office, its antique furniture surrounded by carved wooden bookcases. Behind a writing desk, this Mature Man, looking neat and agreeable, sipped the salt of his own tears. He wiped his nose with a pink Kleenex and said, as if he had known this man for many years, "Very well, Espitia, ¿and to what do we owe your visit?"

"I'm here to cry," he said, his eyes brimming.

"I'm only going to warn you of one thing, Espitia," Mature Man said as he pulled out another Kleenex. "We're not going to help you. We're not going to tell you your daddy didn't want you, or your mother was a wretch, or that you're irredeemably mediocre. Not at all. You're going to cry all by yourself, without anyone helping you. But first, tell me, ¿why do you want to cry?"

"Because I feel very bad. Life doesn't mean anything— it's hell," Espitia said, convinced of the strength of his arguments.

"Please, Espitia, that's a vulgar theory. One cries

because one cries, period. Don't confuse matters. It's possible what you need is psychoanalysis. Lots of chances for tears there. Or even better—three friends and three bottles of rum, or a dog that'll bite you. But let's get on with it. Make yourself comfortable in that armchair. ¿Kleenex or handkerchief?"

"A handkerchief, please."

Fatso offered him a brand new strikingly white handkerchief. Espitia felt along the edge of the armchair and put his elbows on his knees and his hands on his face, in the classical position of the weeper. He began with timid little moans as if he did not want anyone to hear them. A minute later, as if all the world's sadness had dropped on his head, he began panting, letting out choked cries, then inhuman howls that verged on hysterics. He slid out of the chair as if its height might have hampered him in spitting out his despair, and he sank to the floor in the fetal position. He kept crying that way, as he hadn't done since he was ten and found out his father would die from trouble with his pancreas, a swollen, useless pancreas, and he was dying too from sadness and rage because his business had fallen into absolute shambles.

Mature Man rescued him from his sadness. "Not bad, not bad. But don't try to impress us. We've dealt with exceptional mourners, men and women who cried masterfully, people who've spent years in a melancholic pit perfecting the difficult art of crying. We've dealt with people who cried for just anything, real Magdalenes at the foot of the cross."

Espitia blew his nose in the handkerchief and cleaned his visibly swollen eyes. He even moved as if he were on a train bound for Morelia and was bouncing in his seat with a motion that was rhythmic, definite, ceaseless.

Mature Man wiped away his own tears and said, "We need some data to fill out your application card and begin proceedings. ¿How often do you cry?"

"All the time." Espitia snorted his sinuses clear.

"Please, Espitia, answer."

"At least three times a week."

"And with a batting record like that—worthy of the Culiacan Tomato-Pickers—you want to be one of us. ¡Oh, Espitia! I believe you're fooling yourself. The least outstanding cry a daily quota. ¿How long have you been crying?"

"Okay, as a kid I cried enough, from one corner of the house to another."

Before he went on, Fatso Mourner put the box of Kleenex near him. Meanwhile Mature Man asked him his age.

"Thirty-three," Espitia answered.

"You do have the advantage there, I admit it. The thirties are the ideal medium for tears, a veritable petri dish. It's a biological matter: Having just left youth behind, you have entered maturity. During those years one cries a great deal, and with admirable force. As for those entering the realm of the thirties—everything—no matter how trifling—makes them cry. Thirty-year-olds feel they have everything before them, that they're in the best time of their lives—and, of course, that's reason enough to cry. On the other hand, at forty, crying loses its drive, although a certain lachrymose wisdom does come about. Even so, forty-year-olds are only occasional, small-time criers. What's worse, they always make use of friends, alcohol, analysts. Besides, they forget the reason for their tears too fast and invariably end up saying they're on the old age train and they've done nothing with their lives. On the other hand, twenty-year-olds cry without knowing why—they're blind mourners, so to speak. And when they cry, just think, they hug each other. It's embarrassing, an embarrassing spectacle seeing twenty-year-olds tightly embracing and lacerated with juvenile griefs, getting each others' shoulders and bosoms wet.

"Then the fifty-year-olds, for their part, suffer a lot when they cry, and it's because they know they're shipwrecks of time: neither young nor old, they cry in the afternoons—unlike the old, who cry at night and in the dark. The old ones have learned that tears are the only truth there is in us, so at night they cry for their children and grandchildren, for the dead husband or vanished wife.

"Now, at whatever age, there may be timid mourners, and shameless mourners. There are also the contained and the explosive—which aren't the same thing as those I've just mentioned. The latter are dangerous because they tend to break things when they sob.

"We also know that in times of birth, death, or separation there are always tears. I'd like to know what kind of crier you are. Cry again, please."

Javier Espitia remained confused; he had already cried as he hadn't since he was ten. He could not repeat the act with the same intensity. Fatso Mourner put a new box of Kleenex near him, but he chose the wrinkled, wet handkerchief he had in his hands. Neat and agreeable, Mature Man assumed a kind look.

"Go on, Espitia, cry, cry in peace, openly."

Javier Espitia threw himself down on the camel-colored carpet and began beating the floor with his fists and set about crying because life was shitty. He kept on crying, with genuine distress, because no one in the world understood him, because he felt himself the loneliest man on the planet, because he worked like an ass and didn't have enough money; he cried because he was frantic about his unfulfilled hopes, and all his shattered illusions and squandered dreams. He cried about love and about rage, he cried about his thirty-three years and his solitude.

"Noted," agreeable-looking Mature Man said, directing his remarks to Fatso. "A case of Shameless Mourner who can spill tears without any grief, as it were. Not bad. Well, Espitia, your public presentation will be tomorrow. The gentleman will take you to your room. You can come and go if you want; this isn't a jail, or a rehabilitation center either."

"¿Can I take a book?" Espitia asked, scanning the bookshelves, and still sniffling.

"¿What are you saying? *I'll take up some little books with discouraging plots, I'll make myself very sad and tomorrow I'll cry as if my mother had died.* ¿Who do you think you're dealing with? You thought: *I'll take up* Madame Bovary, read the suicide chapter, remember too those days when I read Flaubert, when I was a young man full of loves and enthusiasms and ready to get with it. Or better: I'll look on the shelves for something by Onetti, I'll read 'Bienvenido Bob' or 'Tan triste como ella,' and surrounded by the ingenuous air of those years when you believed life was like that, reading and writing like Onetti, you'll go into such a depression that tomorrow you'll give us a historic cry. Not at all, Espitia. You're going all by yourself to your room without books or music, without a single poem. ¿Or what? ¿Do you want us to give you 'On the Death of Major Sabines' in order to pass the night? ¿Do you think we're stupid?"

On the way back to the corridor of colonial arches he'd entered through, Javier Espitia saw coming toward him a young woman, thirty-six and crying with infinite sadness. Without saying anything she hugged him as if she were his sister. They cried together for several minutes with a profound, inexplicable grief. Farther on, as he went up the stairs which led to the rooms, a man hailed him in the distance while he wiped dry some large melodramatic tears.

The room was very much like a room in a colonial-style hotel, perfect for rest and happiness: period furniture, wide bed, secretary for writing letters, indirect lighting, thick curtains with symmetrical pleats, bathroom with a tub, and TV-radio fixed to the wall.

Espitia threw himself, fully clothed, on the bed and turned off the light. Before going to sleep he recalled the days when his mother had taken him to school and fried tortillas in oil to make tostadas when there wasn't any money in the house. Extending that branch of memory, he drew into the darkness of the room the very afternoon when his father carried him to Chapultepec Park with a soccer ball and showed him the chanfle, the magical spin-kick. That was the day he was sure his dad was a wise, unconquerable, happy giant, and felt proud of having him and no other father. Not knowing how, he came to the point where he saw him again, this time afflicted with business troubles; the creditors came one morning to take away the living room and the dining room and the flowerpots before the undaunted, proud gaze of his mother who had tended them with such exceptional diligence.

Espitia could not hold the machine back: he had seen his big brother go to Europe with a suitcase full of illusions and books and dreams of triumph; he had seen his sisters on a corner, scared to death, kissing a suitor who was filled with some unlikely certainty of the Sixties. He saw the women he had wanted, those who had forgotten him, those he had dropped.

He cried all night, until he heard the first steps outside and light filtered through the pleats of the curtains. He got up from his bed then, put his shoes on, fixed his hair, fixed everything that needed to be fixed before leaving the room. He went in the bathroom, turned the cold water faucet like one opening the door of hope. He felt the cold water on his face and, turning to the mirror, told himself, "I'm ready."

*—Translated by James Hoggard*

*Severino Salazar (Tepetongo, Zac. 1947) is one of Mexico's outstanding regional voices and the author of four novels; the first,* Donde deben estar los catedrales, *was awarded the Juan Rulfo prize for a first novel. His most recent book is* La arquera loca *(1992). The following story appeared in* Las aguas derramadas, *a collection published in 1986.*

# 'JESUS, MAY MY JOY BE EVERLASTING'
## Severino Salazar

### I

*W*hen *Adelaida Avila died of old age, all of us in Zacatecas thought this meant the end of her house, that house sitting high on that hill, always there as if exchanging glances with the city day in and day out. That house through which so many of us women had passed over the years. But no, the house had more to say on the matter. Tino González, her successor, brought new life to the house and reopened it a few months later with the savings of the deceased Adelaida Avila, who had been his mistress, though in name only. Tino González did not serve her as a man, for he had been rotting ever since his youth; he only—and this he did do—protected her and managed her business. Now the house was smelling of fresh paint and newly bought furniture; it shone once again*

61

*atop the same hill. And the man had given the house a new attraction: he extended the bar onto the terrace, enclosed it with windows—wide, tall windows that reached the lofty roof and looked implacably onto the city—and built an enormous dance floor of polished cement that looked like water with a raised section for the band. On Saturdays there was music and dancing all night long; the gaiety lasted until the roosters started crowing and the light of dawn began to encircle the house. By that day and age the Zacatecans knew perfectly well how to behave in a place like this. They didn't start fights or cause a ruckus: they minded their business and we all had a good time. But suddenly, who knows from where, Don Tino González pulled out a dancer and singer, complete with husband. Some say they arrived from the north, although when they showed up in the brothel, no one cared where they were from. (The conjectures all began when the man disappeared and the woman no longer sang or danced.) From the moment she set foot on the dance floor of the house now belonging to Don Tino González, she was received enthusiastically and all the men wanted to see and hear her. She sang on Fridays, Saturdays and Sundays. The singing lasted the whole weekend, stopped on Monday, and began again the following Friday. Her fame quickly raced through the state. She attracted people like a powerful magnet, irresistible, no matter how far away you are. Zacatecas is the hub of many highways and has many attractions, like its movie theaters and its awfully big stores. Which is why it wasn't long before she had to sing and dance every night. Don Tino González's house was always packed on the weekends; by midnight there wasn't even room to breathe. The girl singer's husband was a boy not more than twenty-three years old, dark, tall and thin; well-formed, sinewy muscles; large, veiny hands; large eyes as well, elongated, with a sad gaze, although he always had a smile on his lips. He didn't have eyes for any other girl, although it was not rare for the girls of the house, behind his wife's back, to try to seduce him. And he would get rid of them as if they were a necessary evil, as if he were ac-*

customed to this happening, and would leave them with a
look of boredom on his face, not letting anything disturb his
inner world. There was even a woman who became obsessed
with the boy—it never fails—the one named Cristina. She
longed to get rid of the singer and take her place, supplant
her in the world that held the two of them, but, disillusioned
that she could not achieve any success and certain that she
could not bear to suffer seeing him every day, so close and
unattainable, she decided to leave for Fresnillo to go to a house
she knew there which was frequented by young miners who
looked a lot like him, so that her life would not grow any
sadder. And she went to search, among the men leaving the
mine, for a man like the one she had set eyes on. You could
see from miles off that Ildefonso—that was his name—was
in love with his dancer, whom they announced every night
as Terry Holiday. It seemed as though he was always thinking of her even when the two of them were together, as if
imprisoned by an insatiable love, as if that woman, her music,
her words, her movements, and her rhythm were forever spinning around in his head like brilliantly colored butterflies.
He was looking in her direction all the time—on the dance
floor, seated at a table, or wherever—while he prepared the
drinks and snacks consumed there. He was the one who gave
orders to the waiters and made sure that everything ran
smoothly at the bar and in the kitchen. But one thing is for
sure: he always had his eyes on his wife. Not as if he were
watching over her, because she didn't have eyes for other men
either; the looks they exchanged back and forth were not
tainted with jealousy; they contained a confidence the Zacatecans found hard to comprehend. They lived in their own
world and carried with them, wherever they went, invisible
threads that always held them together. No one was ever able
to penetrate that universe, so small and yet so large, or to
break those bonds, so strong and yet so fragile, especially
given the place. They lived here, in two modest rooms at one
end of, and nearly detached from, the ranch house. They slept
nearly the whole day through and would arrive at the dance

hall just after eight, the two of them holding hands, fresh and recently bathed, the woman dressed to sing and dance three sets until four in the morning. She was tall and dark as well. Someone said they looked like twins. Along with the legend of being a good singer and dancer, another one spread that she was an incorruptible woman; perhaps that was the root of much of the fascination she aroused in those who came to see her dressed scantily and with two large, pink ostrich feathers adorning her head. I never took a liking to that woman. She seemed very distant. She would look at us as if we weren't for real, like a fish from inside its fishbowl, or from inside death itself. Who did she think she was? She never spoke to us or told us her sorrows or let us tell her ours. As if we weren't equals, as if we didn't live off the same thing and in the same place. Her songs spoke of an inner world—violent, delicate and beautiful, fragile as the perfumed flower of a prickly pear that grows and spreads its petals onto the spines pointing up like swords—that made her body writhe on that hot, smoke-filled dance floor redolent of liquor and pierced by spotlights. Music, love, passion and gaiety were the elements that made up the atmosphere contained within Don Tino González's house, to the back of which went the pilgrims who climbed the hill every night. And through Terry Holiday, it was as if each person discovered his own separate world, that world that had remained undiscovered for so long. Terry and the boy were very young—we were all very new then. They were just beginning to enjoy their lives; each had the other and the two of them were one. You could see that fate was shining magnificently on them. If anyone had asked them if they wished to be something more or have more in life, they would have looked at each other in puzzlement, for they never would imagine that a human being could come to feel such tremendous uncertainty. Tino González's house was the place to be. That's the way things were until one night, when General Aniceto López Morelos appeared. Then our lives all took different paths.

## II

(They would say to me: Florentino, tell us how General Aniceto López Morelos turned up here, during the *cristero* rebellion.* Someone would always ask me when we'd be standing here at the entrance to Tepetongo and we'd see him going to Zacatecas or going back to the Víboras Hacienda to the south. This town had the cursed luck to have suffered him so nearby, with only a long irrigation canal to separate us from him, and the road that skirts the canal leads right into the center of the hacienda. Well, to fill you in on a little bit of history, there we were fighting in the rebellion as it neared its end. First, General Montalba arrived in a train to Calera. No sooner had he got his troops out of the boxcars and cattle cars than he was defeated. The brainless fools propped their machine guns on mules and fired them that way. The poor animals, like pinwheels gone crazy, rushed at their own soldiers, firing on them: they defeated themselves. As one might expect, they had sent for him from Mexico City, and that's when, a little while later, Aniceto López Morelos arrived like one of those tornadoes that brings bad weather in its wake. He came in by the Valley side, killing people to his heart's content, already sowing the legend of cruelty and terror that would follow him to the grave. He was a wicked person with no remorse. As he made his way, he burned entire towns to the ground, killed many priests, and finally tortured the priest Juan Chorrey without mercy, revealing what the imagination of a depraved man is capable of. He was an example of villainy, of what the devil himself would do, for by all indications that man was possessed by the devil. He made us tremble and reflect a bit on the evil running loose in the world. He came to the Víboras Hacienda driving ahead of him everything he had rustled along the way. The last remaining daughter of the owner of the hacienda joined him.

---

*cristero* rebellion: a clerical antirevolutionary uprising that began in 1926.

I think it was more out of fear and to keep from losing what she had. And since she was a woman already advanced in her years, she soon vanished from the earth. She was buried in the beautiful Víboras cemetery, where all her ancestors lay. Legend has it that the old man frightened her to death. In any case, the general remained in charge of this zone, previously one of the most rebellious in the country. And soon he was feared throughout the region. One of the men who also arrived with him was Salvador Chávez, nicknamed "Cowboy," but he only lasted two years, thank God. Imagine what it would have been like to suffer under two men as evil as them, for the so-called Cowboy was like the general's twin brother, his righthand man, just as mean and heartless. He had helped the general fight the *cristeros* and rustle the cattle with which he filled the pastures of the hacienda: dairy cattle, fierce bulls, and herds of horses. There were so many cattle, they were coming in from every direction: stolen, I used to say, from nearby and from far and wide. General Aniceto López Morelos's appetite knew no bounds. And there would always be the person who came to claim his poor lost animals. All those people would mysteriously disappear. There are people buried all around Víboras. Nor could anyone enter the pastures: they were tightly guarded by his soldiers. From then on, his was the arm of the law throughout these parts. He installed the municipal presidents and his vote was very important in deciding who would be governor.

The prison in his barracks was empty: capital punishment was always the only sentence. He was feared throughout the region; he desolated it. There weren't even thieves around anymore. We were at peace, the truth be told, but you couldn't even take a deep breath. He was a thief himself and couldn't stand to look at one. He didn't forgive anyone anything. Miraculously, one man escaped his soldiers and tells that a mile or two behind the walls of the hacienda is a thick, black wood, and everywhere men are hanging from the trees, some nothing but bare skeletons and others with a few shreds of clothing still stuck to them. And the man who visits a landscape like that never makes it out to tell the tale. In short, this general was such an outlaw that he even stole heaven, but that's a horse of a different color. In any event, Cowboy helped him a lot in constructing his world, his empire. When we *cristeros* were finally given amnesty right there in Víboras, we came down from the hills to hand over our animals, saddles, bandoliers, rifles, ammunition, and all our gear. Cowboy filled a granary with all that stuff, and we went back to our homes by streets and paths. Some disappeared once more over the hills. Until one day when Cowboy was running around drunk – he too was full of vices – and like a revelation he got this hunch: the general was going to get rid of him. So, as the general was out around Zacatecas, Cowboy availed himself of his absence to steal some horses and other goods and take refuge in the sierra, declaring himself a rebel. Actually, no one ever figured out why he did it, since the general held him in high esteem; he would have forgiven him anything, for he felt a strange love for the so-called Cowboy, the kind that is only felt in prisons and between criminals. In any event, more men joined up with Cowboy every day. He would ride between Víboras and Tepetongo in the middle of the night and we would scarcely even know it. I'm sure that on those nights the general would sit up in his bed listening for him to pass by with a touch of fear and joy, going over the crazy moments of their friendship. Cowboy knew the whole state and its mountain ranges like the back of his hand. No army could have beaten him. Until one of his own men betrayed and killed him and the band broke up. Meanwhile, the general's fortune was taking on fantastic proportions. It was said he had safes brimming with everything he had stolen and now what the hacienda produced, for he made soldiers on the state's payroll work his land and take care of his cattle. Until a soldier arrived whom they called "Boss." He was a tall, thin man, with small eyes and red hair. And he certainly sized up the general. A friendship began between them that we found inexplicable. The

general held him in very high esteem, for he had arrived at
his moment of greatest need.)

### III

By then, the general was an old man. Squat, fat and beardless,
his face shone like the blackest patent leather. His hair was
short and thick, graying, and so straight it lay flat; his voice
was sly and shrill like a woman's. And he was unable to say
more than three words in a row without sticking in another
three curse words. General Aniceto López Morelos had never
set foot in the whorehouse despite the fact that he spent the
night in a hotel in Zacatecas all the time. I had paid a visit
with the sergeant and other soldiers shortly after being sent
to the barracks here. What would be the point for a man like
him, who could have any woman he chose at any hour of
the day or night and fill his hacienda with them? But that
very day we had arrived in Zacatecas in pursuit of this other
woman who had left him. The thing is, that poor old guy,
he couldn't even get it up anymore. She was a really pretty
girl he had stolen from a store in Jerez more than two years
earlier. Everyone in Víboras said that the old bugger was really
in love, because he would take her wherever he went and
even showed her the combinations to the safes, dumb as a
doddering fool. One day he caught her in Boss's quarters and
we all thought this was going to be the end of the so-called
Boss and his old lady. But no, the general forgave them. And
afraid that she was going to escape with the soldier, he
became very friendly with the two of them. That's how we
discovered Boss's real duties, why my general loved him so.
But in the end, she didn't run off with Boss, but with another
soldier who truly loved her—who risked everything—taking
with them a bag full of money. They were nowhere to be
found in the hacienda when the sun rose, and they left no
trail. The general ordered Boss to bring us to Zacatecas, and
he put on the ring he used—so he said—to banish sadness.
The diamond in it was huge. We crossed Tepetongo, Jerez

and Zacatecas by jeep, followed by another truck filled with soldiers. My general was in search of a woman he loved and who had left him all alone. We didn't find hide nor hair of her. At night, since the old man was depressed and feeling sad all by himself and it was a Saturday at the end of September, he asked us to take him to Tino González's new house. "I want to remember Adelaida's empire," the old queer said. We got there around eleven at night. The place was packed with customers. All the tables were taken. *Don* Tino himself had to put a table practically on the dance floor where the general, Boss and three of us sat. Moments later the lights went out and the band stopped playing. A trumpet announced the singer and dancer, lit up in the middle of the floor by a spotlight of the whitest white. "Here is Terry Holiday! . . ." a smooth voice full of enthusiasm was saying into the microphone. There she stood — one arm raised over her head in a gesture of greeting to the audience, smiling, showing two rows of nearly transparent teeth, so white and perfect. She was slim and extremely tall, her height exaggerated by her high heels; her skin was smooth and the color of cinnamon, her dark hair fell in jet black waves over her shoulders, too wide to be those of a woman. Her hips were small and her breasts too, hidden by the lace of the silvery dress which hung in two strips — one in front, one in back — and barely held together by a metallic belt. She had that air women have today and it made her resemble the one who had left the general. Accompanied by the music, Terry Holiday covered the floor singing and moving her body in time to the melody, to the words of her songs. The movement of her body, her words and the music were all one and made each person's heart leap with joy inside his chest; beautiful and profound sentiments rose to the surface of our skin and all of life, in a flash of lightning, felt easy and beatific; everything suddenly became happy and full of life. The woman, singing and dancing, made us all look only at the good side of existence. After seeing her perform, anything could happen, as if life came into focus for a moment, like in the center of the barrel of a gun, and one could pull the trigger, die with no regrets or go on living. . . . The world of all that is distant and impossible looked close and possible; the world of fear and hate, it was like they were wiped away forever. The general was moved, he seemed beside himself; his beady eyes were shining out of sheer enjoyment. "I feel the same yearning as when I met my first wife," he told us soldiers. "You, go tell Tino that I want to have a chat with that chorus girl," that dirty old man said to me, staring at the diamond on his ring as if in a trance. I waited for the artist to finish her number. Through the smoke, the reek of alcohol, the music, and the light, her body moved like the body of a fish. I went right up to where she stood. She smiled at me and I told her that the general would be honored if she would join him for a bit. She looked at the old man's table and then at me. She nodded yes. A while later, there she was chatting with him. But before anyone knew it, he was suddenly holding her hand. She wanted to free herself and was struggling, looking toward the bar. All of a sudden, her man leaped from behind the bar. Next thing we knew he was standing in front of the old man and punching him right in the face. In less time than it takes me to tell you, it turned into the Last Judgment. Chairs and punches were flying and we were getting out from under everybody. Boss fired his gun once and somehow calm was restored. *Don* Tino's house began to empty, like someone letting the air out of a balloon. Everyone left except for the body that lay stretched out in the middle of the dance floor; the spotlights that previously made Terry Holiday dance now bathed him in light, like a dead fish at the bottom of a fishbowl. The dead man's blood covered the diamond of the ring, which rolled on the floor without anybody noticing. We immediately left with the general and Terry Holiday for the Viboras Hacienda. And there were those who, from that night on, never set foot again in that house on the hills overlooking Zacatecas.

## IV

Since the trip from Zacatecas to the Víboras Hacienda is long
and takes nearly three hours, to pass the time I began counting the shooting stars that night. But the rumble of the truck
in which we were escorting the general made me drowsy.
I couldn't stop thinking about Terry Holiday and what she
had sung for those two hours. In my imagination, I was still
seeing her, listening to her voice, so clear over the monotonous hum of the motor. It's said that she and the boy wrote
her songs together. And this night, she had started to sing
a new song in front of the general; it spoke of a man who
is sowing and finds an untended plant thriving among the
furrows of his field, with thorns that enhance its beauty. But
the sower takes a stick and, full of rage, destroys the plant,
just because he has heard that the sap flowing through its
stem is poisonous. But the plant is there, thick with beautiful
and untouchable flowers and it does no harm to anybody:
not to the insect that spends its life running over the sur-
faces and byways of its stems and leaves, nor to the rodent
or lizard taking pleasure in its shadow and protection. It
adorned the landscape and was in harmony with all of nature.
Then there was another of her songs, a while back, which
she brought down from her house and began singing to all
of Zacatecas: "A Moment's Love." It was a melody people
whistled in the streets, sang in the cantinas, and hummed
at home. It spoke of a flower that opened its fragile, irides-
cent petals in the morning, as if it too were a tiny piece of
the sun, and was extinguished with the day itself, with night-
fall. Then it went on dying all night long, never to open again.
The memory of that flower, so ephemeral, caused a suffering greater than its entire existence. The song ended with
a question posed by the singer amidst desperate, inconsolable
cries: why was its death longer than its life, and why was its
memory more fragrant?

That very night, Terry Holiday vanished for all of us —
or did we all, along with the general, make her disappear?

She vanished with her music, her movements, like the fragrance and the flower of her songs, that flower that only lasted while the day was light. Extinguished with her was her voice and the song I liked the best. The one that said that love is like building an avenue of crystal cathedrals along the pathways of the soul, and then, when it goes, we are all like the city: we carry an immense glass cathedral deep in our soul, but so fragile, perhaps so ephemeral. Later, that memory accompanies us throughout life, like the ghost of a cathedral that had stood within us.

That song made me remember how, whenever we passed in front of the cathedral, the general always had the jeep stop for a moment, and from his seat he would look at the facade and then at the towers and would say to himself, almost secretly: "What a marvel, what a marvel. . . ." And since the general was not a believer, we didn't understand what he was saying. But I did know that if he had lived during the time when the cathedral was being built, he would have been one of the slaves working to the tune of a whip. You could see from miles away that he was nothing but a thick-soled Indian.

## V

It was just about dawn when we went to sleep in our tents with the novelty that an early frost was moving over the pastures and orchards of the hacienda. As we arrived with Terry from Tepetongo you could already see the irrigation canal, which almost rings the hacienda, letting off this cold vapor which the wind was sweeping slowly over the fields and which wound through the dead corn stalks and trees and gave the night a leaden, mysterious quality. The water in the troughs in the corrals had hardened. The cows and calves were lowing sadly, as if carrying on a mournful conversation from pasture to pasture through the darkness; the horses were stamping the ground, restless in their stables. Dawn would find the fields of oats and wheat plastered to the ground, the frost-burnt trees would drop their tiny fruit, festering water as if the whole countryside had gone slack, as if Nature had suddenly lost all her strength. . . . But that same morning— before the sun rose to melt the petrified water and cause it to circulate again through the canals, to animate the world, which for a moment had remained paralyzed—prompted by a sudden hunch, the general made a decision before dawn: to get rid of Boss, at any cost. He simply told him, without any explanation, to leave the hacienda and his life forever that very day and never return; that he no longer needed either a driver or an overseer.

## VI

*We got the news from Tepetongo: for one reason or another the general didn't like her anymore. But it didn't strike them as particularly strange over there because they knew the general was an infamous man. So the soldiers had amused themselves with her the whole night, until one of them had the idea of taking her to the dam and throwing her into the water naked. The night being very dark, they lost sight of her and thinking they had drowned her, went back to the barracks feeling somewhat disappointed because the amuse- ment had ended so suddenly. What the people of Tepetongo found strange was that the general never had forgiven anyone before, and he had actually let Terry Holiday escape, God only knows why. They said that something was not quite right with the poor old man. Now, many years later, she walks around Zacatecas altogether changed, asking for coins with the other beggars that scour the train station and the bus terminals. But even so, every Saturday she would come to Don Tino's house (which, even for us, wasn't the same: we were older women, ourselves; we had fewer and fewer customers). Very few people dared to make the climb up here, for it cost a lot to get drunk; also, they said they would leave the place feeling depressed. And even though a few years have passed, Terry Holiday still comes by, still visits us; she hasn't forgotten the way, the slope that leads her up here. Her bust shriveled up or she never really had one, a few long hairs have grown out on her face and they're starting to spread over her chin and jaw. She still wears that dress with faded sequins and her feathers too, now discolored. And she sits here very straight for a few hours, proud and sure of herself—beautiful and mysterious like a cathedral in ruins—with a brandy on the rocks in her hands, smiling undoubtedly at her memories as if no time had passed and she was just waiting for the moment to go out and sing on the dance floor. You can still sense in her the presence of a different kind of woman— how can I put it?—aristocratic and refined, yes, respectful, polite. But decrepitude and decadence make her a sad, poignant figure who, for those of us who watch her, shakes deep inside us the scales we use to weigh life. Sometimes, smiling, she gets up from her chair and starts to sing in that horrifying voice that lacks any tone or rhythm the story of a man who was sowing seeds and who cut the flower off a thorny plant with his stick because people said it produced poison, or the one about a flower growing in a jail cell, or the one about a city filled with crystal cathedrals. Then she sits down and looks around; her face lets us know that she is looking at that other time in the past, and when she has finished her drink, the expression on her face changes, as if the drinks have brought her clarity and she realizes that she lost everything: she lost her youth, she lost her Ildefonso, she lost her love, and all this made her lose her mind. She is completely adrift, perhaps forgotten by God, if it's possible for God to ever forget anyone. It's the first time I've laid eyes on someone who had no attachments to life. And I've seen my share of people passing through this house. You can see how evil has marked her: her body is the battlefield for nothing less than the war between evil and life. She cries without any tears running down her withered face, she cries inwards. And before it gets any later, she leaves the place very slowly, without saying goodbye to anyone. She goes back to the city alone, perhaps ashamed of having dared to come* and rummage through her memories. She begs her way through life, collecting the necessary money to come on Saturday. And on those days she leaves me wondering: "Why get so upset? Why look for things in life that aren't there? Why go crazy over life trying to find them?" Terry and all those men who come here for my company and who frequent this house make me dizzy with their comings and goings, the way the pigeons must make the towers of the cathedral dizzy. Life, after all, is what goes on between the pigeons and the stones of the cathedral.

## VII

General Aniceto López Morelos passed away one afternoon – a cloudy afternoon swept by the cold wind of late November – in a city hospital in Zacatecas, many years later. By then he had long forgotten one of his greatest crimes, one that still has not come to a close. As his misdeeds became increasingly sporadic and less obvious, by the time he was an old man there were people who truly loved him. He died attended by nuns and doctors to whom he gave great sums of money and other favors. But in Tepetongo there was a man who never forgave him, for he had been the victim of one of his crimes. And that man commented on the very day of his passing: "The general was such an outlaw he even stole heaven." All because he knew that at the hour of the general's death a group of nuns were praying around his bed. And from the cathedral, in the afternoon, a melody spilled out that invaded the city like a very fine perfume; a choir accompanied the organist who endlessly played "Jesus, May My Joy Be Everlasting" with all the stops out on that monumental organ. And it wouldn't be surprising if one day in the not so distant future the state came up with the idea of erecting a statue in his memory. But, fortunately, these poor eyes won't see that day.

And so Adelaida's old house and the three human beings who were bound up in its story are dying out. Many small details and doubts that were raised later, when the events had grown cold, were never cleared up. Only that, the day after they stole Terry Holiday from Zacatecas, a man arrived naked in Tepetongo very early in the morning; he was badly beaten, wounded and covered in mud, freezing to death and begging for human compassion. He was mute with terror. He surely had escaped from the Víboras Hacienda also. Another of that old wretch's crimes, said a man named Florentino in Crescencio Montes's store.

But despite the years that pass, the house continues to emerge from the shadows every morning, like a ship floating on the rolling hills of the city, having drifted all night over the vast sea of the mountains of this state, propelled by gaiety, music, alcohol, and our passions. And then, as it rests here quietly anchored for the day, we passengers on this ship cannot get out of our minds the awful thought that for each of us, alone, separately, sooner or later, our shipwreck will come.

The grave of General Aniceto López Morelos can be found today in one corner of the beautiful cemetery of the hacienda that was his. The grave of Terry Holiday—no one remembers exactly when she died or when she was last here in the house—is also in a corner of our personal cemetery. That place where we secretly bury all those pieces of life that die on us.

—Translated by Mark Schafer

*Silvia Molina (Mexico D.F. 1946) has published short stories, novels, essays, and books for children. Her first novel,* La mañana debe seguir gris, *won the Villaurrutia Prize in 1977; her most recent is* Imagen de Héctor *(1990). She has participated in the International Writing Program at the University of Iowa.*

# AN ORANGE IS AN ORANGE
## Silvia Molina

They sat at a corner table in a bar on Avenida Principal. A small bar, almost empty. He sported a new black leather jacket and stone-washed jeans. He smoked nervously. Sonia wore her hair pulled back in a ponytail, and a blouse under which he could see the leotard she had worn at the rehearsal. Sonia remained silent. Words refused to come.

It was one of those hot summer nights, humid under clouds that threatened to unload on the city.

He ordered another Herradura straight. She remained silent, trying to hide her pain. Paralyzed, like the biblical statue of salt, she couldn't move.

She stared past him, her stubborn hands around a glass of rum. She wanted to think about something else, about the couple at the adjoining table, the dance she was choreographing, the waiter, whatever . . . but again and again his words kept coming back to her.

He had been brief, almost curt. "I can't lead two lives. You understand?"

She understood perfectly, though she hadn't been prepared for this or any other dispute that might lead to a break up.

The reality could not be changed. She thought, "There is no magic spell. An orange is an orange."

He didn't want to hurt her. Only to say good-bye without saying it, with nothing to indicate if he meant good-bye for now, forever, or until who knew where or when.

It seemed Sonia had always known him, since the first time she saw him in her parents' apartment building. He occupied the studio on the roof. When he moved in, he was an unknown painter. Her father found him entering one morning with a handful of brushes and spoke to him. The two men became friends.

"This man is an artist," said Sonia's father after seeing his work. "A real artist. The man has talent and style."

The artist began making a name for himself. Sonia's father read in the papers of exhibitions in Mexico and abroad, heard about them on TV.

Sonia and the painter ran into each other in the lobby, in the parking lot, or on the stairs: "Good morning." "Good evening."

One day he told her, "I'm going to have a show."

Sonia's father was right. The images seemed to have more power in his canvases than they did as concrete objects. At the opening she understood that an orange was not what she had thought, but a symbol he played with, the meaning of which she was supposed to discover.

That night, they hardly spoke. The painter thanked her for coming to his exhibit. Sonia left without saying good-bye.

"I went to your friend's opening, Papa," she said on her visit the following Tuesday.

"How was it?" he asked.

"Strong," she assured him enthusiastically.

"I told you so," Sonia's father said proudly, as if he were the father of the artist.

On another day she met the painter on the stairs.

"I enjoyed the orange," she said, "because it represents something inside of you."

Pleased by her observation, he extended another invitation. "Would you like to see what I'm working on?"

They went up together. Sonia saw clusters of brushes in jars, tubes of paint. His studio was order within disorder. The floors and tables were stained, but the jars, palettes, brushes, cloths and rags seemed to have been placed, deliberately, in the best possible spot for them. An unfinished figure of a woman rested on the easel.

After putting on a Mozart CD, he showed her paintings and an etching collection of which he was proud. Sonia liked one by Francisco Toledo, which he set apart, then offered her some coffee. They talked easily, as if they'd known each other all their lives. When he pronounced "vermillion", she exclaimed, "What a lovely word."

He took a sheet of blue paper and wrote with India ink, "Vermillion is happy because you like it."

On leaving, she took the Toledo etching, which he had placed, firmly, in her hand.

The following Tuesday he was waiting for her at the entrance to the building. "Can we walk a bit before you visit your father?"

They walked all afternoon and then began seeing each other on Tuesdays. They'd meet at a cafeteria far from the apartment house so that Sonia's father wouldn't suspect anything and get upset or interrupt them. Together, they explored the city, lingered in museums, went out for dinner. They talked about everything; but mostly about themselves. A familiar story.

One afternoon, out of the blue, the painter confessed that, in spite of the impossibility of it, he loved her.

She couldn't bring herself to say the same so soon.

Instead, she stopped meeting him on Tuesdays. But he sought her out insistently and she couldn't resist the joy of seeing him. Nevertheless, between them there was a distance, a boundary that inflamed her unsatisfied desire, and grew with their increasingly frequent encounters.

He plied her with colorful words, as if rendering a sunset in a painting, made her float blissfully through life, like objects carried by the wind in his canvases.

He had just finished saying that she would understand. *"I can't live two lives. You understand?"* And that was that.

Sonia made an effort to move, to speak, to find a word that might hold him there, until, at last, she said what he didn't want to say.

*"Assez."*

He looked confused.

*"Assez."* She rose. "That means, 'Enough.' "

He sat in silence.

"You're right." Sonia turned to leave. "My husband expects me home for dinner."

*—Translated by Paul Pines*

*José Agustín (Acapulco, Gro. 1944) is a robust social
critic and the leading figure of the literary movement of the seventies known as La Onda. His first
novel,* La tumba, *appeared in 1964 and* Ciudades
desiertas *created a sensation in 1982, bringing him
the Colima Prize. He has received a fellowship from
the Guggenheim Foundation (1977), a Fulbright
grant, and is a frequent guest at U. S. universities.*

# MOURNING
## José Agustín

Her mother's death is no more than
a vague memory, overshadowed, more than anything, by the
looming figure of her Aunt Berta. She had commanded the selection of the mourning clothes with a sharp tongue and her frigid
glances were everywhere to be met. Before she lost her mother,
Baby had never given a thought to Aunt Berta, an excessively
thin woman who spoke little, mainly to scold, complaining constantly of the disorderliness of Baby's family.

"Let them say what they will, but there's no name for the
mess that Cecilia is making of that daughter of hers." Her aunt
took a sip from the bottle of Delaware Punch and went on. "Of
course, Cecilia has always been a little cracked. She was fortunate to have made a marriage that good, but after Christian
died, Cecilia and that girl have gone from bad to worse. Why

she should have enrolled her in such a school is beyond me
... what's the name of it?"

"Helena Herlihy Hall," proffered Teresa timidly, having
always wanted to go there.

"Yes, *that*," and another sip.

Still, Baby is surprised that she had never heard her
aunt saying if I were to raise this girl, with me this girl would
get on the straight and narrow, and so forth. That's why it
came as even a greater surprise that her mother, on dying,
should have asked Aunt Berta to take charge of her and
("Dammit to hell ...!" Baby spits on the ground) to administer
her inheritance.

On another occasion, the aunt said: "It seems to me
her being called Baby is a very harmful thing ... I don't know,
but it's a silly name, senseless."

On the other hand, it was a constant source of pleasure
for her that Baby's father should be called Christian, which
was a very virile name ("Stupid old bat!" Baby comments),
that had a ring to it, and was so christian ("I could puke!"
she adds). Baby couldn't care less what her nickname or her
father's name was ("Leave me alone and call me whatever
you like!" Baby insists, taking a deep drag on her cigarette).
She was used to it by now.

Baby was twelve when her mother died. She cried more
from the surprise than the pain. She remembers how her
Aunt Berta led her along. A dry, bony hand, a dangling rosary.
Baby cried bitterly at the funeral as she clung to her aunt's
black skirt. The bony hand managed to brush Baby's head
before the family, in their compulsion to console, seized her.

Nor did she ever hear her aunt say, now that this child
is under my care she'll learn the meaning of the word decency,
or anything of that sort. Baby simply looked on in alarm as
they packed her clothes and almost before she knew what
had happened found herself at the Motolinía boarding school
which her cousin Teresa attended.

"I did everything rotten I could think of," laughed Baby.
"I inveigled Tere into smoking, got her to put on long stock-

ings with me, and to spend time looking out at the little streets of Colonia del Valle. If those lousy nuns didn't throw us out it was because of their *regard* for my Aunt Berta. They were as sinister as she."

Picture Baby: smiling maliciously, she talks Tere and some of the other girls into it, and they invite one of the new teachers to join them. "Just a Pepsi, so's you won't feel lonely here. After all, you're practically our age."

The teacher has just finished training and is on trial at Motolinia. She realizes at once that the "Pepsi" is practically pure rum but is so scared that she swallows it all without a word and ends up running through the school.

"You nuns are crooks. You pay me 400 pesos and I work like a dog. God'll punish you witches!"

She pulls up her dress and shows her panties in front of first-grade pupils.

"Señorita, this is disgraceful."

Baby applauds.

The outraged directress nun complained to *Doña* Berta and Baby received a long letter (". . . you are possessed of the devil . . . the fact that I'm not there . . . you pervert your cousin . . . the family name . . . my sister Cecilia would die of shame . . . you have no breeding") and her punishment was the denial of weekend passes ("Big deal! I never took a *single* weekend pass," Baby makes it clear and adds, "I wiped myself with the letter when I went to the toilet, even though it scraped.") Teresa was also reprimanded (to a lesser degree). Teresa is Aunt Esther's daughter and remained at Motolinia.

Baby finished a commercial course (at seventeen, because she did not go to high school) and her aunt could find no excuse to prevent Baby from living in Acapulco where the family home is.

In Acapulco, Baby refused to work or study anymore. She had to live with her aunt and saw Tere, who was working as a secretary at the Hotel Caleta, only on weekends.

She got up very late. Her daily before-breakfast cigarette finally drove her aunt up the wall. Baby asked them

to buy her a car and when they refused, she practically com-
mandeered the battered Hillman that had been her mother's
and which they used as a taxi. Every day, even out of season,
she went to the beach where the boys met.

Baby got on with them all but Jorge was the only one
able to talk to her.

"He's a nitwit," she said, "but he's funny."

At home she was accused of being incorrigible, out of
her mind, a slut, and so on, but, in fact, Baby was very strait-
laced. Admittedly, she necked with Jorge once in a while,
but . . .

"That doesn't count," says Baby airily.

She went partying, frequently stayed out till all hours,
and responded monosyllabically to her aunt's recriminations.
She smoked filtered Raleighs and drank vodka martinis. And
yet, she was rarely capable of missing nine o'clock mass (Sunday after Sunday).

There came a time when she stopped speaking to her
aunt and all communication between them was via servants
or family members.

Every once in a while Tere, stammering, would plead
with her for improved relations with her aunt.

"Look, Tere, you're practically a retard but I have a soft
spot for you anyway, so do me a favor and plug up that drain
you have for a mouth and never mention that old hag again."

"Baby, how can you be like that!"

Aunt Esther made her inexorable weekly prediction:
"Baby, you are sinning against the law of God, of Saint Peter
and Saint Paul. You must make up with Aunt Berta. Don't
you realize that you are killing her?"

"Knock it off, once and for all!" Baby burst out one time.
"And stop bothering me or I'll kick you. Don't *I* realize? Don't
*you* all realize that she's robbing my money, that she's a
monster, that who knows what she gave my mother to get
legal authority over me? I vomit on the old witch. I'd like
to sink my nails into her eyes, pull them out, throw them
on the ground, and stomp on them."

"Calm down, Baby."

Baby got in the habit of strolling the beach by herself when it was empty. At some point she would let herself drop.

Baby made sand piles and threw them mechanically into the sea.

Listen, Aunt—she said to the sea—you can't take me in that easily. You're used to running the whole family, but you're not going to put it over on me. Now, listen to this. I've found out *everything*. You poisoned my mom. You poisoned her. When she was dying, you made her sign that filthy paper that gives you legal power over me and the right to administer my dough. My mom was very agitated, she was clawing at her neck, and looked at you not believing you were capable of murdering her. Because that's what you did. You murdered her. And now you want to kill me. I found it all out, didn't I? Why don't you say something, you old dodo? Deny it if you dare! You can't put anything over on me.

Baby spit into the sea.

"But you can just imagine what she said to me one time," Baby explains, eyes on the coverlet, face quite pale.

Controlling herself, Berta said, "Look, *girl*, I've done everything to make it possible for us to get along, but it's not possible. God is my witness. You are a fiend. I want nothing to do with you. I can't leave you your money until you are 21."

"Is that so?"

"You know it. There's only a year and a half to go. Don't you want to go to the United States meanwhile . . . or wherever you like?"

"Yes, but not till the money is mine. So, get out first yourself and leave me alone."

"What a hypocrite, isn't she?" Baby comments. "Besides, I was having my period then and couldn't go to the beach because the Kotex would show. I didn't want to see anybody. I was *wiiiild*."

Jorge, Malena, the Headsucker, Rodolfo, Tomás, and Baby went to El Rebozo. Tomás was the mayor's son and considered himself Acapulco's Don Juan. He led Baby to the dance floor as Jorge looked on, swishing his drink around in the glass to make the ice cubes tinkle.

Baby was back shortly, scowling. Smiling, Tomás took Malena out on the floor. The group had been playing a rumba for the last eight minutes. Baby polished off her vodka martini in a gulp.

"What's wrong, Baby?"

"Nothing."

"Did Tomás say something to you?"

"No."

"Latched on, did he?"

"That's the way we always dance."

"He groped you?"

"No."

"Hey, let's fuck?"

"No."

"Aw, come on."

"Don't be a pest, jerk."

Jorge launched on a lengthy, detailed recital about his parents: they wanted to put him to work. Bored, Baby went to the beach.

I'm not leaving it at this, Aunt, she said to the sea.

"I didn't know what to do anymore," Baby explains as the nurse offers her orange juice. She was fed up with everything . . . .

It took everybody by surprise when Aunt Berta died (diagnosed by the doctors as a heart attack). Berta had been looking strong, gnarled, still with a long way to go. The wake was held in the house and Baby refused to leave her room. An aunt or a cousin knocked on her door every five minutes. You've got to attend. Come out. God will punish you.

"Go to hell!" mumbled Baby, pale, nestled at the head of the bed, sleepless, listening to the sounds of the wake. All Acapulco attended.

On the next day . . .

She simply came out of the room, the aunts and

cousins trooping behind, looking her over, criticizing.

"What did I care, anyway?" explains Baby, smoothing the sheets. "They could say whatever they pleased and it made no difference to me."

Morons, she said to herself, they're nothing but morons.

She put on a black bikini with a red blouse and passed by the window so they could see her. She realized at this point that she had no idea what to do with herself. I'm going to the beach. She headed for a phone booth. A coin, buzzing, a sleepy voice.

"Jorge?"

"Yes, who's this?"

"Baby."

"Dammit, Baby, stop the crap, what a time to be calling!"

"It's a quarter after twelve."

"Much too early."

"Will you come to the beach with me?"

"Hey, didn't your aunt die?"

"Looks like it, yes."

"Isn't the funeral today?"

"That's what I heard. But forget it. If you don't want to, that's okay. Ciao."

"Wait up, don't flip."

"Then you'll come?"

She began to look for a taxi. She thought of getting the Hillman but that meant going back to the house. All at once, Tere had caught up with her. Baby cursed Acapulco taxis.

"They're never around when you want them."

"Don't be like that. You must go to the funeral."

"Tere, in spite of your crap, I like you. Better knock it off."

"Do you realize what you're doing? You weren't at the wake last night and right now my mom and my Aunt Cruz are saying the *worst*."

"So, let them, kid. With luck, they'll soon be having funerals I won't have to go to either."

"Then, you don't think, really don't think, you'll go to the funeral."

"No. Look at the blouse I have on. I'm going to the beach, want to come?"

Tere remained frozen as Baby got into the taxi.

Jorge didn't discuss the matter and she couldn't help feeling grateful. They found the boys at the beach ("They were surprised to see me, of course," Baby relates, as she examines a medicine bottle) who asked a few questions. Baby answered evasively.

They went up to the restaurant where they ordered beers and she a vodka martini, murderously dry, please. The combo banged out something intended to be a surf but nobody was very demanding.

"Hey, Baby," howled Tomás, "in celebration of your new-found wealth, let's surf to end all surfs."

Baby wasn't absolutely annoyed but, scowling, got up to dance. Tomás, showing off, danced without deigning to look at Baby. Some tourists took snapshots and commented, *"Those guys sure are stoned."* Fatigued, Baby sat down, and Jorge began harping on the usual.

"You can't deny it, the bimbos have all emigrated from Acapulco. Whatever happened to the good old days when you could find a floozie under every table? We're just horny old goats."

"Old? Your *modder!*" they yelled.

In view of this, Jorge recounted his adventures as a bellhop at El Presidente. He almost grew sad. Jorge has known Baby since they were children.

"Jorge," Baby insists, "is a moron, too."

She went to the beach. She watched the waves breaking with repressed violence over her feet. She was seized by a need to walk on and on ("Until I tired myself out"). She strayed farther and farther from frequented areas, kept walking and stopped only when the beach ended at some rocks.

She dropped. Her fingers made little piles of sand and, smiling bitterly, she sprinkled them on her legs. I don't want to think about anything, I'm free now, now I can get away from my lousy family, I'll be whatever I feel like, I'll be able to know what I feel like wanting, I'd rather be alone, and live in peace, and live in peace, and live in peace. But she didn't feel at peace, her nerves were bristling, the water lapping at her legs tormented her.

"I felt *awful* because the sand clung to my blouse, the bikini, and my legs when I stood up," said Baby, smiling, as she toyed with the medicine bottle, covering and uncovering it.

Afterwards, she was infuriated by some characters who kept staring at her from a distance. She walked a few steps and sat down again, resting her head on her knees, feeling her eyes beginning to smart and that she was going to end up crying.

"Crazy woman, stop making such a fool of yourself," shouted Jorge, immediately regretting it. "I'm sorry, Baby," he said as he approached her.

Moron.

They returned to the restaurant together where an exodus to Tomás's house was imminent. They were all drinking like lunatics. ("I stayed sitting on the floor in a corner with a glass in my hand," says Baby.) She refused adamantly to dance and with scathing barbs drove off whoever tried to join her.

Baby found herself good and drunk when Tomás climbed onto a table.

"Rodolfo just called me from jail, the jerk got himself hauled in for offenses against so-called decency. Springing him is in order, right?"

Tomás faced off with somebody who seemed to be the judge.

"My friend, we know that on account of political intrigue in high places, a buddy of ours by the name of Rodolfo Radilla has been thrown into the clink and we are here to demand his immediate release."

The apparent judge replied that the young man Radilla would have to pay a one-thousand peso fine ("A thousand pesos!" all howled) because he was apprehended while committing offenses against decency right on the beach with a young girl who managed to get away.

"I was in very bad shape by then," explains Baby. "I can only remember that Tomás threatened to notify his dad, the mayor."

Reluctantly, the judge released Rodolfo. He was received with applause and catcalls. Baby, totally drunk, had hung onto her glass.

"I offered a toast. Can you beat that?" says Baby, with a smile and modest blush, the medicine bottle still in her hand.

Baby followed them to the cars and sat between Tomás and Rodolfo.

"Say, didn't your aunt die?"

She looked into his eyes, her mind lost somewhere, blinking damply, until she finally managed to mumble: "Yes, I have to get to the funeral."

"Yes, I said that," Baby admits, staring at the sheets.

She asked them to stop the car and got out into the street, staggering and wanting to throw up.

A taxi.

The funeral was already over and many bunches of flowers lay on Aunt Berta's grave. Baby had no idea what she was doing there. The sight of the mound of earth and the fragrance of the cheap flowers on top made her feel sick.

"Word of honor, I couldn't control myself, couldn't, couldn't, couldn't," whispered Baby, clutching the sheets. The nurse stepped behind her.

She tried to hold it back but wasn't able to and vomited for a long time over the flowers ("I threw up like a half-wit," Baby specifies), afterwards letting herself drop to the ground, muttering in the direction of the grave, "Dear Aunt, we're just family now ... explain it all to me."

But she remained on the ground, waiting for her aunt to open the conversation.

*—Translated by Asa Zatz*

*Agustín Monsreal (Mérida, Yuc. 1941) has pub-
lished six volumes of short stories, most recently
Lugares en el abismo (1993). Los ángeles enfermos
(1978) was awarded the Premio Bellas Artes and
he was the recipient of a grant from the Centro Mexicano de Escritores, 1976–77. Infiernos para dos, a
new collection of short fiction, will appear in 1995.*

# THE ORIGIN OF MIRACLES
## Agustín Monsreal

Look: In that village there was sad to
say nothing to do except waste time and energy watching the
construction and destruction of those complete shapes that the
clouds, when there are any clouds, usually invent up there in
the sky; and walk around the outskirts of town as constrained
as a prisoner pacing the courtyards of a jail; and greet the same
old faces and watch the sun rise and set in the traditional loca-
tions. Everything very tedium, very tranquility, not even a couple of pretty faces to lust after, not even a billiard room or a
beer hall or a nice little house on the edge of town where the
women sleep all day and spend the nights perfuming the land
and the air with their laughter, no, not even. A village from
another world, and I say another world because of how static,
how transitory, not because I've ever known a village from

91

another world, you understand.

The fact is that for reasons I won't go into because our intention here is not to scandalize anybody, I was obliged to stay there, crowded in with relatives who tolerated me because of some kind of vow they made to my mother before she died, but who really didn't give a damn about me; and since thanks to my dear departed I possess a fairly cheerful disposition, and since I'm adept at love songs and verses to ladies who deserve them, and since the aforementioned village lacked the vital energies for the exercise of such virtues, you can certainly understand that I found myself more regretful and nostalgic than the recently deceased in a cemetery, may God forgive me.

And one night, just because boredom is the father of many a senseless act and since by nine in the evening all the few inhabitants of the village were safe at home and sleeping like souls free of sin that they are, I left my bed and unbarred the door and walked out into the darkness holding a candle in front of me and after some two hundred meters and stumbling approximately the same number of times I put it down fervently at the foot of a tree that to my mind bears a certain resemblance to the image that churches offer us of poor martyrs in agony.

The next night, simply because I'm so stubborn, I repeated my expedition to the little hill with identical emotion and care, and with as much determination the night after that, hoping to see the wink of a little flame like mine emerge from the shadows; but ten days and nothing, and twelve and fifteen, until on the one we'll call number sixteen my perseverance was rewarded by two candle holders placed anonymously and of course with some prayer about "Help me, you who work miracles;" and I say of course because on the day we'll call thirty-five, the little flames had multiplied by the dozens and hanging on the precarious branches of our martyr there had appeared the kinds of objects with which people usually give thanks for wondrous help they've received; by day fifty-three it was common knowledge that the tree on the little hill possessed divine powers to alleviate the sorrows of humanity not to mention diseases and even matters of the heart, as proven by the widely discussed fact that in less time than it takes to tell about it a couple of young women who were hopelessly ugly if truth be told each found a suitor, which until then had been considered impossible, thanks to the overwhelming number of candles they deemed it wise to offer to the dying martyr.

As the days passed, life in the village was taken over by a most extraordinary excitement, discreet but expectant in the men, all exuberance and mystic sensuality in the women, who slipped away from their work four or five times a day and like vehement hens kept pecking and searching for what I'd call hope and pardon at the foot of the redeeming tree; they would stay there for several minutes in an imploring attitude, very serious and filled with emotion, praying to it with unobjectionable devotion and asking in passing for who knows what outrageous things; but besides that and as a way of saying thank you they surrounded it with an abundance of appropriately white and yellow flowers and inserted into the bark, because there were not enough branches for so much communication, nails pins and pegs for hanging rosaries and little silver ornaments and figurines of children kneeling as if they were taking their first communion and miniature golden arms and feet and ribbons of many colors and small handkerchiefs embroidered with "To the Blessed Tree" and little bronze hearts and countless other calamities which the martyr endured with typically vegetal stoicism and which produced in me a strong feeling of surreptitious delight, then astonishment at seeing how the world impoverishes us, and after that extreme consternation, although to be perfectly frank it was never as severe as that suffered after six months by the village priest, who at first struggled to convince his straying flock that what they were doing was an atrocity, a sacrilege, for there stood the holy temple with all its holy saints and virgins of proven authenticity ready to attend to the requests of the faithful; but in the end, after evaluating the situation with barometric precision, he decided to respect the equally holy will of the people and came to sprinkle the tree with a little holy water and kneel before it and remain on his knees with his head bent for too long a time, and who knows if he was praying or simply pretending to as he thought it wouldn't be a bad idea to have a collection box placed next to the divine redeemer, an idea that indeed was put into effect a short while later.

As time went by, and as everybody knows it goes by without legs and flies without wings, the fame of our martyr in agony spread beyond the deforested hills, following their curves and lines to the highway, and when we finally became aware of that, it was on its way back bringing with it a constellation of pilgrims and beggars from neighboring towns and ones even farther away; then the urgent necessity arose to construct for the redeemer a wrought iron fence so that the human avalanche would not damage it and in an ecstasy of emotion even knock it down and leave us without a miracle worker. By now veneration of this wonder had also stimulated significant tourism, which was both natural and understandable and in turn gave rise to the novelty of a camera shop and our first hotel, both of which were opened with the solemn cooperation of the priest and the mayor.

So much prosperity was justified, it seems, since from the very first this famous discovery of mine had adopted the custom of granting miracles, a celebrated virtue that logically enough brought more than happiness to its fanatical devotees who in a kind of righteous gratitude spread the word regarding the gift received and encouraged the arrival of other fanatical devotees, and these, in order not to be left behind, also proclaimed at the top of their lungs the favors granted them, attracting even more fanatical devotees who were not inclined to value themselves any less than those who came before, and since our purpose here is not to offend or fatigue anyone too much we'd better cut this commentary short. And so one morning, spurred on by my disbelief and the behavior of the population, I left my bed earlier than usual—I mean just before noon—and set out for the little hill holding a candle in front of me, and further in front of me was an encircling swarm of pilgrims holding their respective lights and mumbling litanies, rehearsing supplications, carrying pious emblems, and taking forever because they were barefoot or on their knees or carried on litters. And so it was not until the sun began to lose its enthusiasm and was getting ready to disappear that I managed to reach the environs of the fence and set down my candle holder, one among hundreds, with the aforementioned plea of "Help me, you who work miracles."

The next morning, just because I'm a fool and have an excessive nature, I repeated the expedition with identical difficulties and internal palpitations, and stubbornly did the same on the day after that, waiting to see how the redeemer would take care of my case; but ten mornings and nothing, and twelve and fifteen and nineteen, until on morning twenty-three I grew tired and said to myself the hell with it. Then, I assume in overwhelming anger at my failure, I took my place magnificently in the middle of the main square and speaking in all candor I told the people how I had started the business of the candles, explaining in detail how I began the farce, trying to destroy their faith in the miracle worker, inviting them to join in the joke, mocking them and their devotion, attempting to demolish their belief, and my anger was approaching laughter at the sight of those simple faces beginning to fall with the pain of ambiguity, and laughter grew into guffaws and guffaws into convulsions and suddenly, sinisterly, into uneasiness because they didn't seem to get the joke and were moving from perplexity to fury and I from uneasiness to fear and from fear to wild flight, stupendously pursued by a multitude of raised sticks and stones whose aim was to break all my bones at the very least and piously crack open my head, which they undoubtedly would have accomplished if the doors of the police station had not stood open waiting for me like paternal arms ready to embrace the prodigal son who has taken so long to come home.

The poor police station, seized by the most justifiable

terror, was obliged to close its loving arms and defend them with every truncheon it could find to save us from the pious wrath of the people; if it hadn't, I wouldn't be here to tell you this memorable anecdote from my own life; another man would be the narrator of the story and it would not have the same authenticity. The priest and the mayor soon put in, as they say, their two cents' worth, and between sips of hot chocolate they discussed whether I was a conspirator or an imbecile and with the last swallow they concluded that probably neither or possibly both and then the chief of police came and with that disturbingly paternal attitude of his said to me, "Well you're really in hot water now Luciano attacking established institutions like that you really have a big mouth, see, so now the only thing we can do is send you for a while to the big jail in the capital because if we lock you up here there's a good chance the faithful won't calm down and one fine day they'll fly into a rage and storm our station and break all your bones and stone you to death."

And then in the middle of a black night, as black as a wolf's mouth according to the sworn testimony of the lambs, they sneaked me into the municipality's own station wagon and ordered "Get down, don't be an idiot," and I went into a crouch and stayed there the whole way and of course I had to take refuge in the infirmary until my muscle cramps eased and I could stand up straight again. And it wasn't until later, when I honestly weighed the good and the bad, that I reached the conclusion that if I was in the capital it was through the mediation and grace of the dying redeemer; I had asked him to help me get out of the village only I didn't say under what circumstances and he simply granted my wish and so it's my fault if the miracle didn't turn out right. Basically, I learned that if you want the professional favors of redeemers to be to your liking, the first thing you have to do is spell out what you're asking for in complete—and I mean complete—detail.

*—Translated by Edith Grossman*

*Sergio Pitol (Córdoba, Ver. 1933) has distinguished
himself in academic and diplomatic circles, as well
as literary. His most recent volume of short stories
is* Cementerio de tordos *(1991) and many earlier
stories have been reissued under the title* Cuerpo
presente *(1990). His most recent novel is* La vida
conyugal *(1991). Pitol was awarded the National
Prize for Literature in 1993 and his work has been
widely translated. He has been a guest lecturer in
European universities and at Brown and Colorado
in the U.S.*

# THE PANTHER
## Sergio Pitol

No magic moment of my childhood
can compare with his coming. Nothing I had experienced up
to then was such a magnificent blend of refinement and bestial-
ity. On subsequent nights I prayed, at first in fun but then fret-
fully, almost tearfully, for him to reappear. My mother had told
me that if I kept playing cops and robbers so much I would
end up seeing them in my sleep. It was true. By the end of vaca-
tion my nights were a riot of outrageous exploits, chases, villainy,
rage, and blood. In those days going to the movies meant seeing the same picture, with slight variations, from show to show:
the invariable theme was the Allied offensive against the Axis
hordes. A single triple-feature matinee (in which with unspeak-
able delight we saw mortar shells pounding a phantasmagoric
Berlin where buildings, vehicles, churches, faces, and palaces

97

dissolved in an immense wall of fire, then epic love scenes and dark air raid shelters in a London full of shattered obelisks and gutted buildings, and finally, Veronica Lake's silken locks bravely resisting Japanese machine guns while a group of wounded soldiers was evacuated from a Pacific atoll) resulted in my room being strafed, then filling up with dismembered bodies and nurses' skulls, all of which sent me running to seek shelter in my older brothers' rooms.

Fully aware of the risk, I invented elaborate games that nobody enjoyed. I replaced our old game of cops and robbers and our new one of Allies and Germans with battles between other fierce and outlandish protagonists. In my games panthers made surprise attacks on villages, or panthers, howling with pain and fury, were trapped by frenzied hunters, or panthers in bloodcurdling melees rampaged against cannibals. But neither the games nor the dozens of jungle adventure books I devoured was sufficient to make the vision reappear.

His image persisted for a time which could not have been very long. It didn't bother me that his image was growing fainter, his features gradually fading from view. The headlong flood of forgetting and remembering we call time annuls the will to fix even one sensation in memory forever. But sometimes I was overcome by the need to hear the message that my ineptness had kept him from delivering on the night he appeared. That enormous, beautiful animal whose brilliant blackness vied with night had traced an elegant orbit about my bedroom, walked toward me, opened his jaws, and, seeing the terror that this movement inspired in me, closed them again, offended. He vanished into the same misty morning out of which he had appeared. For days I berated myself for my cowardice. I reproached myself for imagining that this beautiful beast would eat me up. His gaze was loving, pleading; his muzzle seemed less eager for the taste of blood than for petting and play.

New hours took the place of the old. New dreams displaced the one that for so many days had been my constant passion. I came to believe that panther games were not only silly but pointless, since I could no longer remember what had given rise to them. I could go back to my homework, my penmanship exercises, and my passion for learning to handle line and color.

Twenty trivial, happy, vulgar, intense, diffuse, foolishly optimistic, despairing, treacherous, and melancholy years had to pass in order for me to reach last night, during which I heard once again, as if in that barbarous childhood dream, the panting of an animal in the next room. The irrational that races inside us gallops so wildly that like cowards we take refuge in those musty rules with which we pretend to govern existence, vacuous canons we fall back on to check the flight of our most profound intuitions. And so, even in my sleep I tried to appeal to a rational explanation: I told myself the sound was coming from the cat, who often went into the kitchen to look for scraps. I dreamed that, comforted by that idea, I fell asleep again only to wake up again a second later on sensing his presence beside me. He was standing beside the bed, looking at me with an expression of pleasure. In my dream I could still remember the previous vision. The years had merely modified the frame. The heavy dark wood furniture no longer existed, nor the lamp that hung above my bed; the walls were different; but my expectation and the panther were the same: it was as if only a few seconds had elapsed between the two nights. Joy, with just a tinge of fear, filled my being. I remembered minute details of the first visit and waited avidly for the message.

The animal was not in the slightest hurry. He strolled past me at a languid pace, describing small circles, then leaped nimbly to the fireplace, stirring the ashes with his front paws, then returned to the center of the room where he observed me fixedly. He opened his jaws and, finally, decided to speak.

Anything I could say about the happiness I knew in that moment would only impoverish it. The words of that dark deity revealed my destiny. My sense of joy reached a degree of unbearable perfection. It is impossible to find anything to compare it with. Nothing, not even one of those rare moments of intense happiness that are a foretaste of eternity, could produce in me the effect of that message.

Emotion forced me awake, the vision vanished; nevertheless, those prophetic words remained alive, as if etched on steel, and I immediately wrote them on a sheet of paper I found on my desk. When I returned to bed and began to dream, I could not help but know that a mystery had been deciphered, the true mystery, and that the obstacles that had made of my days a time without horizons fell away, completely vanquished.

The alarm clock rang. With a thrill I saw the page with the twelve clarifying words. The easiest thing to do would have been to jump out of bed and read them. But such directness seemed out of keeping with the solemnity of the occasion. Instead of yielding to impulse I went into the bathroom and put on my clothes slowly and carefully, with affected nonchalance. I drank a cup of coffee and only then, shaking with excitement, read the message.

It had taken the panther twenty years to return. My amazement at both appearances could not have been gratuitous. The paraphernalia this dream was decked out in could not be written off as mere happenstance. No; something in his gaze, above all in his voice, made me think that he wasn't merely a crude image of an animal but the possibility of connecting with a force and an intelligence that surpassed human limitations. Despite all this I must confess that the words jotted down proved to be nothing but a string of bland, trivial nouns that made no sense. For a moment I doubted my sanity. I read them again carefully, changed the order of the words as if I were solving a riddle. I made all the words into one very long one; I studied every syllable. I invested days and nights in minute and sterile philological combinations. I could get nothing clear. Except the fact that the mysterious signs had been eroded by the same folly, the same chaos, the same incoherence that erodes the facts of every-day life.

Meanwhile, I know that one day the panther will return.

*—Translated by Jo Anne Engelbert*

*David Martín del Campo (Mexico D.F. 1952) is a journalist and the author of several award-winning novels, among them* Isla de lobos *(1982) and* Alas de angel *(1990); his most recent novel is* Las viudas de Blanco *(1993). A second volume of short stories,* Los hombres tristes, *is scheduled for publication in 1994.*

# LITTLE MISTER CHAIR–MAN
David Martín del Campo

They bring me here every afternoon. By the time the shadow of the market hits my side of the street, they are wheeling my chair out there so I can keep an eye on things. Before, when I didn't understand what was going on, people used to stare at me and laugh. And I didn't know why. But then I found out.

The first one to get here every day is Leocadia. She's wearing her tight green dress that shows her knees. The other one, the blue and white, she saves for weekends though sometimes the green one lasts through Saturday, her big day.

Friends? I have none. Well, what people call friends, I mean for real, no, I have none. It used to make me sad, angry even, that they would never play with me. But it's so hard for me to keep still. The good thing is that I recognize the difference

102

between me and others. Even if I have no friends, I still know plenty who could be my friends. They don't know it but I pretend they're my friends and that we play even though it's impossible. So I spend the mornings thinking about the people I see and the guys who work in the market. And of La Tigra.

This is the time of day more or less when business begins. If today were Saturday I would have already marked down more than a couple of crosses on the list *don* Manuel brings me. Yeah, two, three, or more crosses would be down on my list. Right now the shadow from the market is just beginning to cover the magazine stand on the other side of the street. The luncheonette where the one called Leocadia likes to stand is in the shade, too, and the toy store where you can see the orange soccer balls and the plastic rifles. And it's like that until six o'clock, unless the weather's bad because then I'm shut inside. But by the time the shadows cover the rooftop of the magazine stand, business is real good and I mark an X about every half hour.

Even if I don't have any friends, it makes me happy when Perico talks to me and rubs my head as he comes and goes to his orange juice stand. He doesn't know it but I've noticed his hands smell of orange peel and his fingers are shiny from so much cutting and peeling and squeezing those pretty oranges that look a lot like the soccer balls across the way, only smaller. Perico's not at the stand today. He probably went to have a good meal at the tables set up in the market place. When he comes by he looks at me and says, "How ya' doin', Mister Chairman?" or he runs by and ruffles my hair and shouts, "Aren't you tired, Mr. Chairman?" That's what they call me, Mister Chairman, because I have to be always sitting here in my chair. But my real name is Miguel. Some people call me "Stillhands," but I don't like them. I hate them because they make fun of these hands of mine that I can't keep still.

Here comes La Elota—they call her that because her teeth look like big kernels of corn on the cob. That one doesn't like me either. She doesn't like me because I cheated once and didn't mark down one of her crosses. The reason I didn't is because the day before she said to me, "Can't you keep still, *Master* Chairman? You make me nervous with your St. Vitus dance." It made me mad, even though she's never been one to call me Stillhands, and I got even by not putting an X the second time she went off with a man. Afterwards she and *don* Manuel came to ask me what had happened. And I told them, even though no one understands me when I try to speak, that I hadn't given her a mark because I was half asleep. That was worse because *don* Manuel was furious and he threatened me; he said that if I fell asleep again he wouldn't come to get me from *doña* Trinidad's house, he wouldn't bring me here to mark the crosses for Chela, La Elota, La Tigra, and all the others. I got real scared. I felt like crying because I don't like being at *doña* Trinidad's. . . . that old woman is so old she doesn't care if I'm hungry or thirsty and she never gets me to the pot on time when I need to pee. Afterwards I'm all dripping and my chair stinks of urine for days. The worst time was when she left me out in the rain and all I could do was make the usual noises trying to speak, and she didn't do anything because she'd fallen asleep listening to her soap operas on the radio. I wanted to move my wheelchair but I couldn't get hold of the wheels because of this jerking that I've had in my arms ever since I can remember. So that's why La Elota is mad at me, because that one time I didn't mark her second cross.

There's a man that comes by every afternoon carrying a lot of buckets hanging from a stick across his shoulders —that's one of the things I like looking at here in the market. The sun glinting off the buckets makes me look every time. Swaying his buckets from side to side, he doesn't even know I'm looking. Sometimes he yells, ". . . pails and brooms," or "tin buckets," and what he means is that he sells tin buckets and brooms. Nobody had to explain that to me, I figured it out by myself.

*Don* Manuel just got here. He got out of his car to hand me the daily sheet, and as he clipped it on the notebook tied to my chair, he looked around to see what girls had arrived. He saw La Elota and Leocadia across the street and Estrella on the corner where the yellow buses turn to go down to the shipyard. *Don* Manuel put the pencil in my hand so I could be ready to make the X when one of the girls leaves with a guy. He's nice, *don* Manuel, he never forgets the caramels. He just put one in my mouth. He's the one who pays *doña* Trinidad for my food and care. He says she's my grandma but it's not true. He's leaving again now and he looks at me, he doesn't really want to but he smiles at me as if we were the same. He tells me again, "Keep an eye out, Mister Chairman," just like he does every afternoon.

The shadows of the market have covered the windows of the stores across the street. You can't make out the soccer balls any more. There's blue smoke coming from the luncheonette when they start grilling the meat. That's another thing I can always tell on the street.

Right now when I was thinking about La Tigra and looking at the smoke cloud drifting up to the sky, La Rusa arrived and right away they picked her up in a taxi. Quickly I mark the first cross by her name on *don* Manuel's list. Later on tonight *don* Manuel or one of his helpers will be back to pick up the list. I don't know what time it is when they come because at night there's no shadow from the market over the buildings in front to tell me the time. What I do know is that it's very late when they pick up the list, and the streets are empty—well, not altogether empty because there will be some girls left and me . . . only I lay my head back on my chair as well as I can but don't sleep.

That's why Leocadia gets here early, because she's the one with the least marks each day. I feel very sad watching her as she walks away cursing and drinking from the bottle she keeps in her purse. She's the one that has the most fights with *don* Manuel. Perico just messed up my hair as he went by. "Still not tired, Mister Chairman?" he said, and I tell him that no, I don't get tired keeping an eye out from my chair, but he can't understand the noises I make when I try to speak.

He doesn't know that I pretend he's my friend and that I help him make orange juice. Once I imagined I helped him make so much orange juice that we filled the ocean with yellow orange juice. I imagined that because I like the ocean most of all.

Two times they've taken me to see the ocean. Once with *don* Manuel and old *doña* Trinidad. It was two years ago when they took me out of the orphanage and before I started making the marks. La Tigra took me the last time. When I feel the damp sea air I feel so happy I go crazy and I squirm around so much in my chair I almost fall over. People laugh watching me but I don't care. It's worth it to see so much water moving around just like me. Once I thought if I could get wet in the seawater, I would be cured, I thought I would even learn to walk and leave this wheelchair forever. I liked thinking about that even though I know it's impossible, that I'll spend my entire life in this chair, squirming like a worm. After looking at the ocean all day long, I felt very calm, almost still, just looking at the waves rolling onto the shore. La Tigra came close and said, "Hey, what's with you? Are you all cured?"

La Tigra is a very good person. She told me once that she was going to save money for an operation so that doctors from the capital could cure me. She said we would live together "like brother and sister." I know it's not true, that she says that to comfort me and to comfort herself, because with her pretty face she still has sad eyes, like the eyes of a dead fish.

La Elota is getting on a bike with a man. Sometimes they take her in cars, sometimes in taxis, sometimes they walk, but never on a bike! She looks so funny sitting on the bike's handlebars. I won't forget to put down her first cross for the day.

I get real happy when I see La Tigra arrive. She gives me candies and sometimes magazines that she buys across the street so I can look at the colored pictures. La Tigra always has at least two crosses. That's natural because she's the best.

I like when she comes to talk to me. She understands me
. . . sometimes she tells me things about her life, that she has
a son as big as I am. She says that when I grow up I'll understand why everyone wants my list to be full of the crosses
I make with this pencil. She says I don't understand, but she
understood that time when I tried to explain that I do understand. I told La Tigra I know why the girls, La Nati, La Rusa,
and herself, even ugly Leocadia, why they go with people
to talk with them, and then come back and do the same with
other people. Because here on the street no one talks, no
one looks anyone in the eyes, and that's what the girls do
with the men that pick them up. They like to talk, just like
La Tigra telling me things while I look at her with my whole
body shaking.

That's what they bring me here for in my chair, to mark
the crosses for La Rusa and La Chela and all the others. The
only thing I want now is not to be cured or to be able to
speak—because, in spite of what *don* Manuel says, that will
never happen. The only thing I'm waiting for is for *doña*
Trinidad to die so La Tigra can take care of me, because I
know some people are born okay and they can be by
themselves. But there's others, like me, are born for being
together because we are carriers of sickness and together we
suffer less, like La Tigra, who just now got here, or myself,
watching the shadows of the market moving across the street.

*—Translated by Joan Lindgren and Imera Pusateri*

*Marco Antonio Campos (Mexico D.F. 1949) is a poet, translator, and essayist on literature and politics, as well as a writer of fiction. The volume* No pasará el invierno *(from which the title story follows) appeared in 1985. He is editor of the* Periódico de poesia *and has been a visiting lecturer at Salzburg, Vienna, and Buenos Aires.*

# WINTER WILL NEVER END
## Marco Antonio Campos

Federico got out of the car on Rio Mixcoac and Insurgentes. The wind was blowing and it raised thin whirlwinds of dust. His head was spinning. He was nervous, pale. At the end of his rope. Horns, speeding cars, squealing brakes, whistles. He covered his ears. Enough! He saw the traffic cop on José Maria Rico behind a tree, and thought to himself with a certain amount of indignation that instead of preventing accidents, he was actually looking forward to them. He crossed the wide intersection of José Maria Rico, and then Insurgentes. He read CINE MANACAR in big rusty letters. He turned and saw the traffic cop almost behind him; he trembled, surprised. The officer crossed Rio Mixcoac towards Avenida Plateros, and Federico breathed a sigh of relief. No, they never laid a finger on him, but it was worse than if they had ... He didn't have any marks on his body, and yet his whole body bore an inward mark. OK, his eyes, hands, chest, legs were all there, but somehow, they seemed attached to another body.

At the beginning he, and only he, knew. Everyone thought he had taken that three-week trip to Guadalajara last month to see a brother who was sick and that his disappearance was explainable. ("One single word out of you, fucker, and you're dead.") Now everything had changed.

Every day, every hour, every minute he grew more nervous, and he had to make an incredible effort to control himself, because he felt as if they were going to charge him again, that they would drag him down again into that room of hallucinatory blinding white, and that each and all of them would denounce him as a "Communist dog." The worst part was that since they had released him, instead of feeling better the delirium had worsened, to the point where he withdrew more and more from his relatives, friends, in fact, from everything. There were moments when he reached such depths of self-annihilation that he felt himself on the brink of a cruel pleasure. He would spend the entire day writing, thinking back, for as long as his anxiety would allow him, fearing over and over that they would take him away, back to that violent whiteness, that cell.

He walked into the movie theater and went to sit down around the third row. He waited for the picture to start. He looked up at the wide curtain. White. Suddenly chilled, he lowered his eyes. "I'm going to go crazy! My God, if I don't get a grip I'm going to go crazy!"

Federico saw the doctor come in impeccably dressed in white, with greying hair and a cardboard tray. The only discordant color was the pale blue of his eyes. Federico marked off the time that he spent there in that five-by-five room, with its white walls, white ceiling, white floor, bed, chair, toilet, the white clothes that they gave him to wear, and the uniform of the doctor who approached him now, looked him in the eye and said, "Communists are pigs." Calmly, deliberately. In

Federico's brain the sentence struck, rebounded, rang and reverberated like an echo bouncing off of walls or mountains, returning and bouncing back again until it diminishes and fades away. "Communists are pigs. . . . communists are . . . are . . . a-a-a-r-r." Ever since that very first morning when four men dressed in white apprehended him leaving his house ("Shut up or we'll kill you!"), put him in the car and put a blindfold over his eyes, . . . sounds, horns, stops where there were probably traffic lights, the speed, the drowsiness . . . he sensed that his life would change for ever.

He didn't know when he woke up (it could have been that same day) but as he did, he felt the dazzling whiteness. He checked himself over ("there aren't any mirrors") from the tips of his shoes to his neck: white. A few minutes later an old ashen-haired nurse came in, her complexion livid. She closed the door behind her and spoke like a telegram: "This is the only time I will speak to you. I will come three times a day to bring you meals. If you wish to go to the bathroom these will be the only times you can do so. You will go blindfolded."

The nurse put down the tray of food. She left. After the door shut, Federico could hear the echo of the footsteps she had left in his room. He would have liked to have asked her: "What are they going to do to me?"

It would have been useless.

Imagining the worst, and shaking, Federico lifted the napkin that covered the tray: onion soup, white cheese, white fish. "God, it isn't possible! They're going to drive me nuts!" He sat down on the bed and pressed his fingertips into his forehead. He understood; you didn't have to be a rocket scientist to figure it out one way or another: the lock up was a consequence of the interviews and articles on the torture of political prisoners that had appeared in the newspaper two weeks ago, in which he exposed police chiefs at the highest levels as specialists in torture. Of course, that was it. "Now they want to break me, but they aren't going to touch a hair on my head."

They would let him go, sure, but when? No doubt from
what the nurse said it wouldn't be any time soon. "I will come
three times a day to bring food." Three times a day. He smiled
bitterly. (If they wanted to kill me they would've already done
it.) No, that wouldn't have been advisable. Surely the newspaper would do a story on his disappearance, there would
be a front-page campaign in bold type. Perhaps his captors
would make him sign a paper giving out some location or
maybe that the other guys had kidnapped him: the mob.

Federico approached the table where the tray had been
left. He had liked the soup and the cheese, the fish turned
his stomach. But now even the soup and the cheese repelled
him, and to top it off, they frightened him. In spite of everything, he ate. "I should just make believe that this is a nor-
mal day, like any other."

"Leonardo? I have to talk to you. It's urgent. Let's get together
at the Café de las Americas. At eight."

Federico had made a date with his friend Leonardo a
week after they released him.

"I needed to get this off my chest, forget for a moment
those three weeks in Hell."

Federico did not stop fidgeting in his chair, his hands
trembled, he swallowed, spoke with difficulty, and felt as if
bugs were making a nest in his stomach. His nerves were
chewed raw by the profound anxiety. He talked to Leonardo
for a whole hour.

"How is it possible that the newspaper didn't start a
publicity campaign about you?"

"They didn't know about it. The newspaper got a call
on the same day as I was kidnapped, and some guy that had
a voice that sounded like mine or that was imitating me, said
that my brother had had an accident in Guadalajara. A very
serious one. The same person called a week and a half later
from Guadalajara saying that they were sorry but that my
brother was in a coma."

"And who was it?"

"I don't know exactly, maybe the police. If it had been the other guys they would have killed me and they wouldn't have put on such a refined and cruel piece of theater."

Leonardo noticed that there was barely a shadow left of the Federico he had known in high school.

Federico grabbed his hair, his face, his neck, he pressed his fingers to his temples, he rubbed his forehead, he clenched his fists. "You sons of bitches, leave me alone! Leave me alone you sons of bitches! Leave me *alone*."

It was white everywhere, above, below, to the left, to the right. Absolutely white. "I can't take it anymore! *I can't take it anymore!*" He paced like a caged lion and, clenching his teeth and his fists, he started to throw punches, to kick the wall, until he hurt his fingers and toes badly. "Sons of bitches, sons of bitches they're going to drive me *crazy!*" He didn't know how long he had been walking until, worn out, he sat back down on the bed. He closed his eyes. White. White. "Oh my God, forgive me for what I've done, but don't punish me for something that I haven't done!"

In the most acute moments of horror there would suddenly appear the image of Julia: her delicately featured face, her long black hair, her sea-colored eyes, her firm and shapely thighs. He did not understand why. He had loved other women, if not more beautiful then at least with more kindred tastes. Perhaps had even loved them more. But something, deep, subterranean, had left the imprint of Julia so that six years later it could come back with cruel intensity. Uselessly. Uselessly because Julia had left him for one of his best friends. "Why the hell did she do that to me? Why did she humiliate me like that?" But the cries didn't find any echoes within those walls where neither punches nor kicks left anything but white marks. He recalled mornings at the university: waiting for her after classes, loving her, wanting her. But above all there was one burning merciless image of that morning in Acapulco, on the beach, in front of the hotel: Julia walking into the sea, the sun falling on her hair and shoulders, her waist covered with drops turned blue and gold by the sea and the sun. He approached and when he took her in his arms he heard that sentence that drained his blood:

"I'm sleeping with Roberto; I don't think that you'll want to see me again after this."

Roberto said he was sorry, ". . . really, *'manito,* she was the one that hopped into my bed. I told her that we were friends, but she insisted that you didn't turn her on anymore." There is no doubt that that is what happened. Just the same it was something that Roberto pursued indirectly or covertly, juggling allusions, indifference, sympathy. The old game, in short.

"You don't have to be a trained observer," he pointed out to Bazin, to prove his point. "Maybe he can fool others but I've known every word and step of Roberto's since we were teenagers." The friendship ended. He never again exchanged a word with him other than the necessary social pleasantries. Nevertheless, everything turned out just as he had foreseen, and even more: a few months later Roberto left Julia and went around complaining sourly to all of his friends that she was sick, trivial. "She's a woman who thinks only about sunbathing, or going to parties, or to the beauty parlor." True, but there lay much of her charm: the way that she built that palace of superficiality that made her different and more fascinating than the other women who concerned themselves more or less with the same things. A world of splendid trivialities, of empty delights, of small pleasures that would cause irritation or even revulsion to anyone with the least bit of sensitivity. Women whom he had ardently pursued over the years, and whose banality he had put up with because of their beauty and refinement.

"You have a tremendous capacity for disappointment," his friends would tell him.

Julia's mistake with Roberto had been one single thing, but a catastrophic one: to have fallen deeply in love. So that afterwards she denigrated him to their friends and their respective families. She resorted to the petty vandalism of wrecking his car; she shut herself up for a month and a half in her room, not even coming down to eat. Federico, besides enjoying the situation (and he did in a certain way), ended up feeling profoundly sorry for Julia.

So then why was it that Julia now returned with such savage intensity when he was pushed to his limit? When in fact her memory could not compare with the purity of Lorena, or the deep sorrow of the long years that followed the break-up with Claudia. What was it then? The only plausible explanation was that he had never fallen in love with any woman in such a sudden yet deeply involved way. Neither had any one of them ever given him such an unexpected and brutal blow. He had never broken off with anyone else with such swiftness and rage. An image came to him, *that photograph:* Julia in the park with the olive-green coat. Her hair loose, her eyes sea-green. Behind her, the trees and the houses. "She was the woman who most resembled desire."

The doctor entered at that moment and Federico rushed at him, but the doctor, dodging with agility, caught his hands, and then almost effortlessly sat him down in a chair. Federico felt as if he had lost his last ounce of strength. As if in a dream (the door had remained open) he heard the announcer far away but clearly talking about the Pope leaving the airport on his way to the Cathedral. "It must be the television." For a few moments he remained still, enlightened, smiling. The doctor, noticing this, went quickly to the door, closed it and came back again, and said to him, marking each word: "Communists–are–pigs." Federico, bone-tired, was barely able to murmur: "I'm not a communist, you son of a bitch!" He cleared his mind, and then like a jab: "COMMUNISTS ARE PIGS." He wanted to repeat that he wasn't one but the doctor had gone, leaving him with the silence, the whiteness, and between them Julia, the trees, and the sky.

Federico looked at the photograph. It was almost the same image that he had in the white room. He had forgotten some minor details, or had failed to notice them closely: the green scarf over the neck, a cord that would have been a cross. After a week of doubting he decided to telephone. . .

"Federico, What a miracle! Where have you been? It's about time I heard from you."

"Let's get together."

"When?" . . .

He felt as if his brain were splitting in two. It was as if he were living between the two parts, or maybe trying to live with both inside the same person.

"Winter will never end," he said to himself.

Federico Elizondo remembered that noon when, with his eyes blindfolded, they dropped him off at the university.

"You've had fair warning, you bastard!"

He stopped across from the gas station next to the newsstand. The Pope was leaving. He took off walking along Insurgentes, on the side of the street along where Tomboy, Sanborns, Vips, Lynnis were. Where the houses from the turn of the century sat, appearing to have aged more out of neglect than from the passing of time. He passed the modern office buildings that served as public offices, and stopped on the corner of Felipe Villanueva.

He saw the crowds gathering.

"Why are there so many people, Señor?"

"Don't you know? . . . The Pope is leaving today."

"We were practically neighbors," he thought to himself, smiling. He kept going along Tecoyotitla and he stopped at the intersection of Barranca del Muerto and Insurgentes. It was packed: people three and four deep, on stairs, perched in trees, on cars and trucks, peering out from the windows of the buildings, and houses, the sun blazing. "A church united will never fall!" "You can feel it, you can feel it, John Paul is here!" The style of the chanted mottoes of the Left on the lips of five-day Catholics.

He focused in on the crowd: the young woman who had wormed her way with agility up to the second row; the townswoman with a child on her shoulders who didn't stop praying; the old crone two steps away who told everyone in front, in back and to both sides of her, "The Holy Father is so kind! Did you notice how he tried to speak Spanish? And when they sang his song how he clapped along!" The clouds in the sky, the sports outfit of the girl, the apron on the maid.

He looked at the clock: five till two. "John Paul the Second, everybody loves you!" People climbed up in the trees, up walls, posts, on the hoods of cars, and the old woman pointed out that an event like this had never happened in Mexico, and that after having seen the Pope, even though it was only briefly and from afar, she could now die in peace.

A clamor arose, then silence, the whispering: "Here he comes! Here he comes!"–the silence, the Pope standing in the open car with his eyes half closed against the strong sun, looking everywhere and nowhere, blessing everyone and no one, two, three, five seconds; and the crowd, satisfied with the visual dazzle, scattered towards La Florida, Guadalupe Inn, and San José Insurgentes.

"How are you doing these days, Julia? I knew that you were working as a model."

"I quit; there was too much corruption. Not that it scares me, but it's just too bothersome. Every fat bald man wants to sleep with you."

"But, you've been doing well all these years, right?"

"Boy, absolutely the best. You have no idea how much I've travelled. It's been terrific. I've been to Europe four times, and to South America three times."

"How strange that you haven't gotten married."

"What for? You have to have some fun first. Could you see me washing dishes at twenty? What a bore. Maybe in another two or three years. How is everyone?"

"Well. Fairly well overall. Bazin has directed his first film; Leonardo is living with a Swedish woman and just published a book on medicine; Xavier got married a couple of months ago to his German teacher and he's going to Frankfurt for two years on a grant; Alberto is in politics."

"And Roberto?" she asked with a bit of painful curiosity.

"I've seen him a bit, very little, but I understand that he's a manager in one of his father's factories."

"Oh. (She took a cigarette out of the pack. Lit it.) And are you keeping up your old ideas?"

"I think so, but I don't think that you'd be interested in that," he responded a bit nervously.

"It bores me. They're all the same, the Left, the Right. The worst, really, are people like Echeverría. It affected everyone the same, the whole middle class. The poor are accustomed to it in any case. Look: everything now is about double or triple. How much does a trip to Paris cost now? You don't even want to think about it. He was the only one to blame. Why did he have to fight with the businessmen? Who is it that has the money?"

"Oh, well . . ." murmured Federico. Looking up he gazed into Julia's eyes and he imagined her naked, sadly knowing that she was out of reach by now.

"Yes, Bazin, Julia is that kind of woman who over the years prepares herself, without the slightest remorse, to be keenly unfaithful. She's fine for men like Leonardo or Roberto. I need women who are less combative, less worldly, that can exercise some self-control, because otherwise the mental torment begins. No, there's no common ground now. To her I'm nothing but a journalist that will reach a certain salary, have a certain car, a certain house. The main problem with her, with women like her, is not so much the physical attraction or lack of 'worldliness'; it's something else: you're never good enough. But the most painful part, believe me, is to have been a mere shadow in the memory of a woman who was so important, and to realize that someone else, who was your friend, who didn't even love her, should be a more intense memory, an open wound. That's what really fills me with resentment and jealousy."

Federico took off on the green light, crossed Barranca del Muerto and headed towards Manuel M. Ponce. He couldn't stand the film, he had walked out. He was blocked, as if a single idea had taken over his brain, and implacably sprouted filthy claws, made him think only about that white jail, about the bright and violent crisis that disturbed him so profoundly. "It's like I'm living outside of life."
     Federico crossed Felipe Villanueva and he remembered the Pope. He looked into the rearview mirror and wondered for a moment if that was a white car following him. He jumped as if he had hit a live wire. He tried to push the white to a corner of his mind, and looked into the mirror once again to check that the color had nothing to do with him. Terrified, he saw two white cars. He started to shake, to feel a dry cold, a fierce anxiety. He thought that it had been an idiotic move, that no, he should not have published those interviews and articles on torture all over again. But he wouldn't, couldn't turn them down. For a whole day two of the men that had been tortured ("couldn't they realize that I was the same, or worse?") pressed him, pleading that he was the only one capable of doing it, that no one else (reporters, columnists) wanted to touch that story. "Look, Señor Elizondo, if you don't do it, they're going to systematically continue with the torturing: they have battered, castrated, raped, killed. Nearly everyone is involved in this mess. Do it, not for the Left, nor for us, but to demonstrate a basic minimum of freedom and honesty."
     He couldn't turn it down. He knew that he would feel worse if he didn't do it, with his conscience bothering him relentlessly. His best adversary, the one who deserved his respect the most, had always been himself. "I don't think that I've done anyone any more harm than I've done to myself."
     At the traffic circle by the church he looked into the

rearview mirror again, and there were three white cars. He
pulled into the building, then quickly, almost desperately, went
up the stairs to his apartment. He bolted both locks. Trembling, he remained by the door for a few seconds. He tried
to see if he could hear anything: footsteps, sounds, doorbell
... all he heard was the blood pounding in his brain, the quick
beat of his heart. His stomach was churning, and he felt like
throwing up, in spite of not having eaten. Bile. At the end
of his strength, feeling all the sorrow of the world falling on
him, he walked cautiously towards the window. He had an
irresistible urge to cry. He drew the curtain back a few cen-
timeters and looked down at the traffic circle.

He froze.

There was a white car on each of the four corners. He
saw two men get out of the car that was in front of the church,
and cross the intersection. He figured that they must be at
the door downstairs. He waited for the doorbell to ring. He
thought he heard the bell. He still stayed for a few seconds
looking at the traffic circle, then he drew the curtain, and
went to lie down on the black settee that was almost in front
of the window, lowered his eyelids and all he could see
through his tears was a distant memory from childhood, when
he was playing soccer and his father would hand him an
orange to slake his thirst.

–*Translated by Charles D. Brown*

*Jorge Ibargüengoitia (Guanajuato, Gto. 1928–Madrid 1983) brought a biting humor to the criticism of Mexican society and government that clearly transcended its original object: his work has been translated into Italian, Czech, Polish, and English, among others. His first novel,* Los relámpagos de agosto *(1964) was awarded the Casa de las Americas prize and later appeared in an American edition, as did* Dead Girls *(1983) and* Two Crimes *(1985). The following story is from the volume* La ley de Herodes *(1967).*

# PIOUS FRAUD
## Jorge Ibargüengoitia

In the course of its cancerous growth, Mexico City engulfed all surrounding villages. One of these to the south was Coyotlán. It has been a stylish place ever since the arrival of the Conquistadores. To this day it has a parade ground, a sixteenth-century convent, tree-lined streets, colonial houses inhabited by millionaires, a view of the mountains, pure air, plentiful water, and so on.

A big house had been wrecked on one of the main streets and the property subdivided into lots. Part of the facade was left standing and a sign on it read: "LOTS FOR SALE. FOR INFORMATION SEE DR. GORGONZOLA."

Gorgonzola's waiting room was a bleak corridor filled with ailing nuns. I spent half an hour there looking at a chart of the digestive system as I waited for the doctor to receive me. When

I entered his office, I found him in shirt sleeves, sitting at a desk. I told him I wanted to buy a lot and he pointed a finger at me as though he had recognized me just at that moment.

"You went to the Marist Brothers' school!"

I couldn't deny it. Gorgonzola got up from his chair and embraced me.

"We're cast in the same mold."

He was a chubby fifty-year-old baby who came up to about my shoulder and had thin–but blond–hair, bloodshot–but blue–eyes, and a big double chin.

He went to a cabinet and took out a plan, as he let me know, "These lots aren't mine. I've taken charge of selling them as a favor for the Company of Jesus."

He explained that the lots were mortmain properties. Their sale was going to be unconstitutional but a very pious act. The house that was wrecked had been a Franciscan school; when the Jesuits returned the San Francisco church on Madero Street to the Franciscans, they had to give them various properties in payment, among them the house in question. Since the Jesuits wanted no houses or schools but money for charitable works, Gorgonzola, who was a devout Catholic, offered to take over the development and sale of the subdivision.

We went to see the lots.

"The price you will be paying for one of these properties is a pittance. In order for the Jesuits to get the permit to make this development they were obliged to install sewerage, electric lines, and to cut through a street that had to be turned over to the city. Do you consider that fair?"

I then realized that Gorgonzola wasn't acting as an agent for the love of it or of the Company of Jesus. On one side of the street "that had to be turned over to the city" Gorgonzola owned an immense lot he had bought very cheap because of its location, in the middle of a block without access, whose value had now tripled or quadrupled thanks to the public improvements made by the Jesuits.

"Making this development was my idea," he confessed to me.

I bought a lot with two trees on it that I liked very much.

"You have acquired the best piece of property in Mexico City," Gorgonzola said to me when we closed the deal.

The title closing was rather a confusing ceremony. Since religious orders have no right to own property but nevertheless do so, every order appoints as trustee a person of unimpeachable honesty and bombproof catholicity. The function of the trustee is to commit fraud on the Nation by posing as the owner of something that belongs to the order.

The property's shady legal background was read aloud by Malancón, the official notary: Señora Dolores Cimarrón del Llano (that is, the Franciscans) had sold to (that is, exchanged with) Señor Pedro Gongoria Acebez (that is, the Jesuits) the tract of which I was now purchasing a portion. The deed was signed by the industrial engineer Xavier Barajas Angélico in the name of the attorney in fact for the Jesuits and by me, in my own.

Señor Barajas Angélico, on signing, had to restrain himself from tacking an S.J. onto his name. I handed over a check for 4,000 pesos to him and he, a receipt for 12,000 to me, thereby consummating the fraud on the Mexican treasury, which brought the closing expenses down very low. At the conclusion of the ceremony, there were handshakes all around between Malancón, Barajas Angélico, absent-mindedly holding his hand out for me to kiss, Gorgonzola, who was very pleased, and myself.

After a couple of years I had enough money to build and took my architect and some friends to show them the lot. Nothing had changed. The facade of the former house had the same sign that said "LOTS FOR SALE . . .", the trees were still there, and so on; but the entrance to the street "that had to be turned over to the city" was blocked off by a barricade.

We were climbing over it when a ragged woman appeared.

"What do you want?"

"What do you mean what do we want?" I stuttered.

"I'm the owner of the lot over there."

"That's not true. Those lots belong to Doctor Gorgonzola."

I was outraged. "Oh, so they're Doctor Gorgonzola's, are they? Then I'll just have to get hold of him and tell him a thing or two."

At that very moment the person in question drew up in a Volkswagen.

"Tell this woman here who I am," I said to him.

But Gorgonzola didn't recognize me despite our having been cast in the same mold.

"Don't let anybody in!" he shouted to the woman and took off.

I didn't know what to do. I decided to ignore the woman and, acting the cicerone, led my friends to the lot. When I was saying to them, "This one is my lot," the woman threw stones at us.

Something worse happened the following day. My architect went to the City Hall to apply for a building permit and came back livid.

"The Building Department says there is no such development."

I went to Gorgonzola's office. "I'm the person who bought a lot two years ago," I began saying as I entered.

It did me no good since Gorgonzola was on the telephone and paid no attention to me.

"I've already told you I can't," Gorgonzola was saying into the telephone. "I'm not in a position to. Be good enough to stop bothering me." And he hung up. "What can I do for you?"

"I'm the person who ..." etc.

"Ah! I have nothing to do with those lots anymore."

I ignored the fact that he had ordered the ragged

woman not to let me onto his property the day before and told him that City Hall wouldn't give me a building permit.

"The thing is, Mayor Uruchurtu has it in for us." He didn't make clear to me who "us" was, whether the Company of Jesus and he, he and I, or all three. "He refused to sign the permit. All the papers have been presented. Only one signature is lacking. But don't worry, my friend, you go ahead and build, with or without a permit."

He stood up, took me by the arm, and we left the office to walk to the property. The ragged woman greeted us respectfully. We passed by my lot and stopped at his, on which he was building a colonial-style clinic without a permit.

"Take my word for it. What's hatched cannot be unhatched."

Having accomplished nothing, I left Gorgonzola and went to Barajas Angélico's office.

The Compañia Industrial Metropolitana, S.A., a front for manipulating Jesuit assets, had spacious, well-furnished offices. Inside were eight desks and a Jesuit in beige. I went up to him and asked for Barajas Angélico.

"He's no longer in Mexico," he said in a commiserating tone, as though I had come to confession.

"What headaches we've had over that development!"

He opened a desk drawer and took out a number of papers. We pored over them for at least an hour. All the records were there showing the disbursements for sewers, lamp posts, and paving, and a receipt "For one street" signed by His Honor. Mayor Uruchurtu had refused to approve the development but did accept and receive the street that had to be turned over to the city.

In order to obtain the building permit, only one change had to be made in the application, indicating that the property was located on such and such a street instead of being specified as part of a development. Uruchurtu had a heart of stone but, fortunately, even the best hunter may lose his prey. The next problem that arose was determining the street's real name.

The deed and the receipt with His Honor's signature
showed North Reforma Street, the tax receipts showed Reforma, the water bills Reforma Alley, and the sign on the corner said simply Reforma.

"There is no such street," the postmaster at the local
branch told me when I went to get his opinion.

He explained to me that there were three Reforma
streets in Coyotlán that had no connection with each other
and that none of them belonged to the place where I said
I had bought a lot. Ten years have gone by and exactly what
the street where I live should be called is still in doubt. The
name Reforma has nevertheless continued to spread throughout the area, there now being two more Reforma streets, one
in the Atlántida sector and the other in Clavos de Cristo,
which are new sections. This is without counting the new
extension of the Paseo de la Reforma in the heart of the city
which is actually the true Reforma Street, the others being
mere imitations.

As my architect was laying out the boundaries of the lot,
Señor Bobadilla, who dressed like an Englishman and drove
a 1947 Ford, appeared. He said he was the owner of the adjoining lot.

"You are encroaching on me."

He took out a plan and a tape measure and proved that
I was in fact encroaching. My architect had to change the
boundaries of my lot.

I went to visit the construction one morning to discover
that a hallway which was on the plan did not appear in reality.

"There wasn't enough room for it," my architect said.

The mystery went unexplained until Pepe Manzanares
had built on his lot which adjoined Bobadilla's and mine. One
day, Bobadilla appeared in his 1947 Ford, dressed like an
Englishman, with his plan and tape measure, and Manzanares
was obliged to knock down a fence.

"I'm missing footage," Manzanares told me, in the belief
that I had stolen it from him.

"What a coincidence," I answered. "A hallway of mine is also missing."

Manzanares, Bobadilla, and I went to the Building Department to request, with all due respect, that a survey be made.

It was a revelation. The street, extension, or alley called Reforma had been drawn on the plans as going in one direction but was laid out on the ground in another. Consequently, Manzanares lost 20 meters, I lost 50 meters and had built a toilet on land belonging to my neighbor on the north who had lost 500 meters. And so on. Gorgonzola, however, who was on the other side of the street, had gained 500 meters.

Manzanares, Bobadilla, and I met over coffee at La Flor de Mexico to decide what should be done. There were three ways we could go: first, sue the Company of Jesus for collecting from us for more footage than we received; second, sue the city for encroaching on our property with a street, extension, or alley; third, sue Gorgonzola for fraud and abuse of confidence. It was a touchy situation because the Company of Jesus would have paid us for the footage we were lacking at the price stipulated in the deed—which was a fourth of what we had paid and a tenth of its real value.

"I'd rather not rock the boat," Bobadilla said, "seeing that I bought the property from a nephew of a Jesuit and he made out the deed to me on a paper napkin."

Furthermore, we had no proof to substantiate a suit against Gorgonzola whom nobody had actually seen bribing a worker to make a counterfeit street. We chose to approach the Building Department and, with all due respect, seek justice, intending that the Department should come down on Gorgonzola. Justice was served by the Department as follows: a) a new survey was made and the lost footage given the status of *fait accompli;* b) a new assessment was made of our properties that raised our taxes and we were fined for concealment of assets; and, c) we were warned that "His Honor wants nothing more to do with this matter."

That's what we got for having bought pious-fraud property. My only satisfaction has been that Gorgonzola was never able to complete his clinic. It is still there, a ruin of an unfinished building in the middle of an immense empty lot.

*—Translated by Asa Zatz*

*Jesús Gardea (Delicias, Chih. 1939) has produced four volumes of short stories beginning in 1979 with the appearance of* Los viernes de Lautaro; Septiembre y otros dias *won the Villaurrutia Prize in 1980. Another collection,* Dificil de atrapar, *is scheduled to appear early in 1995, together with Gardea's ninth novel,* Juegan los comensales.

# ONE FOR THE ROAD
Jesús Gardea

## I

We stop under a tree. The old man is tough, full of the hardness of the climate. He's wearing a white T-shirt and blue pants. Ravaged blue. The shadows are his refuge; fire burns in his eyes. I met him just this morning, when he opened his front door and looked at me the way one looks at the burning thorns on a mesquite. He had a sweat stain on his T-shirt. He regarded me without saying a word. The stain reached his belly button. The silence was a taut cord between us.

"Five days ago . . .," I began.

A blast of sparks shot from the old man's eyes. "The days of charity are over, my friend," he said, cutting me off.

"I want to work."

The sparks fluttered around in the darkness, flew upwards,

128

disappearing behind his skull.

"Anything," I said.

"There isn't even any of that left, my friend."

The drops of sweat rolled slowly down my body. They wrapped me in their spiral. The old man lifted the dampness of his T-shirt from his skin.

"What can you do?" he asked me.

"Everything."

The old man plucked at another section of his shirt. "Have you taken a look at the sky?"

"Yes."

"It's white. Like hell itself."

## II

I seek the shade of the tree's branches. He is already there.

"Clear this rubble," he tells me.

I take a good look at the lot. It looks like a landslide. Rocks. Cans and empty bottles. Pieces of wood. Scraps of iron. Rags. The bottles sparkle. They stab at my gaze. The old man warns me: "Don't go mixing things together."

That whole world must be boiling up.

"I don't understand."

"Rocks with rocks, my friend."

I look at the old man.

"Glass with glass," he adds.

I vow to charge him more than what he offers me. Making order out of disorder costs extra.

"Where do I put the piles?"

The old man surveys the disaster. "That's up to you, my friend."

"When do you want it done by?"

The old man looks up at the sky. "Whenever you finish."

I'm also looking up. There isn't any air above us. The sun has eaten it.

"By six," I promise.

"Agreed. I'll be waiting for you at my house. We'll come

take a look."

The old man starts to leave. But I stop him.

"Can you give me an advance?"

The old man looks deep into my eyes, blasts me with the fire inside him. I don't run from the blaze nor does my face reveal any apprehension.

"How much, friend?"

"Cigarettes. A soda. That's all."

The old man hands me a crumpled piece of paper. He drops it in my open hand which receives it as the plain receives a drop of water. And then, already on the other side of the tree, he warns me: "It's still light out at eight around here. Remember."

"I'll remember."

"That's when the air begins growing again. The blue grass, friend. It's the best time for putting your back into it without danger."

### III

He leaves. Vanishes from sight. I lean up against the tree where the branches begin. From there, I see a store to my left, not very far off. I abandon the feeble shade.

The storeowner is sleeping. He cradles his head in his arms on the counter top. I wake him up, calling to him in a soft voice.

"What do you want," he says, his eyelids damp.

"A soda."

"The sodas are lined up along a shelf."

"Which one?"

The bottles are identical no matter what the flavor.

"That one," I say, pointing at the center of the row.

The storeowner stands up. Gets the bottle. With one hand he brushes off the dust.

The storeowner sets the bottle on the counter. And then, after yawning, he says to me: "The bottle opener is next to you."

The soda is hot. The gulp I take doesn't taste like any known fruit.

"Cigarettes?"

The storeowner reaches his hand to a package sitting on the same shelf.

"These are the only ones I have," he explains, and shows me the brand.

"I'll take them."

"Matches?"

"No thanks."

I pay. I hardly get any change: three filthy coins, each one bearing an eagle. The storeowner sits back down on his bench behind the counter but is no longer sleeping. I start smoking, my back to him, looking along with him at the street, the lot. I slowly mix puffs with swigs, as if the cigarette and the liquid in the bottle were eternal. Amidst the rubble on the plot of land, like fire between the mounds, the bottles shine, are shining, brighter than before. The glass is rearing up, for now the sun has ignited its very core. And the accumulated brilliance creates a radiant mist above the trash, a smoking layer of milk; the danger the man told me about. The storeowner drums his fingertips on the wood of the countertop. But not with impatience. Perhaps he feels the silence between us has hardened; perhaps he is thinking of a nut and how to crack it.

"Does twelve o'clock last long here?"

He stops his drumming. I tap the ashes from my cigarette. They fall in one piece. They smash on the floor like a column. One finger returns to the board, followed by the others. They peck at it again, the little chicks. The storeowner didn't hear me clearly or he doesn't want to answer. I take a swig. The air smells like burnt fingernails. Why did they let the tree die in that lot? Didn't anyone think about the mist? I flick the cigarette butt into the street and immediately pull out another one from the box on the counter. The cigarettes don't have any taste either. The tobacco is bone dry, soulless. It must surely be as old as the tree; perhaps even as old as the old man. You don't find that brand of cigarettes anywhere nowadays. Not even in the worst backwater stores. I smoke and I feel as if I'm smoking the dry bones of the years.

## IV

"That tree over there, out in front," I say to the storeowner, "died of thirst on you."

The storeowner's fingers are quiet.

"It died on the person who planted it."

I take a drink. Take a puff.

"No. It died on all of you."

"Same thing."

I shake the liquid in the bottle. It's getting hotter and hotter from the heat of my hand which has hardly let go of it. I miss the flies. A summer without them is like that tree out there. I look for them in the air, in the shadows, on the cardboard signs hanging from the ceiling, and on the floor. There are traces, pockmarks on the cardboard.

"What did you do," I ask the storeowner, "to drive away the swarms of flies?"

"Nothing. They come in waves, suddenly. They last several days, many days. But then death starts thinning them out. It doesn't even respect the little babies. What I do is sweep up the bodies."

I shoot a stream of smoke at one of the pieces of cardboard. The sign starts to swing.

"They crowd together on that advertisement," the storeowner tells me. "They hold their ground there. Once I saw some people on an island, in the middle of a swollen river. The flies sitting on the pieces of cardboard remind me of those people."

## V

The brilliance of the bottles in the lot grows leaner.

"Noon lasts how long?" I ask the storeowner again.

"Yes, I heard you the first time. I was thinking. It lasts until three or four in the afternoon. Easily until six in August."

"We're in August."

"The first days."

I ration the soda. I'm taking tiny sips, that is to say just dampening my tongue and the smoke a little. Six is a long way off. If only it weren't August . . .

"Are you a friend of Bayona?" the storeowner asks me.

"Bayona?"

"The two of you were standing under the tree. I could see you."

"No. I just met him. I didn't know his name."

I turn halfway around at the counter. The storeowner notices the soda.

"The dregs are like a laxative. Want another one?"

Looking at the bottle and its cloudy liquid, I answer: "I don't find the dregs to be a laxative. They're like a concentrate, a tonic."

I leave the bottle on the counter. Then I ask the storeowner: "Where did you get the cigarettes"

"Bayona sold them to me."

"They're stale."

"Bayona told me."

The old tobacco burns like gunpowder. I will have nothing left to smoke and it still won't be six o'clock. I should put a cigarette away for later. To light as the sun goes down.

"Bayona is a good man," I tell the storeowner.

"He's all kinds of things."

I take a cigarette out of the box and drop it in my shirt pocket. I catch a look of slight mockery, of teasing in his eyes.

"A souvenir?"

I laugh. "One for the road."

The storeowner also laughs. Reluctantly. And I stand again with my back to him. I continue smoking. If the layer of mist vanishes before six, at five, at four, I'll go out to haul rubble.

"Bayona is all kinds of things," the storeowner says

again. "He sells. Buys. But he isn't established like I am. Are you trying to sell him something?"

"Nothing."

The sun passes over the bottles like a sleepwalker. The conflagration is unimaginable. When the sun falls into the pit of the plain, will the tiny tree come back to life?

## VI

I look over my shoulder at the storekeeper. "Been dried up for long?"

He seeks my gaze at the edge of my shoulder. "Bayona?"

"The tree."

"It's anyone's guess. No one here records the dates of deaths like that. Not even the deaths of the living. They slip away from us. Ask Bayona about the death of his woman. You'll see. Ask me about the death of mine. Around here, the years, time, they have no handles to grab onto."

I look back at the lot. The tree's shadow is stretching toward us. It approaches as if stumbling, as if wounded, as if in flight. They could leave a bucket full of water for it in the middle of the street. The storekeeper. I have no soda left except for a single gulp. I should have asked the old man for a few more *centavos.*

"You don't like him?"

"Bayona?"

I nod my head and my head lets off the smoke from the cigarette.

"Bayona," the storekeeper responds, "is a poor bastard."

Then he gets up. He opens and closes a drawer. He says, "Look how time flies. I'm leaving."

I turn around to look at him as if he were sending me into the lion's den. He continues, "I never miss my siesta."

He comes out from behind the counter. He is holding a padlock in his hand. He reminds me of my change. "Don't forget. I won't be held responsible."

I gather up the coins. "Well," I say to him, "I was thinking of going out to clear Bayona's lot anyway."

The storekeeper hears what I say. "Bayona's lot?"

"That piece of land with the tree. The rubbish pile."

"That doesn't belong to Bayona. Who told you so?"

"He did. He hired me."

The storekeeper looks at me with eyes like a devil's. "I'm telling you," he stresses, "Juan Bayona is a poor bastard. The lot belongs to the municipality."

"To the authorities?"

"To the municipality. And if you clear it, you'll be doing it for free."

The storekeeper's words leave me dazed.

The devil stands there watching me, amused. We are standing in the doorway. I look at the counter, at the bottle, and at the empty box of cigarettes. Then, pulling out the one for the road, I say to the storekeeper, "All right . . ."

And I light the cigarette.

*—Translated by Mark Schafer*

*Enrique Serna (Mexico D.F. 1959) has published*
*two novels,* El ocaso de la primera dama *(1986) and*
Uno soñaba que era rey *(1989). His collection of*
*short fiction,* Amores de segunda mano, *published*
*by the University of Veracruz in 1991, includes the*
*following story.*

# EUFEMIA AND
# THE CURSE OF WORDS
Enrique Serna

Dazed, parched, her eyelids crusty,
Eufemia installs her public secretarial office in the plaza colonnade. The clock in the church tower strikes eleven. She has
lost her best customers, the housewives who line up at dawn
to buy milk. Serves her right, she figures, for sleeping too late
and drinking too much. With the utmost care, feeling the weight
of her own bones, she positions the plank across two crates,
covers it with a soiled cloth, and from a string bag draws the
tool of her trade: a Remington the size of a car battery, old, battered, and with its alphabet keys nearly rubbed out.

A pitiless sun heats the air. It's a year since the last rain
and the dirt streets are beginning to crack. On these streets pass
starving dogs, mules loaded with firewood, *campesinas* carrying infants in their shawls. Eufemia breathes with difficulty. Her

mouth tastes like copper. After placing next to the Remington a sign announcing the price per typed page (she prefers to point to the sign rather than engage in conversation with people—she has never liked talking with people), she collapses on her chair with a sigh. Time for breakfast. She casts a glance left and right to be sure no one is looking, pulls from her bag a bottle of tequila, and takes a long swallow, desperately long. Nothing like tequila to restore the agility of one's fingers.

Feeling better, she wipes the crust from her eyelids with her little finger and observes the idlers who doze or read newspapers on the benches of the plaza. Lucky ones, they can take it easy. She's been a week in Alpuyeca and pretty soon she'll have to move on. She already knows the faces of everyone in town. A few try to get friendly with her; that's not to be permitted. It always happens when she stays too long in one place. People are so grateful for the letters she writes. (The more ignorant they are, the more grateful.) Sometimes they even invite her to eat barbacoa, as if they'd known her forever. They just don't realize that if she goes from town to town, like a lost mare, if she never passes the same way twice, it is precisely in order *not* to soften, *not* to let anyone dilute her anger and disgust with false affection and empty attentions.

A girl coming from the market stops and asks the price of a letter.

"Well, ¿can't you read?" The girl shakes her head. "Right here it says 500 pesos a page."

The girl studies the sign as if it were written in hieroglyphs, searches in her purse and produces a silver coin that she puts on the table. Eufemia's authoritarian voice inspires terror in the girl.

"¿Who's it going to?"

The girl's face takes on a purplish tinge. She smiles timidly, showing her beautiful teeth. She is pretty and, in spite of her youth, she already has the figure of a woman.

"¿Is it for your *novio*?"

Writhing with embarrassment, the girl indicates that it is.

"¿What's his name?"

"Lorenzo Hinojosa. But I call him Lencho."

"All right then, let's put 'Dear Lencho," Eufemia announces, examining the girl's face in order to measure by the brilliance of her eyes the force of her love. Yes, she's in love, poor idiot.

" 'Dear Lencho', ¿what else? Hurry up, now; I can't spend all morning with you."

"God willing, this letter finds you well, and all your family."

Eufemia's fingers race over the keyboard. The girl watches, astonished.

"God will-ing, this let-ter finds you well, and all your fam-i-ly. What else?"

"I miss you so much. Sometimes I cry because you are not here ..."

REALIZE *YOUR* AMBITION said the little balloon coming out of the mouth of the blonde model who was taking dictation from her athletic-looking boss: THE COMMERCIAL COLLEGE "MODELO" PREPARES YOU TO SUCCEED. The trolleybus was full of passengers but Eufemia, installed in her de luxe office, was immune to the annoyances of the trip and to the mixture of sweat and perfumes, until a sudden braking woke her from her reverie, well past her stop. Her distraction cost her a seven-block walk, but she alighted convinced that she had the stuff to be a secretary. The blonde with the face of a princess had pricked her pride.

I want to be *her*, and to be *there*, she thought that night, and for several nights following, afflicted with the fear that her personality did not rise to the level of her dreams. With her savings, she might pay the tuition at the school, but she feared that if she didn't walk, if she didn't dress, if she didn't think differently, in short if she didn't change her skin, they would never allow her to work in an office like the one in

the advertisement, even though she had her secretary's certificate. Her fears diminished when her mistress, *doña* Matilde,
offered to pay her registration fees and lend her a Remington
for the typing exercises. This help made her feel more secure,
more a part of the family than a servant, and she entered
the Modelo Commercial College with the firm determination to triumph or die.

She was eighteen years old, a body that had begun to
bloom, and a timidity that was proof against wooers. Since
she firmly believed that men were not for her, nor was she
for them, she applied to her studies her best virtues (the ones
that no lover would ever know how to appreciate): responsibility, a spirit of service, a mad self-abnegation. She finished
her chores at four in the afternoon, returned from school
at eight in order to serve dinner, and from nine until past
midnight was glued to the Remington: asdfgf, asdfgf, ñlkjhj
... She did each exercise three or four times, managing to
keep her shoulders straight, as the teacher had demonstrated,
and when she made a mistake she became so angry, so filled
with the fear of being a failure, that she would jab a pin into
the offending finger.

Sleeping and waking, her mind was on the keys of the
machine, on the symbols in her shorthand book, in the verses
of Kahlil Gibran that she would hang on the wall of her future
office, and she imagined a paradise of impeccably ordered
files in which she would reign like a good and helpful fairy,
receiving the warm congratulations of a boss who looked just
like the leading man in the 9:30 soap opera. In the first year
of her training—which she finished at the top of her class—
she only once failed to turn in an assignment, and that was
not through her fault but the fault of the Remington. The Remington and the miserable fellow who took three days to come
and fix it.

His name was Jesús Lazcano. He wore a tag with his
name on it, pinned to his jacket, a detail that made a good
impression on Eufemia—like everything related to the world
of offices—but it only took two words with him to discover

that his professionalism was all facade. He didn't even apolo-
gize for the delay. He climbed the service stairs in slow motion, stopping four times to shift his toolbox from one hand
to the other. His slowness was even more disheartening
because it seemed to suggest a certain disgust with the whole
idea of work. When he finally arrived on the landing, where
Eufemia had for some time been waiting, he flashed her a
smile that was both cynical and bold and asked her *"por favor-
cito"* (the diminutive sounded vulgar in his mouth) to hang
up his jacket so that it would not get wrinkled.

She complied with a mixture of indignation and
perplexity. ¿What could this imbecile be thinking? He was
a grimy mechanic and behaved like an executive. If she hadn't
needed the typewriter fixed as soon as possible, she would
have shouted ¡arrogant clown! While she showed him the
problem—the ribbon wouldn't return—she noticed that Lazcano, instead of fixing his attention on the typewriter, looked
her directly in the eyes. From the impudence of his gaze, she
gathered that he considered himself irresistible. ¿How many
girls must he have seduced with this landslide of the eyes?
Certainly more than a few, because he was good-looking for
sure, that she couldn't deny. But neither his dimpled chin,
nor his honey-colored eyes, nor the curled lock of hair that
fell across his forehead gave him any right to be so bold. When
Lazcano set to work, she felt relieved. He might be a slick
one but he knew his job. Terrified by the idea that the Remington was seriously damaged and would have to be hospitalized in the repair shop, she got so close watching the operation that her thigh brushed the mechanic's hairy arm.

"Don't get so close, sweetheart, you'll make me nervous."

She was the one getting nervous. More: she felt a burning sensation in her belly. She jumped back and tried to calm
herself by counting to one hundred, but Lazcano believed
the ice was broken, and while he finished oiling the Remington he submitted her to a series of attentive questions.
To all his questions (age, place of birth, plans for the future)
Eufemia responded with arid verbal economy. Spurred by her

hostility, Lazcano wanted to know if she had a *novio*.

"¿And what's it to you?"

"Just curious."

"I don't have one and I don't want one."

When Lazcano finished with the typewriter he approached perilously close to the corner of the room where Eufemia had taken refuge to conceal her embarrassment. It seemed incredible to him that such a pretty girl would not have a *novio*. ¿Was it possible she never went out? Eufemia handed him the hanger with the jacket, suggesting that she expected him to leave immediately. Instead, Lazcano took her by the arm and whispered in her ear an invitation for the following Sunday, a bit of boldness that cost him a slap.

"Get out of here or I'll tell the *señora*."

"O.K., princess," Lazcano caressed her cheek, "but I'm going to come for you anyhow, in case you cheer up."

Eufemia dedicated her Sundays to the reading of a book that had been recommended at school: *How to Develop a Triumphant Personality*, by the psychologist Bambi Rivera. She underlined those portions that might help her overcome her timidity, to be less shy and aloof with others, promising herself to put these principles into practice as soon as she might escape from her surroundings, so that if in fact they helped her "to face life's challenges as if each obstacle were a stimulus," she would not give herself too freely to "excel in the most important aspect of all, those interpersonal bonds that contribute to your self-realization."

She was memorizing this passage when she heard a protracted and sentimental whistling, quite distinct from the perfunctory trill of Abundio, the butcher, who stopped by to pick up the maid. Feeling an emptiness in the pit of her stomach, she peeked out at the street to confirm what she suspected: Lazcano had fulfilled his threat. Leaning against a lamppost, he eyed the terrace with his arms folded across his chest. He seemed to have the confidence of a pouter pigeon. ¿Did he really think she would come running like a dog at his master's call? No, he could just settle down and wait. Eufemia hid behind a planter so she could casually watch him. He wasn't dressed up, but he wore a jacket of faded denim that suited him nicely. It seemed he had two disguises: one the executive, the other a sporty kid. ¡What a compulsion to be something he was not! She despised him for a *poseur*, vain and conceited, and as she had no intention of going to him, any more than she had of telling him to stop bothering her, she remained motionless in her observation post. The serenade lasted more than ten minutes. When Lazcano finally gave up and walked away, with his mouth dry from so much vain whistling, Eufemia felt some compassion for him. ¿How could one not be grateful for such persistence?

*Doña* Matilde congratulated her on her grades, wishing in front of others that her own children had turned out so studious, but in private reproaching Eufemia that her work was suffering on account of school. She toured the kitchen, inspecting every corner, and whenever any dust in the cupboard sullied her delicate index finger she improvised a sermon on unappreciated generosity. She was tired of such carelessness. If she had permitted Eufemia to study, and even paid for repairs to the typewriter, it was because she had confidence in her; but in return for these privileges she expected a little responsibility. Let her go ask how servants were treated in other houses. She didn't ask much: only that the work be well done.

In order to satisfy her without neglecting her studies, Eufemia worked sixteen hours a day. Every typing exercise became a test of endurance. She no longer battled with her painfully disciplined fingers but with her sleepless eyelids. Her school desk became her pillow. She heard her classes in a half-sleep and dreamed that she was learning. Seeing her fatigued and hollow-eyed, *doña* Matilde gave her a bottle of vitamin pills. "Take one after each meal, and if you feel tired don't go to school. The world won't come to an end if you miss a day."

Eufemia threw the vitamins and the advice in the trash. She was sure her mistress was trying to wean her from her studies in order to keep her a servant for life. She didn't real-ly take pleasure in Eufemia's successes. In her congratula-tions there was a strain of mockery, a subtle belittlement, based on the belief that a servant, however much she burned the midnight oil, would always be a servant. This disdain pained her more than a thousand scoldings, because it matched her own fears. She didn't have the character to be a secretary. If she wanted to disappoint *doña* Matilde (she savored in her dreams the triumphal scene of her resigna-tion, diploma in hand, a job already lined up), first she would have to modify her mental habits, as recommended by *Doc-tora* Rivera.

In Tuxtepec, the town where she was raised, Eufemia had had many friends, but in Mexico City she only got together with her cousin Rocio, who had come with her to the capital and now worked in a beautiful house in the Polan-co district. Wild and flirtatious, Rocio sported a *novio* and a fashionable dress on weekends, smoked like one con-demned to death, dyed her hair blonde, and persecuted Eufemia by telling her over and over that if she wanted a chance to be a secretary she might better find herself a rich old man and stop suffering. As part of her strategy for culti-vating her secretarial character, Eufemia stopped talking to Rocio. Such friendships were not for her. She changed her hairdo, her perfume, her diction. She no longer said "Y'know" and "C'mon," or "this Pedro" or "this Juan," or "He went" when she meant "He said." But nobody appreciated her linguistic progress, because after she lost touch with Rocio she re-mained alone in her perfection: a jewel without a case, a man-nequin without a shop-window.

For lack of a friendly ear, she vented her tensions on the Remington. She had been told many times not to hit the keys too hard, but once embarked on her practice she lost control of her fingers and struck the letters with crushing fury. One Sunday, after a week of complete isolation, she discovered that even after her assignment was done, there remained a desire to keep typing. She put down the first thing that came into her head: words mixed with graphic outbursts, words of songs, vulgarities, even numbers. She filled half a page with a shower of indecipherable signs, heedlessly mashing the alphabet, and without any intention began to string together malignant phrases—*Eufemia pitiful piece of meat STUDY DROP DEAD BITCH!\*@*—phrases that turned against her as if the Remington, to revenge itself for her pummeling, was dragging from her a drastic confession of her impotence: *keep on working keep on preparing yurself for the grave misierable idiot!??\*&!& bloody your fingers in your little garret worthless alleycat without Triumphant Personality nobody wants you useless virgin whore ¡¡Take what you deserve!! stupid/take . . .* She hit five keys at once so that the machine swallowed its words, but the torrent of insults continued to pour out, the paper kept filling up with purulent sores and she had to silence the Remington with blows of her fist, to make it vomit up screws, nuts, springs, to shake it to pieces so that it would know who was in charge.

The following morning she phoned the repair shop. Her remorse at having ruined a machine that didn't belong to her welled up again when she heard the voice of Jesús Lazcano. ¿Had she thrown that tantrum simply in order to see him again? With a petulance born of her rejection, Lazcano made her beg before he agreed to attend to the little job in about a week—and only because it was her, because now he repaired only electric machines. She hung up furious. She had caught a double meaning in his remark about electric typewriters. ¿Had he said it in order to suggest that he was going out with women of more class?

Just in case, the day he came to repair the Remington, she had on her best dress. The *señora* had gone out with the children to Mass and the silence of the house gave Lazcano the courage to get right to the point almost as soon as he crossed the threshold: Eufemia grew more beautiful every day; too bad that she wasn't even aware of it. ¿Why couldn't she put herself a little out of commission, instead of the machine, so he might give her a little check-up?

He arrived half-drunk and with his tie off to one side. His words of flattery were daring but he uttered them without affectation, as if drinking had restored his humility. When he laid eyes on the Remington, he gave a loud laugh. He repaired machines but he didn't work miracles. Poor little machine, ¡how your mistress has mistreated you! That's how cruel she was with anyone who loved her, he could vouch for that.

Eufemia asked him please to stop dilly-dallying.

"I'm not dilly-dallying, *chula*. This thing is no good. If you like, I'll replace all the broken parts, but it'll cost you a bundle. You'd do better to buy a new one."

Eufemia turned pale. It was her *life* that no longer functioned. She fell across the bed and hid her face in the quilt so as not to cry in front of a man. Lazcano took her by the shoulders, gently, trying to make her turn around.

"Let me go, please. ¡Let me go!"

"Don't work yourself up. ¿Did I do you any harm? ¿Is it on account of the machine?"

With a sharp intake of breath, she said yes. She drew a handkerchief from her purse and while she tried to put a stop to her tears, she explained to Lazcano, between sobbing and beating her chest, that the machine was the property of her mistress and while she desperately needed it to achieve her career as a secretary she had ruined her chances, her whole life, for a silly whim. All her wages went to pay the costs of her school; she had nothing left over for clothes, never mind the cost of a new typewriter. They might as well expel her, *doña* Matilde might as well run her off . . .

"Calm down so we can straighten this out," Lazcano said, caressing her cheek. "As for the typewriter, I can help you there, don't worry about that."

"I'm not asking for your help." She gave him a dignified look. "I know what you men expect in return."

"Shut up, stupid." Lazcano was beginning to get impatient. "Someone tries to give you a hand and all you do is grumble."

"I don't want anything from you, I already told you. ¡Now get out or I'll call for help!"

Before she could let out a cry, Lazcano surprised her with a kiss, holding her chin in his hand to prevent her from turning away. Eufemia took a little longer than necessary before slapping him.

"That makes two. ¿Why don't you give me the third one? I'm beginning to get a kick out of this little game."

Lazcano returned to the attack. With a suspicious slowness of her reflexes, Eufemia reacted to his kiss when it was already a *fait accompli* and she felt inside her mouth a tongue that moved like a hot rotor blade, leaving her breathless. There was a brief struggle during which Lazcano endured bites and scratches. Eufemia weakened little by little, gave ground without retaliation, numbed by his turbulent vigor. The strength to resist was still there but her body betrayed her; it had its own way like the perfidious Remington. She closed her eyes and thought about herself, about her youth which she had spent like an industrious zombie. She pictured Lazcano whistling like a veteran in his sporty jacket and the image awakened in her a burning appetite, a tremendous desire to do nothing. Immobile and with an absent gesture, she let her dress be lifted, her breasts caressed. She could acquiesce to all of it, all except the infamy of collaboration with the aggressor. The kisses of Lazcano died on her hard and hostile lips; he, knowing he had vanquished her physically, insisted on a surrender of the emotions, even while he fought, with more force than skill, to undo the tight knot of her thighs.

The obscene squeaking of the bed silenced the deep lament with which Eufemia bade farewell to her virginity. She took pleasure guiltily, thinking about the repair of her typewriter in order to pretend that she was prostituting herself from necessity but the impetuous attacks of Lazcano and her own palpitations, the effervescence that rose in her, and the supreme pleasure of feeling herself wicked, left her without pretexts, without rationalizations, limply defenseless in the onslaught of pleasure.

The Remington and Eufemia both emerged like new. Lazcano repaired both of them free of charge, receiving in exchange a companion for Sundays. At one stroke, he accomplished what Bambi Rivera, with all her science, had not been able to do: he cured Eufemia of her timidity and her tendency to underrate herself. *Doña* Matilde noted with surprise that she hummed while she did the chores, and that she spoke looking her directly in the eye. Her performance in school improved too: her charitable attitude during exams (she no longer considered it a fraud on the state to allow someone to copy) erased the image of a hard-nosed and self-absorbed puritan that she had created out of a fear of others. She began to spend time with a group of girl friends with whom she would linger, chatting after school, careless of the fact that *doña* Matilde would scold her for arriving late to serve supper. She no longer harbored any doubts about her future. The accounting instructor, impressed with her speed and neat handwriting, promised to find her work as soon as she finished the course. She had only one cause for alarm: Jesús had made no formal declaration and her relationship with him, while happy in the essential part, continued in a dangerous state of indefinition during the first two months of what Eufemia would like to have called their engagement.

Words meant nothing to Jesús. He talked with his hands. He touched her everywhere, and at all hours, with or without onlookers, under the solitary tree where they took leave of each other every Sunday, after making love in a hotel in San Cosme, or on a bench in the Alameda, surrounded by children, grannies, beggars and police. Thoroughly occupied by her love, Eufemia had no time nor desire to dwell on her fears. It would have been mean, a crime against love, to doubt a man who gave his soul with every kiss. Together they agreed to extend their Sunday pleasures and to see each other during the week, when Eufemia went out to buy bread. The whistling of Jesús made her nipples erect. And it was heard so often in the street that *doña* Matilde began to get annoyed. "Tell your young friend that if he wants to see you I have no problem with that, you are free to choose your friends, but that he ought at least to have the decency to ring the bell. ¿Or do you find these mule-driver customs attractive?" Lazcano was proud and took offense when he heard *doña* Matilde's opinion of his behavior. He resigned himself to ringing the bell, so that she would not think him a mule-driver, but he would not agree to make conversation with her now and then, as Eufemia suggested. "No way, *chula*. If we start catering to that busybody, pretty soon we'll have her as a nursemaid."

Although his warnings seemed justified, Eufemia suspected that he had other reasons to avoid *doña* Matilde. Jesús was terribly antisocial. He didn't even like going out in a group with her school friends. They were always alone, enclosed in a suffocating intimacy. He talked a lot about his friends at work, with whom he played soccer every Saturday, but he hadn't introduced her to them. ¿Why couldn't they be a couple like other couples?

It cost her a dozen sleepless nights to resolve the mystery. Jesús' love for her was a pastime. If he had no interest in formalizing their relationship, or, to put it another way, he had an interest in *not* formalizing it, this was because he was thinking about leaving her whenever he got tired of going to bed with her. That's why he avoided any social life as a couple: the miserable sneak was preparing his retreat and didn't want any witnesses to his treachery. And she, really blind, really stupid, had believed herself loved and respected. "He believes that I am his whore, and I deserve it, for having given him everything from the first day."

The following Sunday she adopted a glacial attitude. At the zoo, she yawned through the parade of elephants, refused to share a cotton candy with Jesús, or to have her picture taken in front of the panda cage. They got on the little train, and when they entered the Tunnel of Love she removed Jesús' exploring hand from her knee. She ate little and poorly, complaining that the sandwiches tasted like plastic, the movie about druggies gave her a headache, and she looked forward with malevolence to the moment when they would arrive at the door of the hotel, where she would refuse to go in. Jesús resented that most of all. He reproached her for the day full of ill humor: the pretend boredom, her bashfulness in the miniature train. ¿Did she have problems with our arrangement, or what? Her answer was a long and sorrowful enumeration of grievances. Jesús didn't treat her right. ¿Why did he keep on lying if he didn't really love her? He treated her like a worn-out floozy, worse yet because floozies at least got paid. She wasn't his sweetheart, or his wife, or his fiancée. ¿So what was she? ¿His little bed partner? Jesús denied all the charges but Eufemia presented them as incontestable facts. She accused him of cowardice, of *machismo*, of being a man without honor. If she was to believe in his love, she needed a promise of matrimony. She had the right to demand it: he had been the first man in her life. ¿Or did he mean to deny that too?

The face of a scolded adolescent, with which Jesús had endured this peroration, gave way suddenly to an expression of resolve. "Very well, we'll get married. But shut up already."

"¿Really? ¿You want to marry me?" Eufemia's tone sweetened.

"Of course I do, silly." Jesús kissed her on the neck, tenderly inhaling the fragrance of her skin. "I was thinking about telling you today, but you seemed to be in such a bad mood that it scared me off. ¿And now you're whining? Quit it, it makes me think you don't love me. C'mon, how about a little smile, a little smile from my little funny-bunny . . ."

That afternoon they made love three times. Eufemia was affectionate and uninhibited, but between encounters she planned the wedding down to the smallest detail. They would get married in Tuxtepec as soon as she finished her course. Jesús was very fickle. She would have to act fast, so he wouldn't have time to change his mind. The first thing was for him to ask for her hand in marriage; her parents couldn't be expected to give their consent without meeting the fiancé. ¿And his parents? He hardly ever spoke of them; most likely he was on the outs with his family. Well, he could decide whether to invite them or not. She'd better speak right away to the accounting instructor about the matter of a job. She didn't want to be a kept woman. Putting their two salaries together, they could rent an inexpensive apartment and buy the furniture on installments – a refrigerator, a stove... Her future gleamed like the coppery skin of the body that was wrapped around hers. She would marry in white, and with her secretarial diploma: a double surprise for *doña* Matilde.

Between preparations for the wedding and the marathon study sessions for the final exams, the three months before the trip to Tuxtepec went flying by. Her parents awaited impatiently the arrival of the young man, whom she had described, with some exaggeration, as a marvel of honor and economic solvency. While she spread the news of her wedding, and occupied herself in locating a judge and making their appointments for examinations at the clinic, Jesús was going through a crisis of catatonia. He drank more than usual ("saying goodbye to party-time," he swore) and when Eufemia mentioned to him the names she had picked out for their first child (Erick or Wendy), he disconnected and his eyes went blank. She practically had to drag him to buy the rings. Far from being upset by his conduct, Eufemia considered it to be a good sign. What would have been bad was having him take the marriage lightly, not weighing the importance of his commitment.

The day of her graduation party, Eufemia went for the first time to a beauty parlor. They gave her an extravagant hairdo more fitting for a forty-year-old and she spent the afternoon trying to counteract it with a daringly girlish makeup. At eight, the *señora* shouted that they had come for her. She rushed downstairs, anxious to see Jesús in the tuxedo he had rented for the ceremony, but instead she found a ragged child who gave her a letter. It was from Lazcano. He thanked her for all the beautiful moments he had enjoyed in her company. Wanting to prolong them, wanting not to kill so soon this pure and noble sentiment, he had made a promise that a man such as himself, accustomed to a life without fetters, could not possibly keep. He was a coward, he realized that, but in the dilemma of losing love or liberty, he preferred to renounce love. By the time Eufemia read this letter, he would be arriving in Houston, where an uncle of his had offered him a job.

She should not take the breaking off of their relationship as a tragedy. They were both young, with plenty of time to begin a new life. She, so lovely, would quickly find the man who would make her happy and perhaps, sometime in the future, she would forgive. For now, he only asked, begged, implored that in the name of the happy hours they had spent together she would not hate him too much.

She gave a tip to the messenger of death and returned to her room with the steps of one condemned. She reread the letter a thousand and one times, repeating aloud the most hypocritical phrases. She had to hear them to convince herself she was not dreaming. She looked at herself in the mirror and the ladylike hairdo struck her as so grotesque that she tore out a handful of hair. Now to face the commiseration of her parents, the disguised satisfaction of *doña* Matilde, the malicious questions of her school friends when they saw her alone at the graduation party. Too many humiliations. She needed to disappear, somewhere far away where no one would know her, deny them all the pleasure of seeing her defeated. She threw her clothes haphazardly into a suitcase, took from the bureau the container in which she kept her savings, made a small bonfire of all her souvenirs of Lazcano, and looked at her room for the last time. She was forgetting the most important thing: the Remington, her confessor and portable gossip.

In the street she hailed a taxi which took her to the South Terminal. She would like to have bought a ticket to hell but at that hour there were only busses to Chilpancingo. In a small grocery store she bought a half liter of tequila, and while she awaited the departure of her bus she drank until she sank to the level of her own hopes. In her seat in the bus, before it pulled away, she read the letter for the last time.

Damned words. It was only necessary to string them together in order to destroy a life. To kill by writing was to kill from behind. One couldn't confront one's enemy and reproach him for being such a sissy. She tore the homicide weapon into shreds and when the bus started up she threw them out the window. The Remington would be her weapon from now on. At last she would get some good use from her excellent orthography, her extensive vocabulary, her dexterity in the organization of these damned words.

Another town. Another plaza colonnade. A conscript with his face damaged by acne reads a letter, seated in the shade of a cottonwood. His hands tremble. He seems not to understand what he reads. He brings his eyes close to the paper as if he were nearsighted. He reads from bottom to top, then from top to bottom, on the point of tears. He examines the back of the page in search of something more, but it's blank. He crumples the letter, furious, and then spreads it out again as if hoping to alter its contents by this magical operation.

> *Dear Lencho:*
>
> *You were wrong if you thought I could wait for you all my life. What had to happen happened. A real man, not a deadhead like you, took that proof of love that you so often asked of me. Now I know what it feels like to be a woman, and I don't want anything to do with you. Goodbye forever. I'm leaving for the capital with my new lover. You will never know my address. Don't get it into your head to try and find me . . .*

*—Translated by David Bowen*

*Paco Ignacio Taibo II (Gijón, Spain 1949) is inter-
nationally known for his noir detective fiction, published in fifteen languages; the most recent is* La
bicicleta de Leonardo *(1993). He has also written
a history of communism in Mexico and the volume
of short stories* El regreso de la verdadera araña,
*from which the following is taken, grew out of ex-
perience with labor organizations during the 1970s.*

# APACHES IN 'LA GRANJA'
## Paco Ignacio Taibo II

"Like Apaches—hiding at night and
raising hell by day," said Severo, leaving the meeting. He stopped
at the corner, hoisted his pants, and scratched his balls. "The
guy's gone nuts."

"I'm with him," answered Bigass. He was sparing in his
words, favored quick decisions.

"Yeah, I'm with him too, but he's out of his gourd—you'll
see. We met with a lawyer about the papers and he told us to
forget it if we couldn't scrape up twenty men; after telling us
to go to hell, this other guy shows up on the stairs and tells
us that with guts and a good plan we have enough to go after
the boss. And that's where we are. And now he starts up with
this Apache bullshit."

"I'm with him," Bigass said. "I'll be a motherfucker if I

153

ain't with him."

"The guy's no commie, just an out-and-out lunatic."

"I'm with him," Bigass repeated with a smile. He stood there smiling (his awful nickname had been pinned on him by all the assholes that worked in the factory), imagining what would go down the next day. And so it went.

Work started at seven-thirty and they had ten minutes leeway. Afraid to be found out, they decided to hook up at Avena Avenue, a block from work, and wait there till seven-forty, to head off like a herd toward the factory.

The factory was a huge open shed some 30 meters long, divided up by nothing more than the walkways made by the heaped furniture; gutted armchairs, looking a bit obscene with metal poles sticking out all sides, stuffing thrown here and there, and tacks all over the place. The floor was quite wet and when it rained, puddles formed all over. The sewing area took up one corner of the shed and had five sewing machines and piled-up bolts of cloth. The boss's office was a steel and glass walled-in cave with a desk and a safe. That's where the phone was. Sometimes it worked, sometimes it didn't. But it wasn't worth a shit since the boss (and foreman) ran the factory in the old style: riding around in a cart with a whip in hand, a bottle to use like a blackjack to pay overtime, a gun in the desk drawer for when discussions got out of hand.

The owner had said, "A union over my dead body." It was a small factory, 21 employees, two of whom were the same or bigger assholes than the boss, so 19 left them one short for a union shop.

"You're too much, my boy," Severo said to Bigass who gaped silently at the crest of eagle feathers on the head of *Don* Ramón, the carpenter.

"¿Should we strip down?" Marcial asked the union organizer, a stumpy sociology student who had come by bike, wearing his disguise, and was now taking off his leg clips for the charge.

"To our bare asses. ¿Ever seen Apaches wearing jackets?"

Severo solemnly shook his head. It had nearly cost him his life to get out of the house with three huge red zigzags painted on his cheeks and a wavy bright yellow line across his forehead. His old lady was convinced he was skipping work, having signed on as a movie extra or going to a TV tryout. Actually, he didn't have the strength to explain, but he had sworn to take part and there he was. Just like the other eighteen. No one was missing; it was the power of an oath, or having hit rock bottom, of always losing, of having seen so many sunrises from the bottom of a barrel.

Bigass was fat, and he had painted three concentric circles on his belly with white paint.

"My old lady didn't want to sleep with me," he said, taking off his shirt.

"¿How long have you been like this?"

"Since yesterday's rehearsal."

"Our weapons, comrades, don't forget them," said the union organizer. He put on some fake glasses to try to look older than his twenty years.

Screwdrivers, kitchen knives, tack hammers, a couple of well-sharpened axes, a few six-inch blades glowed in the light.

"All set. Everyone knows what he has to do."

The column moved down Avena Avenue. A drunk coming out of the Vencedora bar messed his pants when he saw them.

"¡Here come the damn redfaces!" he went off screaming, not believing what he had seen and swearing to St. Judas Tadeo that he would only drink good brandy from now on.

During the confusion Crazy Gerónimo tried to scurry off as they passed the paint shop. Severo jerked him back.

"Don't be a fag. ¿Are you comin' or not?"

The bosses of small Mexican firms had survived on pure instinct during those years; and at that moment, the infamous Mieles, fifty-year-old owner of *Mieles y Maderas, S.A.*, walked out of his factory into the street, pushed along by the bad vibes he was feeling. He bumped up against his nineteen employees dressed like Apaches. Prudently he backed off, nearly pissing in his pants.

He took off running and ended up locking himself in the shipping room.

"¡Get him, get him!" Severo shouted, playing his part to the hilt.

"Don't finish him off just yet, comrades, now it's my turn. Phase two—" the union organizer said.

The furniture-making Apaches ran over to the shipping room's windows brandishing their blades and knives, axes, and painted faces. Their faces contorted as they pressed them against the glass. With a serious expression, the union organizer knocked very softly on the door.

Half an hour later he came out with a signed contract and a 65% per piece salary increase, a promise to build brand new bathrooms (with toilet paper), to open the stopped drains, and to re-tar the roof. Best of all, he had even gotten the company to give the workers 10,000 pesos for them to buy candies for the children of the poor on the Day of the Child.

While the union organizer read the contract aloud, amid Apache howls, the boss was in his office taking three aspirins, not altogether sure of what had just transpired.

"There's just one hitch, my friends," said the union organizer waving away the workers as they tried to lift him on their shoulders. "¿What the hell are we going to do next year when it's time to review the contract?"

"We'll think of something," said Severo, letting his imagination begin to drift. He tried holding back the tear that threatened to smudge the red zigzags on his cheeks.

*—Translated by David Unger*

*María Luisa Puga (Mexico D.F. 1944) is a novelist*
*and essayist who has lived in Europe and East Africa*
*and maintains her distance now in a small village*
*near Pátzcuaro, Michoacán. Among her works are*
Pánico o peligro, *which was awarded the Villaur-*
*rutia Prize in 1983, and* Las razones del lago *(1992);*
*her seventh novel,* La viuda, *will appear in 1995.*
*She has produced two collections of short fiction;*
*this one is from* Accidentes *(1981).*

# THE TRIP
## María Luisa Puga

"We're nothing but a mass of con-
tradictions," he was saying, just as we met the truck and felt
the rush of wind buffeting our tiny Volkswagen. It was a narrow road and neither vehicle had slowed down. The word "contradictions" hung on the air for a second. I thought, "That's what
we are all right." But then what? What are we to make of it,
I was wondering, at the same time sensing we weren't on the
road any more, though we were still following the route it traced
perfectly calmly.

"What then?" I asked.

"Well ..." and by now we were coasting along some
distance from the road, chatting away despite the oppressive
midday heat, resigned to the miles that still lay between us and
Mexico City "... you simply have to accept them."

Aha? So all one had to do was to accept them? Recognize them, identify them, then leave them be? Take them seriously, pay them attention ... that seemed fair enough, as we glided towards the green hills. I couldn't understand why E. was bothering to steer round the bends or change down, when we were floating along so serenely.

"That's odd," L. commented from the back. "We've left the road."

"The best thing to do," A. recommended, "is to try not to think about it. To let yourself go. Otherwise, things may turn out far worse."

I didn't believe him. His tone of voice—I couldn't believe it. It was cold, not dispassionate. I could tell he was as disconcerted as me. As all of us, probably.

"Of course," said E. "It's not so hard. Simply try not to see yourself in any exact location. Let yourself go."

"Like we are doing now," said L., though it sounded more like a question than a statement.

"Correct," A. agreed. "Anyway, there's nothing else we can do."

"Well, if you say so, you must be right; but I can't help feeling there's something odd in all this," I insisted, glancing out of the car window.

E. was driving along at a leisurely pace, listening, but absorbed in his own thoughts. We all had things to do in the city, so we were happy to drift along, in no hurry to arrive.

L. was the only one who still seemed to find it strange that we had left the road. "I don't know about the rest of you, but this looks weird to me. The trees seem so close."

"That's what's nice about it," E. said. "You mean to tell me you don't like them?"

"If you look closely," A. pointed out, "you can see they all have different expressions. Have you noticed? That one over there is so solemn, for example."

I couldn't see which one he meant. I wasn't particularly looking for it. I wasn't so much interested in our surroundings as in the new state we found ourselves in, which seemed to have something to do with those contradictions. All the same, it was impossible not to notice that we were getting farther and farther from any point of reference, that is, the road.

"Where is this leading us?" L. wanted to know, but the question seemed completely inappropriate.

"Wherever you wish," E. reassured her. "It's for you to choose."

"I'm fine," A. said. "I'm happy to carry on as we are."

"Me too," I lied.

"What about you, L.?" E. asked.

"I feel ill, a bit sick, but don't let that worry you."

"Where were we then? Anyone remember?"

"Contradictions," I said. "What color are they, do you reckon?"

"Red, of course, though sometimes they have brownish tinges."

"No, they're blue," L. put in.

"Trust a Pisces to be so categorical," A. said. "Don't listen to her."

"No, I don't think they're blue at all," I objected, staring at the horizon. "That doesn't sound right."

"No? Well, red and brown it is then. Here and there. Nothing's nothing," he chuckled. "I mean, none of them is entirely one thing, is it?"

"Agreed. I am though," A said.

"I'm trying to get a picture of them," I said, not yet convinced. "Or could it be I have never acknowledged them before? How are you feeling, L.?"

"Actually, I don't feel at all well. I'd like to get out for a while, if that's possible."

E. studied her face in his rear-view mirror. Then he looked to his left, slowed down, and said, rather bewildered, "I'm not sure we can stop here."

"I'm not sure we can stop, period," I corrected him.

"Try to hang on, L.; it's too complicated to stop right now," A. said.

"OK, but how much farther is it?"

"I've lost all notion," E. admitted.

"Why can't we pull up near that hill over there? What d'you say, E.?"

"Yes, I wouldn't mind stretching my legs."

"Great idea," said L.

The car began a gentle descent. E. was steering with one hand, stroking his moustache thoughtfully with the other. He pulled up beside a tree and switched off the car engine. He sat for a while before opening the door.

"Right," he said with a yawn. "Here we are. Who's for a little stroll?"

All of us.

Such a strange sensation to stand up. To stretch one's legs, feel oneself walking, to look around. I was trembling, but it wasn't an unpleasant feeling, simply a new one.

"What time is it, by the way?" A. asked.

For a moment, I had to think hard what the question meant. I had to try to imagine what A. could possibly need to make him ask such an extraordinary question as "what time is it?" I saw E. glancing at his watch, and recalled a similar gesture on my part. L. was leaning against the car trunk, gazing out absent-mindedly as though she hadn't heard A. E. and I replied in the same breath, "My watch has stopped."

"That's strange, so has mine. That's why I was asking ..."

"Where are we?" L. butted in.

"I couldn't say for sure, but I reckon we must be about half way there, don't you? How long is it since we left Cuautla?"

We were all struck speechless. Cuautla. When on earth had we been in Cuautla?

"I used to go to Cuautla when I was a little girl ... I went once with my parents," I volunteered.

"I go more often," E. said. "My folks have a house there, but I haven't been in months."

"You were the one who brought it up," L. put in. "It's

the first time I've ever heard the word Cuautla."

"You must have heard of Cuautla. Remember, you have to cross it to reach Cuernavaca."

"For all those who know . . . the shape . . . of things to come, here on WFM," came faintly from the car radio.

"We went to Cuernavaca six months ago, on that other trip, didn't we?"

"No, it was before that."

"What a strange place this is," L. murmured.

"Why?" I wanted to know.

"It looks to me as if none of the greenery has any stems. Look at the grass, the trees."

I took a good look round. All I could see was green. Green everywhere, shapeless, dense, unending.

"What do you mean, the stems? I don't get you."

"Just look at the grass. It's completely flat on the ground. Look at the leaves on the trees. I've never seen anything like it."

In the distance, the trees seemed weighed down by their exuberant foliage. A green swelling in the skirts of the hills. L. was right, the grass did seem like a cloak of moss stretched out on the earth. Nothing stood out. It was as if everything was lying flat, featureless, though the color was extraordinarily deep and intense. The land was like a padded mattress. Suddenly I noticed another strange thing: The horizon had vanished. We were entirely surrounded by the flat green plain, which gave way in the distance to equally green hills.

"Hey," I called to E. "This is really a weird place, isn't it?" I tried to point into the distance realizing as I did so that I was searching for the dividing line between earth and sky. My hand traced a circle, inviting the others to follow it. E. obligingly did so. "It's beautiful," he said.

L.'s jaw had dropped. "I'd like to move on now," she suggested.

E. looked sad. Then he looked at me and said, "How come the four of us can never really be together? If it's not one, then it's another; there's always someone who wants to be off, who puts an end to the moment ..."

"And that's with just four of us. Imagine what it's like with a whole society."

We all laughed, but our expressions had changed. I could sense the difference in my own by looking at the others'. They were all pale, anxious. All of them peering nervously around. I stared at them (probably too much of a coward to look at what they might be looking at). But their faces gave me some indication of what must be happening to me.

"What shall we do now?" I asked E.

"Move on, I guess—what else?"

So easy, of course, to get back into the car and drive off. But suddenly I for one couldn't imagine the car or any idea of leaving. It was all so crazy, so ridiculous, like when you're already in bed, asking, what time shall we go to bed? I decided the others must be playing a trick, so I started to laugh. Then they all joined in, peals of laughter, doubled up, sprawled over the car, toppling onto the grass, wiping away their tears (which only brought twice as many to my eyes). I slipped down with the rest of them, letting myself go in a fit of uncontrollable hilarity that was born as an echo of their laughter. I think that for a split second I thought of the future and how I had missed my last chance of knowing it, but the laughter was pressing so hard inside my chest that as I gave in to it, I had to sadly relinquish a whole host of fresh intentions. Yet that moment when I lay down was exquisite. A real arrival where I belonged. My own place.

"I can hear voices. Someone's coming," said E.

We'd laughed so much we couldn't sit up.

"You're right," A. said. "I can hear them too."

Then I also heard sounds in the distance, like a happy crowd. It reminded me of when I used to live near a theatre. The noise the audience made as they left after the last show at two in the morning. I would wake up, and their laughter, their chatter, the sound of car engines, was a gentle disturbance, like someone coming to tuck me in.

"Oh yes," I said, "they're leaving the theatre."

The others burst out laughing.

"Don't cackle like that," I protested, "they'll think we're having a party or something."

That sounded lame even to my own ears. By now the others were writhing on the ground.

"Be quiet, dammit, who will they take us for?"

Idiots. Weeping with mirth. And the people were getting closer. Bringing with them their own noise, from their side. A sudden panic gripped me. "Please," I begged the others, "be a bit quieter, or they'll realize we're here."

"If they're headed this way it's precisely for that reason, because they've spotted us."

"It can't be," I said, more and more terrified. "We must do something, E., they're almost here."

"It doesn't matter. They'll understand," he soothed me.

So then I relaxed and fell silent, laughter still tickling me, but the fun was gone. Waiting to hear the simple words:

"Yes, they were all killed, poor souls."

*—Translated by Nick Caistor*

*Inés Arredondo (Culiacán, Sinaloa 1928 – Mexico D.F. 1989) was an essayist and screenwriter who also published four volumes of short stories.* Rio sub-terráneo *(1979) won the Villaurrutia Prize and* Los espejos *appeared in 1988. She received grants from the Centro Mexicano de Escritores and the Fair-field Foundation.*

# PUZZLES
## Inés Arredondo

Mornings were boring until it came time for breakfast. Besides, she had to be careful of her white batiste dress and the upright blue bow on top of her head. Later she would go to the "school" and make strokes and characters with colored crayons that only she understood; there would be songs, rounds, stories, games with her girlfriends. But until then she didn't have anything else to do, except snoop around the house, because they could call her any minute and she would have to do whatever it was.

But since they got in the habit of taking him out for some fresh air at the time when the sun wasn't so strong, everything had changed. They would seat him in the back corridor, near the garden, next to the aviary, and they would go to sweep and dust. So Teresa would be left completely alone in front of him and she would watch him, cautiously. She would sit at a distance on the floor and study him with impassive eyes. She never touched him, just looked at him, she would stay motionless for long periods of time, watching him. At times the birds distracted her or she would draw figures with her fingers over the glistening floor, but without haste she always came back to pay attention to him and continue studying him until the time came to go to breakfast. Sometimes, at night, when she was already in bed, she would think about him, and she would have liked to talk about it with somebody, ask her mother, but she didn't know what to call him. Then she would sigh and forget about him.

The rest of the day there was nothing, or almost nothing, that she could remember about him. She knew that he was in the room adjoining her mother's and that a nurse was in and out of that room with things that didn't interest her, and that was all.

But one morning when she was sitting on the floor, keeping her distance from him, her mother appeared and began to scream incomprehensibly. At first she came toward her as though she were going to hit her, but then afterwards broke into sobs saying, "Don't look at him like that, don't look at him like that," and at the same time she beat her breast with her fists. Her father came up very frightened and took her mother away. Teresa stayed where she was, terrified and hurt, what had she done? La Cuca came smiling and took him away as quickly as possible. But she didn't even touch him ... She heard them call for the doctor, then she got up and went to the garden. She walked along looking at the roses and the little flowers among the grass, absorbed in what was happening at the house: in the arrival of the doctor, in the comings and goings of servants, in the voice of her father.

From where she was she could see perfectly and be seen, but nobody was looking for her, they didn't call her to breakfast, they didn't even look at her when they passed by. She was hungry. Walking slowly, amusing herself here and there, at times turning her head a little, she crossed the garden, then walked among the fruit trees, and finally, disheartened, crossed the patio where the geese were, and yet before entering the granary she turned around and stood looking at her house: she saw the portico with the aviary far away, dark, between her and it a great space with plants, trees, and the animal's patio. Near the portico, in the kitchen, she could hear the strident voice of la Cuca, even though she couldn't see her, but la Cuca was talking to la Paula or to Manuel, not to her. She drew back the bolt and pushed the large door with all her might. She didn't like that place. In the patio, the one that all the doors of the storerooms opened onto, there was nothing; it had an adobe wall on one side and the little low rooms on all the others, nothing else. She went in through the room where the threshing machine was, walked around it, but without coming very near it. When they were threshing it was nice to be there, with Chuyón laughing and letting her turn the crank, and all the men bring-ing and carrying out sacks; it was nice to see how the corn and beans fell everywhere and lay strewn in the dust of the patio as though it didn't matter to anybody. But now the lit-tle rooms were full of grain, the floor completely clean, and nobody ever went there, ever until the next harvest.

Something was hurting her, a lot, in her chest. She put both hands on the threshing machine and pressed hard, the hinges creaked, the mechanism was too heavy for her. She stopped a moment, expecting that someone would shout, scolding her, someone who might be hidden, watching, but after a pause she pulled away her hands, little by little, without haste. She went back to the patio and tried pushing the doors, the windows, making a little bit of noise, skipping on one foot, but continuing to feel that she wasn't able to breathe well, and that strange hurt. She came upon a high small win-dow that appeared to be open, climbed up to it, pushed it carefully and got into one of the little rooms: it was filled with corn up to the middle. She took off her sandals and threw them through the window to the patio. She liked walking on the shiny grain. For a long time she made little mountains

and roads, and when she got bored she made a ditch and
buried herself up to her chest in the corn, but this was making her more and more sad, until she couldn't stand it and
with a little cry she tried to leap out away from that horrible
hole, she had to fight hard for the power to do it: she was
slipping desperately in the grain. At that moment she would
have liked to leave the little room and go back and climb
the guava tree or see the aviary, but none of that was possible, she wasn't able to go anywhere, she wasn't able to do
anything more than stay put in this dark and ugly little room.
Dirty, with her face full of streaks made by her tears and the
corn dust, she curled up in a corner looking at the light that
came through the half-open window. At times she fell half
asleep, but would awaken with a start, feeling as though someone was putting their hands over her throat and choking her.

In the silence the whistle from the factory sounded announcing that it was twelve o'clock. Sometimes she had gone in
the car to pick up her father and saw the workers pour out
to stretch themselves, like a river, as soon as the whistle sounded, as if they were waiting, out of sight. The door to the factory was never closed, but the whistle was a magic curtain
that closed it and opened it, invisible, every day of every year,
except for Sundays. Also they would hear it screech in the
fields, far, far away; it came on the air like a serpent, and the
peasants would seek out the shade as soon as it passed, open
their lunch sacks and sit down and eat. Now that the whistle had sounded, outside it was midday, there was activity,
the men were returning to their homes, the children were
coming out of the school . . . but for her all this didn't mean
anything. She hadn't eaten all day, nor was she going to eat
now like all the others, she was outside the power of that
sharp sound, just as she was outside everything, alone in that
horrible place, outside. She crossed her arms across her chest
and she squeezed herself as hard as she could. She felt fear,
an enormous fear. She was breathing brokenly, the same as
after having cried a lot, but now there were no tears on her

face, just her body quivering with that dry kind of sobbing.

After a long time she heard different voices that cried "Maya," "Teresa," but she couldn't answer. Those voices weren't directed at her, nor could they succeed in reaching her. She continued trembling, with her eyes fixed on the ray of light that entered through the small window, far from them, buried in a room of corn. "Mayita," a man's voice said very near her, but she wasn't able to respond, she couldn't. The door opened with a dry thump and light entered the room like a wave. In the door below, the black silhouette of her father appeared enormous, overwhelming. She hid her face behind her crossed arms. She heard the corn run toward the outside and saw the efforts of the men to keep from sinking in the grain that escaped toward the patio. Her father drew near to her, drew near sloshing through the corn. Teresa trembled and shrank back, she wanted to make herself little, so little as to disappear. "My little daughter, my little daughter," the man said almost next to her, and Teresa with her eyes shut let out a long, rending moan, and without knowing how, found herself sobbing, filling her face with tears, against her father's breast. "Mayita, my little one," said the mouth that lightly touched her hair, meanwhile his arms rocked her rhythmically. She felt very tired. Her father went out with her in his arms, walking gingerly through the corn that flowed around him each time he took a step, and Teresa thought once more that there was corn flowing into the patio and to her father it didn't matter.

"Mama is sick, she's expecting a new baby, she's very nervous on account of that . . . you must behave yourself . . . It was bad that you hid yourself all morning long, you frightened everybody. . . ."

That wasn't true, nobody had hunted for her until they came home from work, but she didn't say anything, now he was here and carried her carefully across the big doorway, across the patio with the geese, across the garden. He carried her back, and that was what mattered.

In bed, her mother looked like a fallen tower. With her loose hair over the pillows, so strong and so beautiful, it was hard to believe that she was sick. She had not seen her for a long time and they had told her that she was being cured in the United States, but she never believed that, nor was she afraid for her: her mother was far away for some other reason that they didn't want to tell her, not on account of being sick. Even now she didn't accept that some unknown malady would be able to attack her; her mother was too proud for something that simple to throw her in bed.

Her father was talking, somewhere between cheerful and sad, and she continued to hold tight against his chest looking at her mother who listened to him without saying a word. It was strange that her parents resembled each other so much physically, were united in some mysterious way, and in spite of this were so different. She felt placed between the two like an obstacle, something that divided them. For example, her father had never treated her in that bizarre way, nor had he beaten his chest shrieking, and now as he was holding her in his arms in front of her mother he seemed to be disapproving of the way Teresa and all the others in the house had behaved. But all that was very vague, what she was feeling most was tired and sleepy.

"Let's go. Give your mama a kiss and promise her that you are going to behave."

She did what he told her, in a mechanical manner and, even though her mother also kissed her, it was a cold kiss. Teresa didn't take her eyes off the bed because she knew that in a place nearby there was the cause of her mother's coming to be like that, things that were never there before.

"Let's go eat, this child hasn't tasted a bite all day. Did you take your medicine? Did they give you soup?"

Her father bent over, still holding her against his chest, and kissed his wife. Teresa held on to him even more tightly and felt very happy when the bodies of her parents touched together pressing her in the middle.

Now it would be more difficult to approach him, to find out about him, because her mother was on the lookout, waiting for the opportunity to complain in that absurd way, that she was watching him. In the mornings, but not every day, she approached the aviary, and putting her fingers through the wire pretended to play with the birds, tell them little things, to be able to glance from afar, when they weren't watching her. During the day she tried to pass frequently by the bed-room next to her mother's and dally there under whatever pretext she could to see how they took things in and out. Only from time to time she met up with her mother's shrewd eyes. Sometimes she was impatient and tried to forget him, but it was too unsettling to know that he was there, on the other side of the wall, jelly like, she couldn't bear it.

One night she thought about him so much that the following day she woke up sick at her stomach, with vomiting and diarrhea. No, she didn't eat green guava apples, nor mangos, she just thought of him and tried to imagine where he came from and why her parents would keep a thing so noxious that it caused her to go to pieces.

But she didn't say anything, rather she suffered the malaise without complaint.

At last Benjamin was born. He was a little red rat that cried and moved his little hands all the time, without any reason. She liked him very much. She always slipped in to see how they bathed and changed him, laughing to see him, covered with talcum, kicking and wrinkling up his little monkey face. He was a precious little baby and her parents were so pleased with him that they lavished kisses on him and kissed each other without modesty. Throughout the entire house you could feel relief and well-being, they even stopped keeping an eye on her. Her mother caressed her when she put out a finger so Benjamin could play with it, and she felt very clear-ly that she loved her once more.

But the other one was still in the house, in the little

room next to her mother's, where la Cuca slept. This continued to torment her. And one afternoon when her father was leading her by the hand along the street she couldn't resist talking to him about it.

"Now that we have a real baby why don't we throw away the other one?"

Her father looked at her astonished and loosened his hold on her hand a little, but made an effort and looking straight ahead answered, "The other one is also your brother."

She jumped free, furious, wanting to hit her father.

"No, no he's not my brother," she shouted with all her might. "He's not my brother, he's not a baby, he's a nasty thing." And she burst into tears.

She never forgot how pale her father became, his face contracted and his eyes pressed shut. She felt the painful shudder that ran over him. She threw her arms around his legs wanting him to hit her so he would cease to suffer, so he might discharge onto her his anger and pain. On the contrary her father caressed her cheek a little, with an effort that was also in his voice when his speech returned.

"He is your brother, he's alive, his name is Alberto."

Her father took her little child's face in his two hands and pressed very hard, while he looked into her eyes with a strange intensity, trying to communicate to her his loving grief. The look terminated with such force it appeared that his blue pupils were going to burst, then turned into something profoundly beautiful and sad, a powerful force that sustained him and tore him to pieces at the same time. The child remained still, devouring him with her hungry gaze. He leaned over and looked at her intently, a long kiss, then slowly let go of her head, and they continued walking in the diffused twilight without saying anything more, tremulous, hand in hand.

*—Translated by Allison B. Peery*

*José Emilio Pacheco (Mexico D.F. 1939) is a distin-
guished poet with nine published volumes, a novelist, translator, essayist, and cultural commentator.
His novel* Las batallas en el desierto *(1981) became
a successful film. Among his volumes of short
fiction are* El viento distante *(1963/69) and* El
principio del placer *(1972). A variety of short-short
narratives are included in the 1990 reissue of* La
sangre de Medusa. *He frequently lectures at universities in the U.S.*

# CASTLE IN THE EYE
# OF A NEEDLE
## José Emilio Pacheco

A man who gives a good account of
himself is probably lying,
since my life when viewed from the
inside is simply a series of defeats.
    —George Orwell

The windows in the hallway looked
out to the sea. When the last class was over and the students
were heading back to the dormitory to get ready for dinner,
Pablo paused before the glass to observe the thrashing of the
sea, the dark gnawing, the uneasiness.

Other nights before falling asleep he heard the galloping
of the wind across the stalks of grain. In the morning his mother
awakened him with breakfast. Afterwards Pablo walked about
the gravel patios in the house. From the wall separating them
from the night and the fields, he watched the road and amused
himself by counting the cars that passed in each direction.

In the early afternoon Pablo entered the kitchen, and his
mother put two or three dishes in front of him on the painted
wood table. He returned to the garden, destroying ant nests and

hunting butterflies to pull off their wings. Weeks went with a semblance of happiness for the boy. Beyond them loomed the return to boarding school at the port, and the duties, the scoldings, the taunts and slaps.

From the first seat in the bus he watched both sides of the road. Soon the marshes disappeared and the fields of grain appeared along with the house where his mother waited for him. He stood up and asked the driver to stop. Thanking him, he crossed the road, squinting at the sun's reflection on the plain. His mother had come out to meet him. Pablo hurried across the grass where peacocks ran loose. There once again was his house, the one next door, the castle in the eye of a needle.

When Señor Aragón and his wife went to live in the capital, the only property they retained was the house in the country where they spent their vacations. It was left in the care of people they could trust: *Don* Felipe, his wife, Matilde, and Catalina, the girl who had served the Aragóns from childhood and who, in an unfortunate turn of events, became pregnant— it was never known by whom—and had Pablo. A childless couple, the Aragóns had taken pity on the boy and from the age of five had paid for the boarding school in the port. Dimly and over a period of time, Pablo had come to know all this.

Pablo had only one friend: Gilberto. He never understood why Gilberto boarded at the school since his parents lived in the same city. Pablo met Yolanda the first Sunday Gilberto dared invite him to his house. The family had just returned from mass. When Gilberto introduced them, Yolanda held Pablo's hand in hers for a moment. Then she went upstairs and was lost in the back of the house.

They went into town by the shore of the lagoon, ate shrimp and *mojarras,* and listened to the sound of harps coming from the wooden house with the tin roof. Señora Benavides wanted the girl to dance: "She dances so well. She's already been on stage, you know, in the school show. Her teacher says she's the best one." But Yolanda refused, looking at Pablo.

Señor Benavides asked his wife not to insist, saying this was neither the time nor place, these people were not of their class. He promptly paid the bill, and as they were preparing to go back to the city Pablo opened his mouth for the first time to whisper something to Gilberto: "Pablo's inviting us to see his house." Benavides tried to decline the invitation but Gilberto insisted he wanted to see the place his friend had told him so much about.

The car followed the road lined with pine trees until they turned in at the curve opening onto the thin asphalt strip through the marsh. Pablo felt Yolanda's body brushing against his own skin, but the girl seemed not to notice. In the front seat Gilberto was reading the adventures of Mandrake, while his mother was absorbed in the social column. Benavides turned on the radio. The wind bent the palm trees. Brilliant green, the fields of grain, too, were bent. Pablo moved imperceptibly closer to Yolanda, who did not reject his proximity. They held hands for a moment. The house, built as a copy of a castle on the Rhine, in the midst of the tropical vegetation on the plain, and partially hidden by the trees in the vegetable garden, the weather vane, and the lightning rod, stood out in the brilliance of the sun's reflection off the windows and the whitewashed walls.

"This is my house," said Pablo and once again his fingers rested lightly on Yolanda's moist hand. The engineer slowed down and turned to enter the gravel path from the other lane. *Don* Felipe opened the gate and greeted them with a bow.

Pablo turned again to Yolanda: "Do you like it?"

No one answered: they were all looking at the gardens, the orchard, and the white building in the background. The car stopped at the entrance. Pablo got out first and hurried to open the doors.

Señora Aragon appeared in the vestibule and greeted

everyone without looking at Pablo: "Engineer, Conchita, what a surprise! You have no idea how glad I am to see you. Please come in and make yourselves at home."

Pablo tried to get Yolanda to look at him, but she turned away, blushing and pretending to be interested in the peacocks. Then Señora Aragon found Pablo: "Please tell your mother to make coffee and serve the children *guanábana* ice cream."

He went out to the road. As he approached the weather vane he broke into tears. He looked into the well but could not find his face in the remote, concentric circles on the surface. At that instant . . .

the wind from the north begins blowing over the fields, bending and breaking the stalks. Lifting from the shore sand that swirls among the palm fronds. Wrinkling the surface of the water in the canals, knocking purple flowers into the marsh. Windows blow open and the wind and the sand take charge of everything, destroying it.

*—Translated by John Incledon*

*Hernán Lara Zavala (Mexico D.F. 1946) is a novelist, critic, and short story writer who also directs the extension program in literature of the University of Mexico (UNAM). His second collection of short fiction,* El mismo cielo *(1987), was awarded the Colima Prize; he has published two novels:* Charras *(1990) and* Flor de nochebuena *(1992). As part of his graduate work in England, he did a study of the English novelist Henry Green.*

# LITTLE SISTER
## Hernán Lara Zavala

Isabel had finished with her reading; Papa was dozing; he was about to be discharged and only had a week left in the hospital. Monica, concentrating on her homework, caught a glimpse of Isabel leaving the room. When she came back, José Luis, in bed and with his leg up, stopped her and peppered her with questions in a barely audible voice: Hey, what school do you go to? Do have a lot of friends? A boyfriend? I don't know yet how long they're keeping me here but maybe we can see each other when I get out, how's that sound? Why don't you give me your phone number? So I can say hi to you once in a while now that your dad's getting out of here, right?

Yes, Papa had gotten into an accident on the highway to Puebla while he was on a business trip. He dislocated his hip and broke both legs. They had to put him in a cast from the armpits down, so he was practically immobilized and in complete rest in the hospital where he'd been for more than three months. On weekends the whole family went to see him: the mother; Isabel, the oldest, who was seventeen then; Luis the youngest one, who was just twelve; and her, Monica, who had just turned fifteen. Because of their household chores and homework, they took turns going to the hospital and keeping Papa company during the week: Mondays, Wednesdays, and Fridays Mama and Luis went. As soon as they were through with lunch, Mama would get fixed up, get Luis to brush his teeth, comb his hair, bring a sweater, his satchel — and don't forget anything since you know that in the hospital we can't get cardboard or erasers or anything to color with — and they dashed off. From where they lived, in Tizapan, they walked to Avenida Revolución. There they waited for the streetcar that would take them to Insurgentes and Felix Cuevas where they'd take the bus to get to Pennsylvania Street where the hospital was. That was back when not many families had cars and theirs had been totaled in Papa's accident, besides which, Mama didn't yet know how to drive. Mama and Luis spent the whole afternoon in the hospital; they came back home a little before eight at night, just in time for supper and for Luis to take a bath, watch a little TV, and go to bed because he was the one who had the hardest time getting up. Tuesdays and Thursdays it was Isabel and Monica's turn to visit. After lunch they cleared their dishes, washed them, picked out their books and school notebooks, and went off to catch the streetcar without even changing out of their Regina School uniforms since they couldn't spare the time.

During most of his convalescence Papa was the only one in his room even though there were two beds. When they got there, Papa greeted them affectionately and said to Isabel, "Let Monica do her homework while you read to me. When you get finished then you study and let Monica talk with me."

Monica was known for being absentminded and she wasn't a very good student; Isabel, on the other hand, was number one in her class and everybody thought she was conscientious and responsible. So Monica stretched out on the empty bed with her books and notebooks while Isabel read to Papa from *Rob Roy, The Antiquary, Ivanhoe,* and who knows how many other novels by Sir Walter Scott, who seemed to be the only writer who interested Papa.

While she was doing her homework, Monica heard Isabel's voice, a little put-on, the model young lady, reading slowly and with good intonation. "The reader cannot have forgotten that the event of the tournament was decided by the exertions of an unknown knight whom, on account of the passive and indifferent conduct which he had manifested in the former part of the day, the spectators had entitled Le Noir Faineant..." So when Monica finished her homework or felt tired or when Isabel had come to something that interested her, like the part where Ivanhoe saves Rebecca from being burnt at the stake, she put down her notebooks and started listening to the outcome, until Papa said, "That's fine, we'll continue again Thursday." Then he called Monica to talk while Isabel, very serious, took up her books and, sitting up very straight, started studying in silence on the other bed.

At seven o'clock at night their father sent them home because even though visitors could stay till eight, he required them to be home by that time. While they were making the trip back home Isabel once asked Monica: "Who'd you like to have been, Rowena or Rebecca?"

"What a question," Monica answered. "Rebecca, of course ..."

"Monica! Are you crazy or what? Rebecca wouldn't become a Christian when Bois Guilbert proposed marriage to her ..."

But Monica shrugged disdainfully and didn't say anything while the streetcar made its way speedily through the broad swath of flowers they had back then south of Avenida Revolución.

Their father got better bit by bit: First they took off his body cast and left just the ones on his legs. It was on one of those many visits, right toward the end of his convalescence, the two sisters found that the hospital administration had put another person in the same room with Papa. He was a young man, about twenty years old, with one leg in a cast and in traction. He had light-colored hair, very white skin, and a hearty complexion. He wasn't bad looking. That day, as soon as Isabel and Monica showed up, their father asked them to pull shut the curtain that separated one bed from the other so they could continue their set routine.

The next Thursday, Isabel finished lunch before Monica and went up to her room to get fixed up. "Hurry up, Moni, or we won't get there on time," she yelled while her sister was still at the table. As they left, Monica noticed that that day Isabel was going on the visit without her Regina School uniform. She wasn't carrying the usual battered briefcase inherited from her father, either; she had done a subtle makeup job, but you could see the difference. Once they were at the hospital Isabel politely greeted the young man who was sharing her father's room and read more correctly than ever. But when Papa let her know she should stop, that they'd go back to it on the next visit, Isabel, instead of turning to her studying as she usually did, started to converse happily and with her eyes wide open, blinking once or twice, and then slipping off to sneak a look at the other bed. She even left the room a couple of times—she, who often scolded Monica when she had to use public restrooms, a frequent habit of Monica's despite her best efforts.

The next Saturday they all found Papa having a friendly chat with the young man in the next bed. He introduced them formally and when Luis found out that the young man was named José Luis, almost the same as him, and that he was a pilot, he made him his hero. "Did you ever fly war planes? Did you ever go on a parachute jump?" Isabel said something, too, and that was when they found out that he had been in an accident: "You know, it's funny really, not in a plane but on a motorcycle. Part of my femur was shattered. The bad part is that after three months of going around with my leg in a cast the bone still hadn't knit right so they hospitalized me and strung me up by the leg." They were going on in this vein when a lady with a serious, haughty face showed up in the room, and she turned out to be José Luis's mother. The lady's eyes went over Isabel, Monica, Mama, and stopped at Papa. The lady managed a cold smile and pulled shut the curtain separating one bed from the other.

That Tuesday, Monica heard Isabel and José Luis talking in a low voice, because Papa was asleep. Monica pretended not to be paying any attention and to be concentrating on her homework; she felt a little sorry for that boy who at first seemed so strong, so good looking, and yet was so hurt, so helpless, so alone, and with such an unpleasant person for a mother ... and she also felt an uncontrollable irritation with her sister Isabel, a vague annoyance (who knows where it came from?) that made all those things that Monica admired about her sister — her self-confidence, her cordiality, even her beauty — seem to her not just disagreeable but downright repulsive.

Papa finally got out of the hospital. At home Isabel was getting frequent calls from her girlfriends and from boys who were interested in her. When the telephone rang both Isabel and Monica rushed to get it; even though almost all the calls were for her sister, Monica was curious to know who was talking to her. "If you already know it's for me, why don't you let me get it?" complained Isabel, who would talk for hours, especially if it was her best friend Cristina. And of course, when boys called and talked to her — Adolfo, who lived in the neighborhood, or David, whom she met in Vanguardias, or José Luis — as soon as they hung up Isabel would call Cristina and tell her, "He spoke to me from the hospital, the pilot, he wants me to come see him but that can't be. I already told him, we'll see each other when he can comfortably come over to my house and pay a call on me, not before." And even if Monica answered the phone, José Luis never asked her anything but to get her sister Isabel and when she greeted him he treated her worse than a little girl.

One afternoon, after lunch, Papa as usual went off to the factory where he worked as chief of maintenance. Mama was going out shopping with Isabel, and Luis was playing in his room with a friend from the same building. Monica figured out the time: She would have to be home by eight if she didn't want to get grounded. She grabbed her keys, took out her bike, left the apartment complex, and pedaled down Avenida Revolución; she went down Insurgentes till she got to the Parque Hundido where she turned in to get to the hospital. Since the staff there knew her, they let her leave her bike in the reception area. She went up to the third floor and knocked on the door.

"Come in," she heard José Luis's voice say. Monica opened the door shyly and came in. "Hi. What a surprise. Is Isabel with you? Or what? Are you bringing me a message from her? To visit me? You? By yourself? I think this is the first time I've heard you talk since I met you. No, of course not, it's not bothering me; come, let's see, have a seat, I'm surprised you came because you're so shy and so quiet that, seriously, I've only heard you talk over the phone."

Monica wanted to seem perfectly at ease, like Isabel, but the words wouldn't come, so she remained silent, with her eyes cast down, playing with her keys. Why did I come, she reproached herself.

"You may find this hard to believe, but a pilot needs more training than a doctor; look, you have to study your whole life long, hey! Plus which, you have to master English, because just imagine if they were giving you instructions from the control tower and you didn't understand anything? And for them to accept you as a student, you have to have perfect vision and be over a meter seventy and it's just one of those funny things but we pilots have a special attraction—the stewardesses always fall in love with you and there are these big parties at night, especially on international flights; I'm still on local runs but pretty soon I'll have enough hours for them to let me have one of the big ones ..."

While José Luis was talking, Monica thought she could tell, without knowing how, that he was nervous, that he was afraid of her. "Listen, stop jiggling those keys, will you? You haven't been paying attention to what I was saying." José Luis took the keys away from her and put them under his pillow. "Now are you going to listen to me? What was it I was telling you? . . . See? You weren't paying attention. I was talking to you about planes, this is dumb, what's going on here is that you're still a little girl . . . Listen, why did you come, if you don't mind my asking? I should give you your keys back? Why? Don't they teach you to say please at home? Oh, now you're leaving. I won't give them to you unless you say please . . . So I won't give them to you."

Monica tried to take the keys out from under the pillow. José Luis grabbed her by the hand. "Let me go. Plee-ease. Let-me-go-o-o-o and give me my keys. Please?" They wrestled. By the time she realized what was happening, he had hold of her by the shoulders, her chest against his. José Luis kissed her on the mouth. Monica slapped him like in the movies when someone kisses a woman without her consent. He pulled her toward him and kissed her again. José Luis's expression had changed. His face was flushed and his eyes were unfocused. He started playing with the buttons on Monica's uniform. No, she said, but she didn't do anything to stop him. José Luis kissed her for the third, fourth, fifth time without encountering resistance. He touched her breast, he lifted up her skirt and stroked her legs, upwards, way far up, and she was going no, no, no, but she let him until she realized that she was kissing him, too, that she was on top of him despite the leg in the air and Monica going no, no, and José Luis stroking and kissing and pinching and his steamy breath hot on her mouth, his breathing hard and his heart bam-bam-bam and his body smelling of disinfectant, iodine, or Vap-o-Rub and bam-bam-bam she heard it again and felt happy it was over her, over her and despite the no,

no, no, he was hurting her, she was letting him and hugging
him and she felt his cheeks and a kiss and then another, what
a big dumb make-out session she said to herself, until he
grabbed her by the shoulders and began to shake her hard,
violently, with his mouth on hers and then she let herself
go and she moaned no, no, no, but he didn't let go of her,
he didn't let her go until finally she felt him go weak and
he lay spread-eagled like a dead man, his eyes half closed,
his face red, as if it were about to burst. Monica seized the
opportunity, slipped her hand under the pillow, got her keys
out, straightened her clothes and her hair, and left the room
without saying a word or looking back.

She hopped on her bike and started on her way home.
Pretty soon it would be eight. She'd get there late. She pedaled hard, rushing along toward Insurgentes, her body swaying and raised up off the seat, when a lazy feeling came over
her: She wouldn't care if she got punished. She slowed down
and began to ride calmly amid the cars' headlights. She got
home around nine at night. Her parents were waiting for her.

"May I ask just where the hell you've been? Out on
your bike ... on your bike ... And didn't you notice what
time it was? Where's your brain? You're grounded. Go to your
room and you're not going out all weekend. And don't let
it happen again, hear?"

Over the following days, she couldn't avoid the feeling that
she'd like to meet José Luis somewhere: in the street, when
she was coming out of Regina School, or at the supermarket.
But that was impossible, at least for the moment, since he'd
be spending at least a month more in the hospital. Then she
comforted herself with the hope that maybe José Luis would
call her on the phone. When it didn't happen in the next
weeks, after giving it a lot of thought Monica got up her nerve
and called the hospital. José Luis answered in an icy tone
and when she asked him how he was doing he answered that
because of her visit his leg had shifted and so they had to
take new X-rays and put on a new cast. He was very depressed.

Monica hung up.

*The big one is as good as the little one,* Monica heard the beer commercial on the radio while she was doing her homework. The telephone rang. For once, she obeyed Isabel's shout, "I'll get it!" as her sister came out of her room with hairclips in her mouth and fixing her hair.

Isabel sat in the chair next to the phone. She was asking questions in a put-on way, with a perky look in her eyes. Suddenly her face grew tense. "Whoooo? Hold on a moment . . . Monica, it's José Luis asking for you," she said dryly and handed the receiver to her brusquely. Monica took the phone: José Luis greeted her nervously. He apologized for having seemed so distant the day she called, but, he explained, he was in a lot of pain and upset over his leg and his mother had been right there talking to the doctor. He had been thinking a lot about her since her visit and he wanted to know whether now that he'd be getting out of the hospital he could see her now and then, at home if they'd let her, or maybe he could ask her out for coffee.

While José Luis was talking, Isabel came out of her room fixed up to go to Cristina's house. Monica listened to José Luis's words and observed her sister: Isabel had lost the ability to irritate her. Now Monica could see her again with tenderness and even with a little complacency. At that moment, she remembered that the night of the visit, when she changed her clothes, alone in her room, she discovered that José Luis had made her bleed. Now, José Luis, despite his affectionate words and the interest he was showing in her, seemed to have faded into a shadowy forgetfulness after having exhausted the curiosity and the desire in her still-green heart.

*—Translated by Naomi Lindstrom*

*Eraclio Zepeda (Tapachula, Chiapas 1937) is a poet, actor, and Mexico's best-known storyteller; some of his works are available only on CD. He has produced three successful volumes of short stories: Benzulul (1959), Asalto nocturno (1974), and Andando el tiempo (1982) from which this story is taken. Following the uprising in Chiapas early in 1994, he was named to the presidential peace commission. He is also at work on his first novel.*

# THE TRUTH
## Eraclio Zepeda

*"H*e who tells the truth has a sweet mouth, as if he were chewing mint leaves, and he has clean, white teeth, because there isn't any mud in his heart," said old Grandfather Juan.

Sebastián Pérez Tul never said a word that didn't embrace the truth. What he spoke was true; it had happened just that way sometime, someplace.

"He who has courage can see at night and can always hold his head up. He who is brave keeps his hands clean; he knows how to harvest his pleasure and his pain. He knows how to accept punishment. He who is fearful runs from his own footsteps and suffers and cries out and the moon can't cleanse his eyes. He who doesn't accept his mistakes knows no peace, and all the stones seem to bloody his step, for there's neither taste in *his body nor peace in his heart,"* said old Tata Juan.

Sebastián Pérez Tul never avoided the punishment which wipes mistakes clean. He never tried to run away from the truth. He never trembled at suffering, and he lived at peace with his heart.

*"He who doesn't remember lives at the bottom of a well, and his past actions turn sour, because he can't feel the wind or the sun. He who forgets can't laugh, and tears dwell in his eyes, since he can't remember the light,"* said old Tata Juan.

Sebastián Pérez Tul lived with his memories and they walked alongside him, and in his company they jumped for joy and also suffered and moaned. Sebastián Pérez Tul never forgot what his hands caressed or his feet destroyed.

*"He who wounds deserves to be wounded, and he who cures deserves to be cured, and he who is a killer deserves to be killed, and he who pardons deserves to be forgiven for his mistakes. But he who harms others and runs away has no love at his back, and there are thorns in his eyelids, and sleep brings him pain, and he can never sing again,"* said old Tata Juan.

Sebastián Pérez Tul agreed wholeheartedly, and he had no doubt that now he must follow through. It never crossed his mind to deny that he, with his own hands, had killed the white man* Lorenzo Castillo, moonshine merchant.

"You killed him, Sebastián. You were crazy with rage but you were the one who finished him off."

"I was the one."

"You followed him, Sebastián, and you called out to him and he stopped."

"I called out to him and he stopped. That was his mistake, he stopped."

---

* The term *ladino* (originally *latino*), which is here translated as *white man*, refers to any non-Indian in Chiapas. Because of the situation of internal colonialism which prevailed in Chiapas for centuries, until recently there has been less intermarriage than in other parts of Mexico; therefore, the term *white* seems appropriate in this especially polarized context.

"You caught up with him and accused him ..."

"Yes, I accused him."

"And you grabbed him by the hair and jumped him and started to hit him ..."

"I started to hit him. But I couldn't see anything anymore, and I just wanted to get it over with."

"And then, when he stopped moving, you let go of him, and the late Lorenzo went rolling into the gully."

"That's right. He went all limp and started rolling. That's right."

"You were the one, Sebastián. But he came looking for it. If the damage had already been done, why'd he come back?"

"Why'd he come back. That's the thing."

Sebastián Pérez Tul was sitting in the doorway of his hut with his elbows propped on his thick, sturdy knees, holding his head, filled with worry and fright, between his hands. He was sitting there with fear drying up his tongue. His brother, Fermin Pérez Jo, was speaking to him, hoping he could talk him out of any second thoughts.

"You warned him in San Ramón, on the outskirts of Ciudad Real. You warned him real good. We all heard it clear as a bell."

"I told him so he wouldn't try to feed me any lies. So he would know where the road started. So it wouldn't take him by surprise. And you all heard it ..."

"But since that's the way he is, or was, 'cause now he's deceased, he didn't pay you any mind, and he just started laughing real loud, down there in San Ramón."

"That's what made me maddest, Fermin; that's what blinded me; he just stood there laughing, not paying any attention to the words."

"Yes, Sebastián, but you warned him."

"I didn't sneak up on him."

"No, Sebastián, you warned him. You warned him in San Ramón."

*San Ramón has one, long street. That's where the wind comes down from the hills to slip into Ciudad Real. It's just* one street, but there's rancor and there's mud, and there's evil. San Ramón is the first sign of white people you run across when you reach Ciudad Real; and it's your last chance to fill your mouth with bitterness when you leave Ciudad Real. It's the last place. That's where the merchants come, the priests, lawyers, prostitutes, old aristocrats, in short all of Ciudad Real. That's as far as they get. That's where they stay.

"It was in San Ramón that I told him. That's where."

San Ramón is named after a saint, but that wasn't the original idea. That isn't its original name, because first the government named it Ramón Larrainzar, but now they call it San Ramón. The white people changed it, because without the protection of a saint sins glow in the dark, and the devil follows the reflection and is guided by the glow, until he reaches the souls of those who have lost their purity.

"That's where I first ran across him. Once again, you might say. That's where I made him see the error of his ways. The harm he had left behind him; and I gave him his warning. I warned that fellow Lorenzo."

San Ramón was the home of Lorenzo Castillo, a fat, white moonshine merchant. That's where Sebastián found him.

"You'd better watch out, Lorenzo. Don't you show your face around there. I let you leave, but don't you dare come back again. I'm warning you, Lorenzo. Don't you dare come back again."

"Shut up, you Indian."

"I let you sleep in my house. I put you up. I let you sell booze in my doorway. But when all of us were drunk, you went and robbed me and then you took my daughter and hurt her, and then you started mocking me. Don't you dare come back again. I'm warning you ..."

"You goddamn Indian! The liquor's making you hallucinate. Why would I want anything to do with your daughter. I'm not familiar with the bitch; but if she's Indian, she must stink like hell," and that Lorenzo showed his dirty

*mouth and his black teeth when he burst out laughing.*
*"I've told you three times. Don't you dare show your*
*face around there."*
*"Is that a threat? Since when do Indians talk to me*
*like they're my equals? That's what I want you to tell me.*
*Oh, fuck off, you wouldn't want me to put you in jail for*
*lying and making threats, right, Counselor?" And the old*
*man dressed in black, standing at Lorenzo's side, nodded,*
*and they both kept right on laughing until Sebastián was out*
*of sight.*
*That's how Sebastián Pérez Tul warned him. He gave*
*him notice. He told him the correct number of times, neither*
*more nor less. That's how he warned him.*

"But he didn't pay any attention, and he came to mock
you, Sebastián. He came looking for you at your house, Sebastián, and he insulted you and made fun of your daughter again,
and said that she looked prettier now than before."

"And he was on notice. I didn't sneak up on him."

"You didn't sneak up on him, Sebastián. You did it right."

*Lorenzo Castillo arrived in this hamlet, with his jugs*
*of moonshine on his three old mules that he used in his*
*trade. He came, falling down drunk, from San Juan Chamula;*
*he had made a good sale there, and he had been drinking*
*to celebrate until he made himself sick and thought about*
*going home. He was headed for Ciudad Real, but once he*
*saw this hamlet, he got it into his head to come mock Sebas-*
*tián. He went directly to Sebastián's house, and he called out*
*to him, and he insulted him and started telling everyone about*
*his daughter.*

"You Indians jump when I snap my fingers!"

"You killed him, Sebastián . . ."

"I killed him."

"It was his fault. Don't feel sorry. Don't let sadness into
your heart."

"I don't feel any regrets. I'm not ashamed. I killed him
because you have to do away with what's bad, with what's
poison, with what stinks."

"But you should run, Sebastián. Yesterday, when we took the dead man in, they said they'd be coming for you today."

"I'm not running."

"Beat it, Sebastián! Your blood tells you to stay, but the cops and the white men know nothing about that. They don't know the tongue or the heart. Run away."

"No."

"Then tell them a lie. Say it wasn't you. We're going to say so too, because they can't understand the heart."

"I won't deny it. It was me."

"Sebastián! Run away. Here come the cops," shouted Rosa Lopez Chalchele.

"I killed him. That's the truth. My words are clean. It was me."

"Sebastián, beat it! They're going to take you away. You'll go to prison."

"I owe it. I killed him. It was me that killed him."

The neighbors started arriving. They formed a semicircle around Sebastián's door. They urged him to go away, to put his feet down on some path and get lost for awhile.

"Run away! You can run away."

"It's my punishment. That's how it should be. My heart is clean but if I run it will go bad."

"He's a white man, so he doesn't remember the truth, and when he encounters it, he mocks it."

"It wasn't your fault, Sebastián. He came looking for it."

"You had given him fair warning. Run away."

"No."

The mounted police came riding over the hill. To one side of the hilltop cross, you could see the big horses scattering stones in their path. There were five of them.

"It isn't too late, Sebastián."

"Hit the road, Sebastián."

"Run away. You have no sin to carry."

"It was Lorenzo who came looking for it."

"It was me. I'm not leaving. I'm not running away."

The policemen's horses came down into the plain. They spread out into a long line surrounding the little valley.

"It isn't too late, Sebastián. Run away."

"You've got a wife. Run."

"If they catch you, you're done for, Sebastián."

"You've got kids, Sebastián. Run."

"I can't. I owe a debt. It isn't a good idea to fool around with punishment."

The policemen took out their weapons. A cold gleam leapt off the rifle barrels. Now they were riding into the hamlet.

"Run, Sebastián. They haven't seen you. After a while you can come back. They'll forget."

"No."

"Sebastián. That fellow Lorenzo was a white man. You're an Indian. Run."

"No. This is the way it should be. I have to stay."

The dogs started barking. The policemen were coming through the streets of the town. Now you could see their faces. They clearly heard the sergeant order his men to cock their rifles; the dry, harsh sound of the bolts slapped them in the face. The dogs kept on barking and one of the policemen cracked his whip at the one nearest him. They saw all this from Sebastián's house.

"Go hide. There's still time."

"No."

"Go hide. They're going to get you good."

"That's my punishment."

"The cops are white men, Sebastián."

"That's my punishment."

"All they know how to do is punish other people, Sebastián."

The policemen stopped ten meters from the Indians, who were watching them fearfully.

"Sebastián Pérez Tul, you're under arrest for murder," shouted the police sergeant.

No one said a word. They stared hard at the ground.

"Who knows the bastard?" he shouted again.

Sebastián got up from where he was sitting in his doorway. He turned toward the policemen. Everyone was watching him. Some people clenched their fists to keep themselves from stopping him.

"Who knows where the fuck the murderer is?" yelled the sergeant. All eyes were on Sebastián as he walked toward the policemen.

"Here I am, Government . . ."

"Who are you?"

"Sebastián Pérez Tul."

"Why didn't you make a run for it?"

"Because I didn't."

"Do you want to go to jail?"

"Yes."

"You don't have the money to hire a lawyer from Ciudad Real to defend you, do you?"

"No."

"OK. Turn around so they can tie you up."

Sebastián turned around. He stood with his back to the policemen and, with his eyes, he wanted to say good-bye to his house, to his wife, to his children, to his people, to his mountains.

Sebastián was calm. His mouth never knew any word that wasn't the truth, and there was never fear in his eyes, and he always held his head up. In his legs there was no dread of punishment.

"Now," said the sergeant.

Sebastián Pérez Tul never knew how it happened. People heard a shot and saw him fall to his knees.

"Why waste our time with him," said the policemen and they galloped away.

"Sebastián, Sebastián, we've been telling you, Sebastián."

Someone kneeled down to pick him up. He ran his hand over the back of his neck and felt Sebastián's blood run through his fingers. His head was shattered.

"We told you so. You should have run away, Sebastián."

Several neighbors lifted the body together.

"*He who tells the truth has a sweet mouth, as if he were chewing mint leaves* . . ." That's what old Tata Juan started to say, but his voice broke and his eyes filled with tears.

—*Translated by Cynthia Steele*

*Marta Cerda (Guadalajara, Jal. 1945) has mapped out a new terrain of fiction, linking short story and novel, in works like* La señora Rodríguez y otros mundos *(1990), soon to appear in a French edition. She is the founder and director of the writers' workshop SOGEM in Guadalajara. Her poetry is represented in the bilingual* The Translator's Workshop *(Long Beach CA 1994) and she was the recipient of a National Endowment for the Arts grant in 1993.*

# MIRROR OF A MAN
## Marta Cerda

He had started shaving at thirteen, when the other children in the family began to make fun of that little moustache, which made him feel insecure. He tried to hide it because it embarrassed him to be looked at like that; it was as if they were seeing him inside, too. The less anyone noticed the change, the better. Even though he was still afraid of cutting himself and then it would be even more obvious.

Now he laughed remembering his shyness, and he liked to play with the razor, making it flash in front of the mirror while he was trying out smiles or hairstyles. By now he had gotten used to his new body, but he still was amazed at the vitality held in by the briefs his mother had given him:

"I saw you needed them so I brought you some."

"Striped?" he had answered stupidly.

"They were on sale and these were all they had. Besides, who's going to see them?"

*Nobody—that's what she thinks. She's convinced I'm still a child. If she knew ...*

After all, he liked to be seen like that, he felt more like a man.

"Memo, telephone for you."

"Who is it?"

"Susana."

He pulled up his pants and ran out of the bathroom. He'd get a telephone to go in his room. He'd been thinking about it since the day his brothers kept him from hearing by joking: "It's Susana. Pretty little Susana. Are you sweethearts?" Those little idiots, what did they know.

"I'm going to tell Susana you wear striped underpants and you named your dog Susy."

*Susana, with her little bunny-rabbit laugh, right in class...*

"What were we talking about, López?"

"López? Oh, yeah, about oxygen, prof."

"Oxygen is what your brain could use some of. Pay attention, you're always off in space."

*Why should they all be telling me the same thing, my parents, the teachers, and even Susana. She can't even imagine what I am. How could she imagine, even if she knows all that anatomy, what a real man is, like me. Why should a guy have to wait so long to prove his manhood with a woman?*

"Yes? Susana? No, I don't know what the chemistry prof gave out."

*And what's more, I don't care. She always has to be the little super student. I thought she was calling me up about something else. They say she likes me, but I never see any sign of it. Susana, red-haired bunny rabbit, if she keeps playing hard to get she'll see. Every night I dream about her, plunging down into her reddish fuzz ... it must be reddish ... and then I wake up wet. I have to go some day with Toni, he says* he knows who with, but first I need to scrape together some money; they'd get suspicious around here if I asked and didn't say what it was for. I'm sick of always asking permission, sick of how they razz me at school: "Memo doesn't dare because he'll get a scolding . . ." I can't take any more of Toni daring me and Mama with her advice, I'll show them who I am.

"Mama, my brother's holed up in the bathroom again and he won't let me in."

"You little tattletale, shut up."

"I told you not to keep playing so long in the bathroom, it's for you both to share."

"Okay . . . Mama, I'm going to Toni's house to study after school."

"When are you getting home?"

*When are you getting home, they coddle me like a girl. Doesn't my mother know anything? Take care of yourself, eat up, study, turn it down, like that's all there was to life. I'll go tonight, I'm a big boy, I know what I'm doing. When I have kids, I won't act like that. When I have kids . . . I have to go, I have to. If I don't, how will I . . .?*

"Now what's this you're coming at me with, don't tell me you're mad at me when you're the one who made me look bad. Boy did you ever blow it, you were acting like some queer. Why'd you start acting like an idiot when they offered you a drink? 'I'm just here to keep Toni company,' and you kept looking and looking at her, like you'd never seen an old lady. Well, what did you expect, butthead?"

*Anything, just not that she'd look so much like my mother. Toni you bastard, you really fucked me over.*

—*Translated by Naomi Lindstrom*

*Luis Arturo Ramos (Minatitlán Ver. 1947) made a
striking debut with his novel* Violeta-Peru *in 1979
and went on to produce* Domingo junto al paisaje
*(1987),* Intramuros *(1983), and* Este era un gato
*(1988), all the while teaching and serving as direc-
tor of the press at the University of Veracruz. He
has been a visiting lecturer in the U.S, most recently
at the University of Texas at El Paso. His 1981 volume of short fiction* Los viejos asesinos *is the source
of the following story.*

# DOCTOR'S PRESCRIPTION
## Luis Arturo Ramos

What caught your attention was the
scar that wound down from just below his forehead to the middle of his cheek. Otherwise he was a run-of-the-mill patient.
Perhaps more ordinary than anything else. Too white to be from
the country; probably from the city, thin, with brown eyes and
a strange lilt in his voice.

He came in during the morning, and there wasn't even
a mist or rain to distinguish the day from any other. They put
him in the emergency room, half-dead from gastroenteritis, his
stomach half-eaten by some malign virus that under the glass
of the microscope was bound to be more interesting than his
pale and emaciated face. If it weren't for the scar.

You asked him his name and address, and sketched
his medical history on the lined hospital paper. You filled

197

parentheses, lines, blank spaces, without looking at the curved ladder of the scar, but seeing it in your memory; or rather, without losing the image of it that was engraved in your mind from the moment you saw it. Pink, smooth between the stitch marks, prominent on the surface of his face like the unbroken row of crosses that represent railroad lines on a map.

They stuck an I.V. into him, gave him something to stop the vomiting, and advised him to stay as quiet as possible. You watched him as he listened to the advice with a look on his face of I-don't-understand, or why-so-much-trouble, if when all's said and done. . . . Later you realized that you were the only one he smiled at, as if you were the only one he didn't remember or didn't believe he remembered. From his case history you knew that Valentin Espinoza ("with a z, not an s"), was a longtime resident of charity hospitals and clinics, and that he was as accustomed to professional faces as he was to the strange pain of a needle in his skin, and to the measured coming and going of the drip in his bruised veins. So you have no idea why he smiled at you that first time; especially since you look more like a musician than anything else, and least of all a doctor. Your father wanted you to be a doctor and you were. You wanted to be a sailor, but never a musician. Nevertheless, when people first meet you, they immediately associate you with a violin case, or right away want to discuss private piano lessons for their daughter who will soon be ten.

*Don* Valentin Espinoza (you use the title "*Don*" not out of sarcasm inappropriate for an emergency room, but rather to give some life and history to the poor little fellow who is over forty in spite of his adolescent eyes and skinny beggar's body) relates his history of illnesses without taking his eyes off the nurse with the nice legs except to smile at you from time to time. You make the most of the moments when he isn't smiling (that is, when he is looking at the nurse) to observe the scar and run your eyes slowly (as slowly as his non-smile allows you to) down the rungs left by the stitches. Then, when *Don* Valentin smiles (that is, when he is looking at you), you glance away and busy yourself with the sterilized needles, gauze, forceps. The autoclave.

They "earmarked" him (and here, in this emergency room run down not so much by the budget as by the bunch of loafers they send from the School of Medicine and from the whorehouse that the School of Nursing has become, that strange word becomes a sick joke) for Room 51, Bed F. Fortunately for him, but who really knows for sure, the bed is next to the window that opens onto the run-down garden with its patches of sandy earth and, beyond the sad old benches and swings rusted from the lack of children, a high railed fence through which you can see women with baskets and busses passing by. Bed F, together with Bed C opposite it, has this advantage–disadvantage. And they assigned *Don* Valentin to Bed F where he will stay for the time necessary for the cheap drugs and the insipid food and the antibiotics to do their job and re-equip him for civilian and civic life. You use the word civilian because the uniform of an in-patient gives the wearer a particular look, as if he belonged to a military organization, guild, or secret brotherhood. In the meantime, *Don* Valentin will be able to see, to his left, the profile of the other two bodies; and beyond his feet, the face, or feet, opposite him. To his right, the most pleasant option, the little garden with swings and worn ruts, the street travelled by women and cars. . . . Well, once there, he will decide.

In Bed F, Room 51, you went to see him once a day, feigning a clinical interest that allowed you to disguise your personal interest. For some unknown reason, the scar fascinates you, as if it were the synthesis of an entire wretched life; as if it were the emblem of the most miserable fortune. But you play innocent, and inquire about the frequency and nature of his bowel movements. You take his pulse, you tap his stomach, and you denounce the band of assassins that masquerade as street vendors behind every taco stand. *Don* Valentin smiles warmly and asks for something to read. Or rather, he asks you where he might get something to read. You become even more interested. You are moved by pale working-class men, with scars and literary intere ... But careful, a disappointment at this stage might be very pain-ful. You first ask him about what he prefers: papers (sport papers?), magazines *(The Enquirer? Musical News? Boxing & Wrestling?)* ... Books? Yes? ... Which? ... He asks you for *One Hundred Years of Solitude* or *The Autumn of the Patriarch*. No, of course not, the clinic doesn't have a library, as much as you'd like it to, but let me see how I can get hold of them for you. You know what, I'll bring them from home. ... Which do you want to read first? ... Yes, I'd recommend *One Hundred Years* so that then you can see how he changes in the other one. ... No, it's no bother, no bother at all. If I can be of help to you, just say so. ... Yes, my friend, of course ... of course.

You leave very happy. You put your watch on the other wrist so you won't forget; a disappointment at this stage would be a real bitch. On the way, you decide to buy new copies, to give them to him as a gift; maybe I'll catch something if I lend them to him. Impossible. Microbiology. ... Anyway, it's better if I buy them for him.

Before he got halfway through the first book, you asked him about his life. You went into Room 51 and you saw him look-ing out the window, the open book to one side of his body. The conversation switched from the crazy escapades of José Arcadio to the past of *Don* Valentín Espinoza as you waited for him to let slip something about the scar. He was from Puebla, he didn't finish high school; he's been living in Mex-ico City for years. You tell him that you also lived in Puebla more or less at the same time. What a strange coincidence, right? ... Yes, it's a small world.

Sometimes you watch him from the door. *Don* Valen-tín scarcely ever speaks with his neighbors; it seems they are jealous of him for attracting so much of your attention. None of the other doctors, not even you, speaks to them other than to ask them where it hurts. But it seems as though *Don* Valentín isn't very interested in socializing with his neighbors

either. He prefers to look through the window or read or just
lie there thinking, like he is now. His hair has grown, and
it bothers his eyes. He has become paler although his general
improvement is obvious. His features have become sharper
and now that you know he's from Puebla, you can better
explain the lilt in his voice. You know he is forty-two in
spite of his boyish body and attitudes, and when you see him
as he is now, musing, not looking at anything, he seems so
grey and absent that you fear he might disappear like one
of those kites you give too much string to, and one moment
they're there and the next they're not and it's sad. For this
reason, the presence of the scar seems stranger and stranger
to you, just as if it were a full-term pregnancy in the body
of a girl of seven. Most everyone would expect pimples
and blackheads.

Valentin Espinoza is now able to sit in the little patio without
getting nauseated. You go and see him there although he is
now out of your jurisdiction. Now he convalesces from four
to six in the sinking sun of the late afternoon. He's already
finished *One Hundred Years* and now he's reading *Autumn
of the Patriarch;* but your conversations haven't gone beyond
memories of Puebla and the odd commonplace. You have
discovered that on occasions you could have crossed paths
with each other, seen the same movie, or attended the same
performance, separated only by ignorance of the future. *Don*
Valentin says that "if we'd had the gift of knowing the future
we would have become friends long ago." (He says *friends*
with a confidence that makes you uneasy.)

"Just think," he says. "You and I in Puebla saying to each
other: in fifteen or twenty years, we'll see each other again;
so good-bye, I hope all goes well for you until then." You both
laugh as if all that could be true. "Have you read Borges?"
you think of asking him tomorrow.

Little by little you realize that the life of *Don* Valentin
Espinoza interests you more and more; you even realize that
you have said "life" and not "scar", and that makes you a

little embarrassed. Nevertheless, you can't bring yourself to
ask him directly. You realize that *Don* Valentín's face is not
one of those it's easy to look straight in the eyes.

Shortly before he finishes *The Autumn of the Patriarch*,
you realize that you almost went to the same school. You
say "almost" because yours was fee-paying and had a blue
uniform and *Don* Valentín's, though very close by, had khaki
and military caps. You both remember the same orange ven-
dor and laugh about the straw hat that all of you knocked
off at one time or another. You remember *Doña* Rafa, the
woman who sold tacos, and the bus route that carried you
in opposite directions. *Don* Valentín smiles and his scar seems
larger to you, as if it were smiling too. His face takes on the
look of an advertising balloon on which you discover the
slogan when it's inflated.

*Don* Valentín asks where you lived and it makes you
feel bad to explain exactly where because that means admit-
ting many other things. But *Don* Valentín understands and
nods somewhat sadly as if saying: "Yes, I thought so." His lank
hair falls over his eyes and makes him look even more of
a boy and you look at the rounded, fleshy scar, at the stitches, and you imagine an accident in the street some years
ago now.

You began to speak to your wife about him barely a
few days ago. Your growing interest demands to be shared
and who better than your dear wife. She listens very atten-
tively and she's thrilled that her very own little doctor is showing such solidarity with the have-nots. You both make jokes
about it.

"What did you say his name is?"

"Valentín Espinoza.... But I call him *Don* Valentín."

Your wife is interested by the coincidences, by the
books he reads; she's a bit ashamed that she never finished
reading *Autumn* and puts her finger on the sore spot—or
rather, on the scar. She asks you how he got it and you say
who knows, but it's obvious that it was some time ago now
and that it is the product of some accident. Not related to

knives or bars or drunken brawls. No, you can tell that *Don*
Valentin is from a good-but-really-modest family. Most likely
he was hit by a bus.

"Oh no! Why don't you ask him?"

You let some time go by and then go to visit him in
the garden. He is seated on a swing looking toward the street.
He smiles when he sees you coming. "How are you feeling?"
you ask. "So-so," he gestures. You sit down on the next swing,
also looking toward the street. The busses make the ground
reverberate; the rumbling rises through the metal supports
and from there moves down the chains and vibrates lightly
against your bodies.

"The busses also passed right by the school. Do you
remember, doctor?"

"Yes. . . . Of course. The whole classroom would shake
like a skinny horse."

You both laugh at the comparison. You are gratified by
*Don* Valentin's laughter.

"Yes, like a skinny horse. . . . We used to throw water
balloons at the busses," says *Don* Valentin.

"We would even throw stones."

You both laugh again.

"Maybe we even saw one another sometime and we
didn't even recognize each other," he says.

"We didn't . . . recognize each other. . . . And just how
could we have recognized each other?"

"Well . . . I mean, in a manner of speaking. It strikes
me that I did see you."

"Me? How do you know?"

"I don't know. . . . But your face seems familiar."

"No. It's just that I was the first person you saw when
they brought you in half-dead. You revived and saw me and
that's that."

"No, I believe it was before that . . . I mean, afterwards
. . . I mean . . . Dammit, now I'm all mixed up."

You both laugh, swinging to and fro. The scar smiles
as well and his hair curves down over his forehead.

Although he is now out of your jurisdiction (you like to use this word) you look over his chart and discover what you already knew by his face. *Don* Valentín is a good little bit better, and they are going to release him in three days' time. They fattened him up, they cleaned him out, and they are going to put him back on the mean streets to see what happens. He made a good impression, got in your good graces. The things he did and said. Besides, you are both from the same place. He likes to read good books, you were almost schoolmates, uniforms aside. You remember the street fights with the kids from his school ("Starving Indians"). The stone-throwing and the returned insults ("Rich bastards"). Boys' games, when all's said and done, it was nothing, only the urge to raise hell. Some of them poor, others rich, others somewhere between the two; but all of them just a bunch of boys wanting to raise hell.

You tell him about your memories. He agrees, remembers, "Yes, boys' games." He admits having thrown stones at the windows of your school. "Boyish pranks, you know?" "Perhaps we even threw stones at each other from time to time." He agrees again: "Yes, you may be right." All this reminds you of a movie: the one where the German and the American meet after the War and realize that they were in the same place at the same time, only on opposite sides. You mention it to *Don* Valentín and he, very serious, once again says yes the situation is similar. You also tell your wife about it and she wrinkles her brow and shows some disappointment. "Ugh," she says, "I thought he was different. Not like that." "Boys' games," you tell her. "Well, I don't know. But don't get it into your head one of these days to invite him home or anything." "No, of course not, how could you think such a thing?" You laugh as you have been laughing since you saw the scar for the first time.

You find out that old Calvo was also his teacher. You find out that the damned old man was giving classes in the other school without anyone finding out. Who would have thought? With all his airs. *Don* Valentín remembers him with affection; or at least it seems that way to you because he smiles when he speaks about him. Although it could all be a trick of the scar; frequently, after this type of surgery, the muscles are affected and they contract unwillingly. You realize, suddenly, that *Don* Valentin could have been smiling all this time without really wanting to.

You didn't like old Calvo because he was a Communist. The old bastard. I don't know why the priests had him at the school. It was said he taught classes at the University.

"I'm sure he told you all kinds of things about us."

*Don* Valentin shrugs his shoulders as if unwilling to accept a reality that is becoming ever more evident.

"So Señor Calvo cracked jokes at our expense."

"Don't blame him," says *Don* Valentin. "He must have done the same with us."

But you don't admit to him that you didn't even know that he taught classes in the public school. Distractedly, you listen to the voice of *Don* Valentin saying something about the railroad workers.

"What ... ?"

". . . he was put in jail."

"Who was?"

"Señor Calvo ... at the time of the railroad strike ... he was with Vallejo and the radicals."

The busses pass along the street and the little garden reverberates and the metal posts shake.

You don't want to tell your wife about it because she'll begin with her "I told you so's." It's better this way—you think over and over again in bed. What a letdown. The good thing is that he is about to leave. And if it occurs to him to ask you for a favor or work or money? This is what almost always happens. Patients identify with the figure of the doctor and then they want you to work miracles for them.

You did not return to the garden or to Room 51. But Valentin found you in one of the corridors. You made as if you didn't see him and gave him the slip. But Valentin by then knew that entire wing of the building by heart and found you again. He was holding in his hand the two books that you had given him.

"They told me that I'll be going home the day after tomorrow.... Would you mind writing a dedication for me?"

No way out. In situations like this there's no alternative. You weren't going to be rude to him either.

You scribbled a few words and handed them back without speaking.

"Perhaps in a little while we can chat."

You said, "Perhaps," and left him standing there.

You were so angry that you had to talk to your wife about it. "Who would think that he read García Márquez?" That night you dreamed of the scar. Your wife put her finger on the sore spot once again.

"You'll be left wanting to know how he got it."

On the way to the hospital you were planning out your attitude for the whole day: to go straight to the point or to act definitively as if nothing had happened. In any case the scar continued to interest you. You leaned forward a little to change the station on the radio and that very moment the child stepped down from the sidewalk; you slammed on the brakes and swerved in the other direction until you heard the sound of other brakes in your left ear. The bus hadn't hit your car but the passengers were crowding the windows and looking at you, and on the other side the kid was scream-ing and the mother was yanking him around and smacking his bottom.

You remembered the other time. The kids from the neighboring public school running towards you and your companions, armed with sticks and shouting, and the Ford lurching forward without you touching the accelerator and ploughing into that pack of louts. then the faces in the win-dow, the open mouths slobbering and shouting, the sticks against the body work and the impact on the right fender and that kid who was thrown back and struck the curb and a spurt of blood that spread over him as if it were wrapping him in a red mat.

When your class found out that he hadn't died, you went to spy on him to see the state he was in. You saw him leaving the hospital, surrounded by his family; his thin face split in two by the gauze bandage, his hair curving down over his forehead. And now the scar and all your interest are explained. You remember the memory: the time he saw you in the hospital and the way in which he deceived you so that you would come to trust him.

Now you realize what's really happening. You know that the arrival of Valentin on a certain day (on which there was neither fog nor rain) was only the beginning of a plan. That everything else – his feigned smile, his bland niceness, the lilt of his voice – was a way of undermining any resistance. A long time he must have waited, preparing himself, and that day without rain, when Valentin saw you again after so many years, he knew that the time had come.

When you arrive at the hospital, your mind is made up. You will walk up to him and without hesitating you'll point to his scar and demand an explanation that will necessarily unmask him on the spot. ("What happened to you? Who did it to you? When?")

He tells you an incredible story. He speaks of sabers, of horses, crowds packing the streets. A story that stretches from his expulsion from the public school until barely a few months ago. In Sinaloa, he says, the police surrounded the place, broke the lines of the strikers, and burst into the building. They weren't looking for him but he was caught right in the middle of it. A soldier split his face open with the butt of his rifle. His companions helped him, they ran, he lost consciousness several times. In their flight, they left him in a hospital. He remembers the black thread and the needle; the gloved hands working very close to his left eye; the smell of rubber, the white gown. But that was many years ago, it was a hospital like this one. The story was not so heroic this time around: he'd been found writhing and vomiting in a hotel room.

You have smiled the whole way through the story. You imagine the cavalry charges, sword in hand, as if you were in Russia. You laugh at the patient's inventiveness. You once again re-live the rock fights in the old street in Puebla, the boy's eyes peering from his bandaged face at the door of the hospital, seeing you also from between the bodies of his relatives who surround him. All the while you pat his back and *Don* Valentin smiles and nods his head. "Don't worry," you say. "It does you no good to think about those things."

You accompany him to his room, holding his arm. "A relapse at this stage ..." you suggest and conclude the sentence with movements of your head. You give him recommendations: they will release you tomorrow. Rest, a lot of rest. Avoid eating in the street. You open the door of Room 51 for him and you watch him take his short steps toward his bed. "And no politics, alright?" you say to him from the door. *Don* Valentin raises his hand and lets himself be convinced. You know that he's still weak and that he'll not give you any problems.

In bed, looking at the ceiling, you tell your wife all about it. She agrees with you: she also mocks the man's explanation. She is accurate, without knowing it, in the comparison. "Only in Russia," she says. You both sleep until three in the morning when the alarm clock wakes you. You drink coffee without speaking. Once in the doorway, your wife gives you some advice you understand as a "be careful."

You drive through deserted streets, shrouded by the reflections of the light that pours down from the lamp posts. Once in the hospital, the duty nurse gives you a sleepy greeting that you answer with a nod. She watches you enter your office already taking off your jacket in order to put on the white coat.

When you open the door of Room 51, a gust of warm air envelops your face; slivers of the light from the street seep in through the cracks in the curtain. A gentle, collective sigh comes from the sleeping bodies. A, C, E, G, and H are emp-

ty, and the rubber shoes also help. From C you take the pillow
and position it gently. You press down until you feel through
the material the laddered scar that has just come to life.

*–Translated by Tim Richards*

Elena Poniatowska (Paris 1933) is one of Latin America's leading literary and intellectual figures, the first woman to receive the National Journalism Award (in 1979). Among her influential novels: Hasta no verte, Jesús mio (1969), and Tinísima (1992), soon to appear in English. She has written strong sociopolitical criticism following the events of 1968; La noche de Tlatelolco is in print in English as Massacre in Mexico. She has made a literary genre of the interview; an extensive collection of these is being published in 12 volumes under the title Todo Mexico. She has been a visiting professor at numerous universities in Europe and North America and was the recipient in 1994 of a Guggenheim fellowship.

# LITTLE HOUSE OF CELLULOID
## Elena Poniatowska

"Magda, Magda, come here!"

She heard childish laughter in the sitting room and leaned over the staircase.

"Magda, it's you I'm talking to!"

The mocking laughs got louder, or that's the way she heard them.

"Magda, come up here this instant!"

"They've gone out into the street," Laura thought, "that really is the limit," and she ran down the stairs two at a time, the hairbrush in her hand. In the yard, the children were still tearing around as if they hadn't heard a thing. Magda's hair flew, almost transparent in the early morning sun, a kite following behind her: that's what she was, a fragile, featherlight, kite. On the other hand, Gloria, with her short curls stuck tight almost

to her scalp looked like a boy, and Alicia showed no sign of
any Wonderland: the only thing she had on was her pajama
bottoms all bunched up between her legs and most likely
smelling of urine. And with bare feet, of course, as you
might expect.

"Didn't you hear me? I'm fed up with this."

She flew at them. The group of little girls broke up, and
they ducked away from her screaming. Beside herself, Laura
caught the one with the long fine hair and with an iron fist
gripping her arm took her back into the house and forced
her up the stairs.

"You're hurting me!"

"And what makes you think all this disobedience of
yours isn't hurting me, too?" In the bathroom she sat her
down beside the toilet. The little girl's hair fell limply onto
her shoulders. Laura began to brush it.

"Just look at all the tangles you've got it into!"

At each tug, the little girl raised her hand to hold onto
the lock of hair, stopping her mother from continuing . . .,
she had to plait it, if not, by the afternoon it would be a complete mess of knots. Laura brushed fiercely: "Oh, oh, mommy, stop, it's hurting me!" The mother continued, the little
girl started to cry, Laura could see nothing but the hair that
hung in flaps mingled with knots; she had to chop it into
chunks to undo them, the locks of hair gave out little groans,
wailing like violin strings under attack from a cunning bow,
but Laura kept up a ceaseless assault, her hand grasping the
brush, its wide bristles reaching a broad swathe of hair, whack
whack whack over and over on the shaggy mane. Now, in
her daughter's sobs, the mother clearly detected fear, a fear
that shook the bony childish shoulders. The little girl had
hidden her head in her hands and the brushstrokes fell lower
down, on her nape, on her shoulders. At the first opportunity she tried to escape, but Laura restrained her with a
definitive yank, timeworn and hollow as a door slamming
shut, and a shudder ran right through the little girl. Laura
didn't immediately notice the moment when the girl turned

round to look at her until she caught sight of a terrified gaze
that goaded her through her eyelids like a spur: a red flash
of lightning that made the brushstrokes fall from some
unknown space, from all those years of dirty dishes and unmade beds and broken chairs, from the peeling rooftop: pro-
jectiles of black bristles and transparent pink plastic following on each other with an inexplicable force, one after the
other, at a speed that Laura neither could nor would control, one after the other, whack whack whack, whack, she
was no longer counting, the hair no longer wafted like a curtain in the breeze, the little girl had curled up completely
and the mother was beating her on her shoulders, on her
back, on her waist. Until the aching arm stopped in mid air
like a disconnected fan and without turning to look at her
daughter Laura ran down the stairs and into the street, her
arm still uplifted, her hand crowned with boar bristles.

Then she understood that she had to go away.

It was only after she started walking that Laura managed to
lower her arm. One muscle pulled on another and everything
returned to its place and she walked steadily on, if she were
beside herself she didn't notice it, she scarcely noticed that
there were tears on her face and she wiped them on the back
of her hand without letting go of the hairbrush. She wasn't
thinking about her daughter, she wasn't thinking about anything. She was rather short in stature and her steps were not
very long; she had never been able to match her husband's
pace—his stiltlegs were way too tall for her. She left her neighborhood and walked towards the green of other gardens that
almost invaded the sidewalk, protected by precarious toylike
fences. In the midst of the lawns, the houses looked white,
even the doorhandles shone in the sun, round locks, little
suns exactly the size of a hand, the world in the hands of
the rich. Beside each unpolluted house stood a smaller replica
with a red Asbestolite roof: the dog kennel, just like in *House
Beautiful, House and Garden, Ladies' Home Journal;* what
cute little houses, most of the windows had blinds made of

green shutters like the ones children draw in their copybooks, and the shutters made her think of Silvia, protected twice over inside her bedroom.

"But it's right around here somewhere that she lives." Laura slowed her pace. There was a time when they never used to leave each other's side, not even at bedtime, since they were *room-maits*. They had gone to High School together in the United States. Silvia! She started to run: yes, it was here on this block, no, the next, or maybe down there at the end of the block on the right, all the houses looked the same with their garage at the side, and their dog's house and their quadrangles of fresh lawn, fresh as the pause that refreshes. Laura stopped in front of the glossy dark green door and it was only at the very moment the door was opened that she remembered the hairbrush and threw it with its bristles pointing skywards into the gutter, into the water that runs constantly along the edge of the sidewalks.

"I told you it wasn't the right sort of life for you, a woman with your talent, your good looks. I still remember clearly when you used to get the first place in the Essay Contests. You used to write so nicely. Of course I can see you're exhausted, and it doesn't surprise me with that dog's life you lead, but a good haircut and a facial will make you feel like new, you've always looked good in blue, and by the way I'm giving a lunch party today and I want to introduce you to my friends, they'll love you, do you remember Luis Morales? He asked me about you a long time after you got married and he's coming, so just you stay right here, no, no, just stay right here, it's a pity I sent the driver for the flowers but you can take a taxi and later on when I'm dressed I'll meet you at the beauty shop. Please take it, Laura dear, aren't we friends? I always loved you very dearly, Laura, and I always regretted you getting married to that imbecile, but from here on out you're going to feel different, come on Laurita, for the first time in your life do something for yourself, think of what you are, think of what they've done to you."

Laura had felt good as she looked at Silvia from the edge of her marble bathtub. She looked so young and healthy in the water and she looked even better when she got out and dried herself exactly as she used to at school, completely shameless, happy to show off her long muscles, smooth belly, firm buns, the perfect triangle of her sex, the equidistant knots in her spinal column, her shaven armpits, her legs bronzed in the sun, her hips—yes, a tiny bit rounder, but just scarcely. Naked in front of the mirror she brushed her hair, healthy and shiny. In fact the whole bathroom was an advertisement: enormous, satinsmooth like the pages of Vogue, always remember to apply your face cream in an upward direction with light little dabs of the fingertips, sweet almonds conserve the natural moisture of the skin, fresh scented like the first day of spring, aerosol deodorants (stay more adorable just for him) green herbal essence containing all the freshness of a country field, of wild flowers, eight hairbrushes and the winner is . . ., a round mirror to amplify the soul, cotton balls, moisturizing lotions, pistolgrip-hairdryer—automatic—with tongs and hood, a pair of combs, everything within arm's reach around the furry white rug, bearfur, ermine, from the center of which Silvia told her: "Sometimes I dry myself by rolling on it, when I feel like playing and also when I feel like feeling." Laura was ashamed that she hadn't had a bath, thought of the tangled fuzz around her own sex, of her uneven breasts, of the hard skin on her heels; but her friend, in an endless shower of words soothing her like the morning dew, smoothing her like little cleansing tissues, took her by the hand and drew her into the bedroom and continued twirling around in front of her wrapped up like a Roman in a huge fluffy towel, the final touch of intimacy, benzol best for feminine hygiene (take care of yourself, pamper yourself, get to know the woman within . . ., only we can understand), perfumed salts, the towel with the greatest absorbency (give yourself the gift that you alone . . .) and Laura noticed on the bed, the spacious bed that smelled a lot like love, a nightgown of sweet abandon—how vulgar, how deliciously vulgar—and a robe wadded into a ball, the breakfast tray, the newspaper open at the Social Section. Laura had never had breakfast in bed again since the old days, and in fact her breakfast tray lay forgotten in the room where she kept all the kitchen utensils. She only brought breakfast to Gloria when she had scarlet fever and the messy little girl somehow always managed to tip it all over the sheet. Now, as she went down Silvia's circular staircase—another touch of Hollywood, the icing on the cake— she remembered climbing up and down another stairway, carrying the tray up to Gloria, weighed down with all that cumbersome china from the Valle de Bravo she'd chosen instead of the melamine or high-resistance-plastic that Beto suggested. Why was it that in her house the drawers and the closets always stood open, revealing clothes hung up any old how, shoes piled up like debris from a storm? In Silvia's house, everything was ethereal, heaven-sent.

In the street, Laura walked to find a taxi, passed through her own neighborhood again and for the first time felt herself to be superior to the people who passed by. Without a doubt, she would have to leave in order to succeed, get out of this hole, away from the thick monotony, thick as the bean soup that Beto enjoyed so much. How grey and inelegant everyone looked, so harried and miserable. She asked herself if she would ever again be able to write as she used to at boarding school, if she could put all her feelings into a poem, for example, if the poem would be any good, yes, it would be, for its desperation, for its originality, Silvia had always told her that was what she was: o-ri-gi-nal, a good hair color would enhance her high cheekbones, her grey eyes washed out like a pair of underpants, her lips still full, make-up could do miracles. Luis Morales? But of course, Luis Morales had a dark, deep gaze, decidedly oriental, and Laura felt as if she belonged to him alone when he stretched his hand out to hers in order to escort her among the sound of so many voices—voices always made her queasy—to a quiet corner, oh, Luis, this is so nice! yes, it's me, at least, I'm pretending to be the person you fell in love with many years ago, are you going to go with the group to Las Hadas next weekend? but of course I'd love to go, it's been years since I last went sailing on a sailboat . . . and I'll launch myself out to sea, further and further and onto the high seas with you, yes, Luis, I love to sunbathe, yes Luis, daiquiris are my favorite, yes Luis, I can't reach my back, put my Sea-and-Ski on for me, now it's my turn for you, yes, Luis, yes. . . .

Laura was pondering so passionately that she didn't see the empty cabs and walked right by the taxi rank Silvia had mentioned. She walked and walked, yes, she could be a writer, the poem was almost done, her name would appear in the newspapers, she would have her own circle of fans and today at the lunch Silvia would feel proud of her because she hadn't forgotten anything from back then, not the tall-stemmed roses, nor the sparkling crystal, nor the eyes that shone with pleasure, nor the champagne, nor the men's shoulders in their well-cut suits, so different from the bulky beflanneled back that Beto presented her with each night the instant before collapsing and releasing the first snore, the deathrattle, the noisy surge of steam under pressure: a beatup locomotive squatting on the rails as it reaches its station.

Suddenly, Laura noticed a lot of trains under the bridge she was crossing over; yes, she would travel, Iberia Airlines, a reclining seat, the stewardess at her side serving her a whiskey, how delicious, such a thirst, the plane traversing the blue sky like someone ripping through a piece of cloth, the same way she cut out blouses for her children, the sky ripped by the plane she would travel in, in her eardrums the Aranjuez concerto, Spain, water, land of fire, from the rooftops of Spain whitewashed and black, in Spain the men compliment women a lot, hey beautiful! how ugly Mexico was and how poor and how dark with its network of blackened hovels all over the place, squashed together way down there at the bottom of the abyss, underpants on the clothesline, a pile of old clothes getting covered with dust and soot and hung out to dry in the filthy air that clings around railway stations, diesel air, layered with grime, stinking, what feeble dwellings, how

fragile was the life of the people who wallowed about down
there below while she headed towards the Beauty Shop of
the Maria Isabel Hotel but why was the beauty shop such
a hell of a long way away? For a long time now you couldn't
see any large expanses of lawn with a house in the middle,
on the contrary, there weren't even any trees. Laura kept going, Silvia's changepurse clutched tightly in her hand, first
the brush, now the purse. She didn't want to accept a handbag, she had lost the habit, she told her friend, yes of course,
she knew that only maidservants carried changepurses, but
she would take the step from purse to handbag later, after
the hairdo. At the moment, she had to take one step at a
time, recuperate her strength slowly like sick people who
when they get to the convalescent stage take careful slow steps
so they don't fall. She was suddenly overcome with thirst and
on seeing a Sanborn's she went in, a Ladies Bar at the back,
without hesitation she ordered a whiskey like the one on
Iberia, what a thirst, spongelike, saliva, semen, yes, if the saliva
that's now dry in your mouth turned into semen it would
create just like a man, just like Beto who simply because he
had a penis and fishy sperm considered himself a Tarzan,
the king of creation, God, Santa Claus, Mr. President, who
knows who-the-devil what, what a thirst she had, what a thirst,
she must have walked a long way to feel so thirsty and to
feel so tired but it would all go away with the loving sham-
poo to come, and at lunchtime it would be such a thrill to
go from one group to another, and laugh, and talk in a dignified
way about the book of poems about to be published, she
looked good in blue, blue has always got her to love herself,
didn't the psychiatrist in that article in *Kena* say that the first
sign of mental healthiness was to begin loving oneself? Silvia
had shown her her blue outfits. The second whiskey brought
a flush to Laura's cheeks, after the third she took a break
and a gringo sat down beside her and offered her a fourth
drink. "And I haven't even had my hair done yet," she thought
with pleasure. In the booth, she stretched her legs out, that's
what the seat opposite was for, right? and settled herself

comfortably. "I'm free, free to do whatever I please."

Now the time was definitely passing slowly and no thought at all raced through her head. When she left Sanborn's it was getting dark and the manager had ordered the long strands of neon light lit in the interior aisles. Laura's body ached, and her uplifted arm, halted in mid air, called the first taxi and she automatically gave the address of her house and as she got out she gave the driver the last cent she had in the purse. "Take the purse too." She thought that the driver looked like Luis Morales or what she remembered Luis Morales looking like. As usual, the front door stood half open and Laura tripped over one of the little girls' tricycles, there seemed to be a lot of toys scattered around the living room, lots of them, big toys, a field full of toys, if she walked through them they'd come up to her ankles. The whole place smelled of bacon and she could see from here the dishes piled up in the kitchen sink. But what struck her the most was the picture of her as a bride standing next to Beto. Beto had cold eyes and she looked at them coldly and they responded with the same coldness. They weren't ugly, but they had something mean about them, they rejected her and they challenged her at the same time, without passion, without desire, lifeless, they were eyes going nowhere; from where she was she could hear what Paco Malgesto was announcing on the television, Bimbo cupcakes, the walls of the house were very thin, you could hear everything and at first Laura had thought that was an advantage because that way she would always know what the kids were up to. Almost nobody turned their head when she went into the television room—they were glued to the guy on Channel 8. Magda's hair hung in a pitiful tangle as always, Beto's back curved bulkily at the shoulder—certain men get old precisely at that point, at the neck, like an ox; Gloria and Alicia were lying on their bellies on the wrinkled and stained carpet, barefoot, of course. Nobody seemed to pay her the least mind. So Laura went on into the bedroom that nobody had cleaned up and was on the point of throwing herself fully dressed shoes and all onto the marriage bed that no one had made when she saw a sock lying beside it and without thinking she picked it up and looked for another one further down and placed it with the first: "Do these make a pair?" She picked up Jorgito's sweater, Quique's backpack, Betito's skate, some diapers impregnated with the ammoniac odor of stale urine and took them into the bathroom to the dirty clothes hamper; it wouldn't be long now before Alicia would be getting out of diapers and then the house would stop smelling of urine; in the bathtub she saw Alicia's plastic ducks, Jorgito's diver and submarine, sailboats and motorboats, a cake of deformed multicolored soap composed of all the leftover bits and she began scrubbing at the ring of grime which bothered no one but her. She took the family toothbrushes from the toothmug and rinsed them; they had toothpaste clogged around the roots. She began to go up and down the stairs looking for the right place for each item. How, in such a small space, can so many useless objects pile up, so much dead matter? Tomorrow she'd have to air the mattresses, tidy away the shoes, so many of them—football boots, tennis shoes, canvas boots, sandals, make a list, Wednesday she'd clean out the closets, just to clean the kitchen cupboards would take her a whole day, on Thursday the so-called library where she once tried to write and where they installed the television set because you got better reception in that room, another whole day mending sweaters, redoing the elastic in underpants, sewing buttons, yes, mend those socks that kept on wrinkling down around their ankles, then on Friday. . . .

Beto got up, went to the bathroom, didn't even bother to close the door properly while he urinated lengthily and as he came out, his hand still on his fly, Laura caught for an instant the coldness of his look and her heart shrank at the hatred it expressed. Then he did a half-turn and hauled his body back to the television room. The children would soon get bored and come down to the kitchen: "Mommy, we hardly got a thing to eat for lunch." They would come down prancing about, she could already hear their hoofs on the stairs,

Laura would open her mouth to scream but no sound would come out, she would look for something to defend herself with, she would try to find a knife, something to protect herself but they would surround her: "Mommy, I want a fried egg and hotcakes and I want a toasted sandwich and I want bacon again," they would raise towards her their milky breath, their hands stained with ink and Laura's mouth would undo itself into a smile and her fingers clenched into a fist, on the point of thrusting them away from her, stiff and trembling, would open one by one as if drawn by the invisible threads of a puppeteer, slowly, gently, oh so wearily.

*—Translated by Irene Matthews*

*Daniel Sada (Mexicali, Baja Calif. 1943) is a strong voice from Mexico's northwestern border region, with a fascination for the intricacies of the Spanish language. He has published four collections of short fiction; the latest one,* Registro de causantes, *won the Villaurrutia Prize in 1992 and is the source of the following story. His third novel,* Una de dos, *will be published in Spain in 1995.*

# THE GREAT CARPENTRY HEIST
## Daniel Sada

When Juventino Treto opened his carpentry workshop (he had passed through the streets just before dawn doing his accounts on his fingers, his gaze fixed on the cobblestones as if in search of the total, any total, right or wrong. He walked with a slight stoop as though following his shadow, lengthened and graceful) in the half light he saw: no workbench, no treadle saw, no hammers, no sandpaper, crayons, or measuring tape. There was nothing, and this emptiness frightened him. They had robbed him in the night. His shop! In all its ten years, never; this had never happened before.

But what an unlikely burglary: they had carried off everything. Some magic, maybe. Suddenly to see himself without . . . What? How could it be? How had they gotten in when all the windows were intact and hooked shut? Both doors were also

221

padlocked. So . . . should he call the police? Would that make sense? You can bet those brown-uniformed types were not to be trusted—and the local ones were worst of all. Ugly, unwholesome-looking characters, armed to the teeth, ready to take on anyone who got in their way. It was well known that in Sacramento when criminals finished their ten-year sentence in the stinking jail, they were given a uniform and credentials, two pistols, a billy club, brass knuckles, and a machete. What a pretty graduation ceremony! But somebody was behind this system, with plenty to gain. That's why there were four policemen in Sacramento, and these four . . . well, why get yourself into trouble?

Whether out of laziness or whatever—call it prudence: not to tell, not to give the gossips a field day, a chance to blow things out of proportion. What was really interesting was that everything had been taken except the money, which had been put in an unlocked drawer, and a machete. It was impossible to explain how they managed, all at once, to make off with the table and five chairs, and all the sheets of Masonite.

Juventino began looking for the opening of a tunnel in the floor, a secret chink in the wall with movable bricks. He was digging the earth from the floor, even scraping with his nails, chipping away with the machete. Juventino was, after all, a very stubborn man. He spent three hours at this labor. By now it was nine and the town was coming to life.

The businesses open now and the trucks arriving, a few people, not many, were in the streets. It was a mild winter, the sun warm on the skin, with many clouds from distant skies. And as Juventino's shop was only three blocks off the main plaza, there was no lack of the morbidly curious who stopped to look in—the unhappy carpenter, in his haste, was too impatient to close the doors from inside to prevent anyone watching his excavation—and of the many passersby one did stop to ask what was going on.

It was a stout woman coming from mass, wearing a black veil that touched the ground.

Juventino reacted quickly, remembering his decision to say nothing about the crime, and without so much as a word or a grimace, he answered by shutting the door in the woman's face, whereupon she ran off with an even bigger story: that the mad Juventino had moved all his equipment out and was digging a well. Rumor followed rumor, even to the point where there was talk of a burglary. Conjectures varied, including that the assistant Juventino had employed for seven months—and whom he had fired in an ugly manner, shouting at him in the middle of the street—was the culprit, it being well known that he had duplicate keys. The trouble was that this guy no longer lived in Sacramento so that the story remained no more than a wild guess.

Ergo, aside from him, who else was there? Following the episode, Juventino had become distrustful; except with his customers and the local kids, he spoke with few people, always work work work. But alone. For ten years it had continued like this.

Maybe he was becoming an oddball because at the age of almost fifty he was still single. That was probably the reason he worked like a burro in a cornfield. It would already be late at night when Juventino went off home, which was about a block away.

The gossip grew within three hours to the extent that the police came knocking at his door. Juventino opened it nervously. It was the infamous four, with stars gleaming from their caps, and one of them said, "We're only bothering you because the word is that you've been robbed."

The carpenter knew nothing about it. In dismay, but attempting to smile, he asked, "What's it all about?"

"It's this. I have to inform you that everyone says that your shop was broken into, and we've come to find out if what they say is true."

In his confusion, Juventino wanted to shut the door on them but ... They seemed to be aware that they were making him uncomfortable. The carpenter's gestures spoke louder than his words.

"No, there's . . . There's been no burglary. I'm pretty sure they're mistaken."

"Good. Well, if there's anything we can do for you, we're at your service."

They left and Juventino, relieved, closed the door after them. Ouf! What an escape! The thing had been within a hair of getting out of hand. Ah! When he went to throw the bolt it came to him, the business of the ungrateful assistant, the ugly circumstances of firing him—and so far it had escaped him—the fact that he had a copy of the key. Well, he couldn't be sure that his suspicions were real, but it seemed certain: He was the one who had robbed the shop during the night! And the rest of that long day found Juventino closed up in his workshop. Pensive.

It might be revenge. But the money and the machete? Why not take everything? That detail made the story improbable. It wasn't him. The police! *They* were the thieves. And between his doubts and his certainties, suddenly it was night. Now his dilemma was whether to stay and sleep in the shop, or—he decided quickly. It would comfort him to keep watch. Maybe just past midnight, those lizards would come to pick up the money—and he'd be ready for them. Actually, the carpenter had not yet counted up the quantity of bills.

There were six of them, six of those colored peso notes, spread out like a hand of cards. A small-town fan! And a heap of small change. The assistant—according to a quick pencilled accounting—had robbed him of five hundred and eighteen pesos—or the police, or both together—and he felt sleep overtake him until he was in this tunnel, which ended in an abyss of random floating tools and people fleeing through the air, and unfinished chairs.

Adrift in a void! And unable to grab onto anything. What was real was that someone tried to force the shop door just after midnight. Juventino, who had slept with machete in hand, hurriedly arose at the sound of the pounding, but at that very moment they gave it up and you could hear steps, soft, as if in tennis shoes, and the noise of a jeep.

A clue? What difference? "The bastards, now they know for sure that I was in the shop," he said to himself, greatly relieved. He didn't even want to open the door to observe their flight. "If one of them gets in, he'll get it from my machete. And if another one kills me with one shot, at least I'll take one to the graveyard with me." In any case, his dream-filled sleep was finished. And soon the dawn found him thinking up strategies. He was forced to think more clearly about what he would do next. Certainly he had unfinished work that ought to have been ready and delivered in less than a week. Certainly now . . . What was he going to do? It wouldn't help to talk to anyone, to ask Tancredo for help, or Felix or Sinforoso, who were good friends when it came to money and who knew the trade. Maybe they—this was a long shot— maybe *they* would turn out to be the long-armed burglars. Thinking about it made him weak in the knees. So he closed the shop and went home.

On the way—indifferent to the looks he was getting from passersby—he was thinking that it wasn't the first time that the assistant had been in there; it was a sure thing that Cayetano had invited his friends in at night to get drunk in the workshop. They probably organized California-style parties, with balloons and streamers, and even invited those women who look like lionesses, kissed by many mouths and still smiling, undressed in front of the men with Tarzan haircuts, smiling and smiling for no reason. Painted hussies, the kind who belong to nobody, while the men are hitting the bottle . . . The good life, and let the rest of the world go to hell.

He was about to go into his house when he noticed three women laughing at him behind his back, making fun of his stoop and the dark glasses he wore to protect his eyes. "Ay, *don* Juventino, every day you get more and more weird, almost interesting. Don't forget that if you get sick any one of us can give you an injection," said one. The carpenter, fiftyish and bad-tempered, raised his hand. "Get out of here, you old *charangas*. One of these days, if you get your tongues

under control, I'll invite you to dinner ..." And they all ran
off in different directions, horrified. Bad timing as usual; what
did he want with easy women, considering what had happened to him last night.

And upon opening his door, he found the house in good
order. He walked carefully through the front room into the
patio, where he found—miraculously—a pig and a goat, from
now on his only assets, aside from a few pesos he had left
around. And thinking how much easier it would have been
for the thieves to get into the house instead of the workshop,
since the patio had a low fence easy to jump over, almost
built expressly to make burglary easy—of the pig and the goat
at any rate. Well, the pig not so easy because with its loud
squeals it would give them plenty of trouble, while the goat,
no, she was easily pacified and would just cry like a baby.
Anyhow, this house was almost always unattended.

The carpenter frequently went off into soliloquies,
possibly because he was a bachelor-philosopher and more
than a little obsessive. He had a favorite corner where he
would go to sit by the hour to smoke, and arch his bushy
eyebrows, and make himself interesting. There, he mused that
it was a miracle, at least a paradox: his house intact, each
object in its place—and the money. Careless. Should he count
it? After what had happened? Needing to relax a bit, Juventino went to the kitchen to fix himself some coffee.

He had time on his hands now. Time to put things
together. And to picture the burglary, done with such attention to detail and in a matter of seconds, the way that they
... But the real problem now was the cost of the equipment.
Should he replace it? He'd have to sell off some of his favorite
things to raise the money. What a complicated business!

Somewhere between indolent and fretful, Juventino
stirred himself to collect the smattering of coins, a hundred
pesos and small change, enough to get himself to the border
with a vague intention of crossing to the other side, cooling
off, for sure, in the waters of the Rio Bravo.

But wait, would it have to be so? No. Because over in

Acuña he had a friend who got by with his English even when
he was drunk, who had his papers in order and was a friend
of some half-gangster gringos. Juventino let the idea turn over
in his mind until it was doing somersaults and took over his
fancy. What a breeze, to get across the bridge with his friend's
help; he wouldn't even need a passport. He was so caught
up in this daydream that he gave no thought to who would
take over the house and shop while he was gone, or whether
to rent them both.

Instead he thought about taking the goat and the pig
with him on his back so as to sell them along the way and
have a few pennies more when he arrived. But first he opened
some peach juice, the kind that comes in cans.

The robbery, at this distance, was pushing him rudely
towards a new and fortunate beginning, towards the unknown.
A new life at fifty. Maybe once on the other side he might
marry one of those blondes with great legs.

Despite this, and with some bitterness, the image of
Cayetano passed through his curly head. Revenge, that's what
it was. And no doubt, even though he had employed him for
fifteen years, he could never cure the man's rebelliousness
and sneering humor. He was often late to work and left when
he felt like it and took advantage when Juventino tried to
be flexible, and seldom had he been pressured to finish the
most urgent jobs.

Next morning there were urgent knocks at the door.
The carpenter, startled and half in a stupor, awakened, dressed
himself and, still dazed, opened the door ... Surprise! It was
three of his customers.

"We found out your workshop was robbed last night.
I, for one, had given you an order to upholster some chairs
for me."

"I had ordered a chest."

"And I a wagon."

Scratching his head, mired in his apathy, Juventino
wondered how to answer them; he wanted to shut the door
on them but he also wanted to move ahead with his plan.

He answered in a grieved tone.

"They've taken everything. So that my business is lost, so that . . . Listen, you know I respect my commitments. I'm telling you that the only thing I can do is to go to the United States to earn a lot of money to pay you back what you left on deposit. All I ask is that while I am gone you take care of my house and my workshop . . . Now wait a second and I'll be back in a flash with a copy of both sets of keys."

So the carpenter left, leaving the customers in a state of confusion. It would have been logical for them to think his decision was precipitous; after all, it would have been easier to go to the City Hall, report the burglary, and leave the problem in the hands of the authorities. He hadn't done that, and the reason—they looked at one another without a word—out of laziness? Too much official red tape? True, the investigation could easily drag on for a couple of years . . . Right! And meanwhile . . .

When Juventino got back, one of them remarked, "And how long will you be gone?"

"I'll be back in a month. You'll see."

"I think it's good, what you've decided . . ."

To this one Juventino turned over the keys and said, "Let's hope I come back with my pockets full of money."

"And if you stay beyond the time, we take over everything . . ." said another.

"Correct."

"We ought to get some legal paper to formalize this," said a third, less trusting voice.

"No need for that," the carpenter assured. "I'll be back sooner rather than later."

"But what if something happens and you take longer? Remember, you're due April second . . ."

"No, really, I go and I'm back, understand? One thing: don't mention government to me. No legal nonsense."

The deal was made. The customers left without saying goodbye, silent. Juventino did not turn but watched, wishing he could undo the bargain, the receding backs of the men to whom he had entrusted his worldly goods, the future of which hung now on an unknown adventure. The doorway seemed to signify an ending, or anyway an improbable return, and the rectangle of sunlight it projected framed the three men as they receded into the distance, gesturing among themselves under their big sombreros. All that day the bachelor-philosopher spent thinking, thinking, about life on the border: the go-go songs, all those hamburgers and hot dogs—Not bad, eh? And those gigantic stores. . . . But the bad part was to be a wetback, and he knew from way back how a lot of his friends had been caught and roughed up for not having documents. On the other hand, whoever got through got rich overnight and almost without working. God willing, his compadre would not refuse to help him. Although . . .

Very early the next day he shook himself awake and hastily threw together some clothes, and in a bag he threw bread and cans of juice and tins of sardines. At that moment he began to think about the goat and the pig, dumping them into a sack, although they would fight like hell. No, better to tie the pig by its big snout, or just let them follow along. He realized dejectedly that to load them up would be awkward, with these suitcases and all; even so, that seemed the best idea.

Well, he was not going to confront his problems with tears; on the contrary, he'd take heart and stick to his goal. Next, then, to get his baggage put together however he could. What took time was getting the stupid animals into the flour sack; then, carrying this trousseau of his, he turned and looked about him, aware that each beloved piece of furniture represented a fragment of his daily labors, a quiet and remote glimmer of his life in this town; yes, an incomplete catalog of his solitary life. And the result? It was the last chapter of an effort that had provided only small bits of happiness, and when he pictured these good-natured comings and goings he felt himself no more than a puff of smoke. "Let's get on with it," he said to himself. "This is some heavy load." Of course the real problem was the flailing of the unfortunate animals: the *me-e-ehs* versus the grunts.

Juventino departed, staggering under the load. He couldn't or didn't want to lock the door with the key. In one hand he was carrying two heavy suitcases and in the other, over his shoulder, the bag of food and the animated flour sack. With great difficulty, he made his way for a little more than two blocks, ignoring the stares of the people, some sharply critical, some seeming to say goodbye. Among the many who stood watching him – children, men, and old folk – were the three women from yesterday, the ones who had flirted with him. Adios. But wait – if he was going to get to the bus station in good shape, he'd better take a breather, during which it suddenly dawned on him: It wouldn't make a bit of difference if he abandoned the sack; after all, the hundred pesos would cover the trip.

With a bump the stunned goat and pig hit the ground, the pig still wearing the knotted rag in its nose. A whole festival of children, men, and women ran after the animals in order to claim ownership ...

Juventino, resolute, refused to look back. Let them work it out back there. He simply passed one valise to the hand already carrying the sack of food, his very important lunch. He walked on rapidly as if pleased with himself, thinking about his future and able to feel that, this being the first time that he crossed the border, destiny was seducing him: marriage, perhaps, and pockets full of money with all its rewards. In the bus station the bachelor made a sarcastic face.

Oh joy!

And the first thing he did was to buy his ticket to Acuña and take a seat on the waiting-room bench, where the image came to him – fleetingly – of his former assistant and his perfect revenge. He said to himself, "God-damned Cayetano, who would have guessed?"

And so he began imagining how his workshop of so many years was going to become a place for wild parties with light women and heavy drinking. Yes, if he did not return quickly from the United States or if they gave him problems for not having blond hair and blue eyes or at least green, all would be lost.

At last, with a triumphal cloud of smoke from its muffler, the bus arrived and Juventino climbed up immediately, yielding his ticket to the driver as if this were some god who would carry him to death or to happiness. Inside, it was already another world and since there were six empty seats in the rear, Juventino had his choice. He selected a window seat. Soon, the motor starting up, his anxieties increased, and then, more relaxed on leaving Sacramento, he had the sensation of turning his back upon a badly-drawn picture that was floating in space. With this, he leaned his head comfortably against the headrest. Then, with a quick glance at his native fields, he opened a can of juice.

*—Translated by Joan Lindgren*

*Edmundo Valadés (Guaymas, Sonora 1915) is a journalist, teacher, and founder emeritus of the magazine* El Cuento. *He is currently director of the journal* Frontera Norte *and working on his first novel,* Isolda de Moscú. *His first collection of short stories,* La muerte tiene permiso, *was published in 1955, yet its title story, below, has the immediacy of this week's news.*

# PERMISSION GRANTED
## Edmundo Valadés

On the platform the agronomists are chatting, laughing. They hit each other with incisive jokes. They let loose dirty stories with gritty punchlines. Little by little their attention is drawn toward the gathering crowd in the hall. They stop recalling the latest party, the intimacies of the brand-new girl in the whorehouse they usually visit. The subject of their talk now turns to the men below, the communal farmers who have come together in this meeting, down here in front of them.

"Of course we must liberate them. We must incorporate them into our civilization, cleaning them on the outside and teaching them to be dirty on the inside ..."

"You're a sceptic, *ingeniero*. You're also questioning our efforts, the efforts of the Revolution."

"Bah! It's all useless. These bastards are hopeless. They're rotted by liquor, by ignorance. Nothing has come from giving them land."

"That is shallow; you're a defeatist, *compañero*. We are the ones to blame. We gave them the land, and then what? We are very pleased with ourselves. But what about loans, fertilizers, new agricultural techniques, machinery? Are they supposed to invent all that on their own?"

The chairman, meanwhile, smooths his upright moustaches and looks through his glasses, impervious to the rhetoric of the technicians. When the earthy, pungent animal smell of the men occupying the benches tickles his nostrils, he takes out a colored handkerchief and blows noisily. He was once a peasant too, but that was long ago. Now, thanks to the city and his position there, all that is left of that earlier life are his handkerchief and the roughness of his hands.

The men below take their seats solemnly, with the wariness typical of the peasant entering a closed space: an assembly room or a church. They speak sparingly and the words they exchange have to do with harvests, rain, animals, loans. Many carry with them their *itacates,* pouches of food slung over the shoulder, ammunition to fight hunger. A few are smoking calmly, in no hurry, as if the cigarettes had grown out of their hands. Others stand, leaning against the side walls, with their arms crossed over their chests, quietly mounting guard.

The chairman shakes his bell and the sound quiets the murmuring. The officials speak first, about the agrarian problems, about the need for increasing production, for improving the tillage. They promise to help the farmers, and urge them to voice their needs. "We want to help you, you can trust us."

Now it's the turn of the men below. The chairman invites them to bring out matters of concern. One hand rises slowly, shyly. Others follow. They speak out about their affairs: the water, the local political boss, credit, the school. Some are direct, to the point; others get entangled and don't manage to express themselves. They scratch their heads and turn around looking for what they were going to say, as if the idea had hidden itself someplace, in the eyes of a *com-pañero*, or up above where the lamp is hanging.

Over here, in a group, a few men are whispering. They all come from the same village. Something serious worries them. They consult one another: they are considering who is to speak for all of them.

"I think Felipe. He knows a lot."

"Come on, you, Juan, you talked that other time."

There is no agreement. The men whose names have been mentioned wait to be pushed forward. An old man, perhaps the village patriarch, decides: "Let it be Sacramento."

Sacramento waits.

"C'mon, raise your hand."

The hand goes up but the chairman doesn't see it. Others are more visible and are called upon first. Sacramento looks questioningly at the old man. One of the group, very young, lifts his hand high. Above the forest of unkempt heads five dark fingers can be seen, crusted with earth. The chair-man spies the hand. The group has the floor.

"O.K. now, stand up!"

The hand goes down as Sacramento rises to his feet. He tries to find a place for his *sombrero*. The hat becomes a vast nuisance, it grows in size, doesn't fit anywhere. Sacra-mento keeps it in his hands. At the table there are signs of impatience. The chairman's voice leaps out, authoritarian, threatening: "Well. The one who asked to speak. We're waiting for him."

Sacramento fastens his eyes on the figure at the far end of the table. It seems as if he will speak only to him, as if the others had disappeared and they were the only two left in the room.

"I want to speak for all of us people of San Juan de las Manzanas. We bring a complaint against the municipal president, who is always fighting us until we can't put up with it any more. First he took some land away from Felipe Pérez and Juan Hernández because it was next to his own. We sent a telegram to Mexico City and they didn't even answer us.

The whole community got together and thought it would be a good idea to go to the Agrarian Commission to get the lands back. Well, it was no use, all the trips and all the papers: the municipal president kept those pieces of land."

Sacramento speaks without any change in the expression on his face. One might believe he is reciting an old prayer which he knows very well from the beginning to the end. "So then, he looked at us with bitterness and accused us of being troublemakers. You would have thought it was us who had taken his land away. And then he came at us with that story about the accounts, these mortgage payments, *señor*, saying we were behind in the payments. And the agent agreed that things looked bad, that we had to pay a lot of interests. Crescencio, the one who lives over the hill, near by the water, and who understands about numbers, figured it out and found that it wasn't true; they just wanted to charge us more. But the municipal president brought some officials from Mexico City, saying they had all sorts of documents, and that if we didn't pay they'd take our lands away. So, like they say, he forced us to pay what we never owed . . ."

Sacramento speaks with no emphasis, with no deliberate pauses. It is as if he were plowing the land. His words fall like seeds at sowing time.

"And the thing about my son, *señor*. The boy got real mad. Believe me, I didn't want that he do it. I tried to stop him. He been drinking and it messed up his head. Even being his father I couldn't do anything. He went out to find the municipal president, to protest . . . They killed him, without warning, then pretended he was out to steal one of the municipal president's cows. They sent him back to me dead, his face destroyed . . ."

The knot in Sacramento's throat trembles. Only that. He is still standing, like a tree that has taken root. Nothing else. His eyes are still fastened to the man at the far end of the table. "Then there was the business about the water. Since there isn't much, because of the poor rains, the municipal president had closed the canal. And since the cornfields were

going to dry up, and the community was going to have a bad
year, we went to see him . . . to give us just a little water, *señor,*
for our crops. And he met us with angry words, because, like
always, he gets mad at us for nothing at all."

A hand tugs at Sacramento's arm. One of his companions whispers something to him. Sacramento's voice is
the only sound in the hall.

"If this were not enough—because, thanks to the *Virgen-
cita,* there were rains and we more or less managed to save
the crops—there is what happened on Saturday. The municipal president went out with his men, a bad lot, and stole two
of our girls: Lupita, who was going to marry Herminio, and
Crescencio's daughter. We were out at work so we couldn't
stop them. They dragged the girls to the hills and left them
there on the ground. When the girls got back, in real bad
shape, beaten up, too, we didn't have to ask what happened.
And people got really furious, fed up with being at the mercy of a man who uses his authority to do evil."

For the first time, Sacramento's voice trembled. There
was menace in it, and hatred, and an ominous determination.
"And since no one listens to us, and we've been to all the authorities and we don't know where justice is to be found, we want
to get a decision here. We ask you," and Sacramento swept
the men at the table with his gaze and stopped at the chairman, "you who promised to help us, we ask your permission
to punish the municipal president of San Juan de las Manzanas. We ask your leave to take justice in our own hands . . ."

All eyes search the men on the platform. The chairman and the others look at each other silently. At last, they
speak among themselves.

"It's absurd. We can't sanction this inconceiv-
able request."

"No, *compañero,* it is not absurd. Absurd would be to
leave the matter in the hands of those who have done nothing
about it, who have refused to listen to these voices. It would
be cowardly to wait for our justice to do justice; we would
never be believed again. I'd rather stand with these men, with

their primitive justice, but justice after all, and assume with them whatever responsibility I may share. As far as I'm concerned, we have no choice but to grant them what they ask."

"But we're civilized men, we've got institutions; we can't just set them aside. It would be justifying barbarism, action outside the law."

"And what worse action outside the law than what they denounce? If we had been offended as these people have been, if the authorities had caused us less grievances than they have been made to suffer, we would already have killed, we would have ignored a system of justice that fails to intervene. I urge you to put their proposal to a vote."

"I agree with you, *compañero.*"

"But these people are not to be trusted. We should find out the truth. What's more, we have no authority to grant a request like this."

Now the chairman speaks. The peasant inside him stirs. His voice admits no argument. "The assembly will decide. I'll take the responsibility."

He turns toward the hall. His voice is a *campesino*'s voice, the same voice that must have spoken there in the hills, mixed with the earth, with his people. "The vote is on the proposal of the *compañeros* of San Juan de las Manzanas. Those who agree they should be given permission to kill the municipal president, please raise your hand . . ."

All hands are lifted high. Those at the table, too. There is not a single hand which has not been raised in categorical approval. Each finger points to immediate and certain death.

"The assembly grants permission to the people of San Juan de las Manzanas for their request."

Sacramento, who has remained calmly standing, finishes his speech now. There is neither joy nor pain in what he says. His utterance is plain, simple.

"Well, many thanks for the permission because, seeing that no one would listen to us, since yesterday the municipal president of San Juan de las Manzanas is dead."

*—Translated by Adriana Valadés and David Bowen*

# TRANSLATORS

*In the order of their appearance in this volume.*

**Margaret Sayers Peden** is among the best-known translators of Mexican writers, from Sor Juana Inés de la Cruz to Juan Rulfo, Octavio Paz, and Carlos Fuentes, including the latter's *Old Gringo*. Her series of interviews with 49 Mexican artists was published recently under the title *Out of the Volcano*. Having been raised in a very small, Bible-belt Missouri town, she recognized the jockeying and games of influence just beneath the surface of Carballido's story. "It is always the translator's hope that these universals will be conveyed *as* universals, yet maintain their cultural integrity."

**John Incledon** has translated, among other works, Salvador Elizondo's complex *Farabeuf,* and *Day of the Winged Lion* by Mario Luis Rodriguez. He teaches at Albright College in Reading, Pennsylvania. He points to Pacheco's stylistic idiosyncracies in this story – abrupt paragraph breaks, unusual punctuation – as a strong clue to the central character's confusion and alienation as he attempts to move in social circles not his own. Mastretta's subtle dialogue in "White Lies" (an untitled story from the collection *Mujeres de Ojos Grandes)* he compares to the work of masters of fiction from Henry James to Manuel Puig.

**Cynthia Steele** teaches at the University of Washington and is the author of *Politics, Gender, and the Mexican Novel 1968-88*. She has published translations of fiction and poetry by Elena Garro, Inés Arredondo, and José Emilio Pacheco, among others. She describes Zepeda's story "The Truth" as a "chronicle of a death foretold, couched in the curiously indirect and somewhat formal speech of the Mayan people. . . . Some subtleties, like the use of the archaic *vos* (a substitute for the familiar *tú,* used by Mayans in addressing one another, by ladinos in addressing Mayans, and sometimes also subversively by Mayans with ladinos) are lost in translation."

David Bowen is the founder and publisher of Corona. After several years as a freelance journalist in Latin America durng the early 1960s, he took a master's degree in Latin American history at City College of New York, and continues to travel widely in Mexico. He recently edited *Columbus and the Crowns* (1992) from the work of historian William H. Prescott.

James Hoggard is a poet, essayist, and writer of fiction, a professor of English at Midwestern State University (Wichita Falls, Texas), and president of the Texas Institute of Letters. He recently produced two volumes from work by the acclaimed Chilean poet Oscar Hahn. He points out the "cartoon-like" effects of Pérez Gay's story, which moved him to render its original title *("Para Llorar")* as "Big Tears."

Mark Schafer lives in Boston and has published translations of Alberto Ruy Sanchez and Virgilio Piñera, and collaborated (with Cedric Belfrage) on a translation of Eduardo Galeano's *The Book of Embraces*. He is also a collage-maker — perhaps a provocative metaphor for translation? He is currently at work on a collection of short fiction by Jesús Gardea, whom he describes as "a masterful writer" who grew up in the sun-baked desert of Chihuahua, "an extreme and desolate environment favorable only to that curious mixture of fatalism and hope expressed in 'One for the Road.'"

The Salazar story, he points out, is told "in a brilliantly conceived chorus of overlapping voices" that poses intricate problems for translator and reader.

Paul Pines is a poet and translator, and author of a novel, *The Tin Angel* (Wm. Morrow). His most recent book, *Hotel Madden Poems*, appeared in 1992. His work has appeared in *Prairie Schooner, Pequod,* and *New Directions Annual,* and in *Nicanor Parra, Antipoems.* He lives in Glens Falls, N.Y. "An Orange Is an Orange," like most of the stories in Silvia Molina's book *Un Hombre Cerca,* has a "dream-like construction," he tells us. "Her stories resonate with what has gone unsaid."

Asa Zatz has been a translator for the Organization of American States and for many international agreements, conferences, and official messages of the President of Mexico. He has translated important Mexican writers in economics, art, and anthropology, as well as novels and plays by Ramón del Valle-Inclán, Alejo Carpentier, Arturo Arias, Jorge Ibargüengoitia, and many others. He lives in New York City.

He considers Ibargüengoitia a Mexican Maupassant and says, "This light short story carries deceptively heavy artillery." Agustin's hues are darker, but both are a translator's delight "for their attainment of maximum effect with minimum verbiage."

Edith Grossman is a familiar name to readers of Latin American literature, as translator and critic. Her most recent publications include translations of *Magroll* (three novelas by Álvaro Mutis) and *Strange Pilgrims* (twelve stories by Gabriel Garcia Márquez). She lives in New York City. Ms. Grossman describes Monsreal as a "proto-Joycean stand-up comic with an unusual gift for reshaping colloquial language into an eccentric, incisive medium for irony and humor."

Jo Ann Engelbert, a Kentucky native, attended Adelphi University, Middlebury College, and New York University and teaches Latin American literature at Montclair State University in New Jersey. She has translated work by Macedonio Fernández, Jorge Luis Borges, Julio Cortázar, Carmen Naranjo, Isabel Allende, and Roberto Sosa, among others. She compares translating a text to crawling under a car to see how it works. Translating Pitol, she reports, is "like crawling under a Rolls."

Joan Lindgren is a teacher and writer in the San Diego/ Tijuana area. Her own poetry and essays on border poetry have been published in anthologies, as well as translations of the Argentine poet Juan Gelman and Costa Rican artist/poet Magda Santonostasio. She taught a Cross-border Literary Translation Workshop at the University of Baja California. The story by Martin del Campo she places in the tradition of Juan Rulfo, and likens it to a glass of water, reminding us "how thirsty we always are for transparency and simplicity in describing our shared human condition." She points out that the story by Daniel Sada is in large part the "doggedly self-defeating interior monologue" of Juventino, the central character. "His attitudes and his language are shaped by the harshness of the Coahuilan landscape, a deep-seated distrust of authority (even the authority of his own experience), and the whine of the Mexican ballad or *corrido*."

Imera Pusateri, born in Mexico of Italian parents, was a member of Joan Lindgren's translation workshop at UABC; she is currently translating into Spanish a book of poems by Margaret Gibson, and does simultaneous interpreting in the San Diego/Tijuana area. Regarding the story by Martin del Campo, she adds that *Sentadito* (the original title of the story we have rendered as "Little Mister Chair–Man") is typical of the Mexican practice of giving affectionate and accepting nicknames descriptive of physical or personality traits. (The literal meaning of *Sentadito* is "little seated one.")

Charles D. Brown was raised in Havana and lived in Mexico City and Guayaquil. He studied sociology and film at New York University before moving to San Diego, where he works as a staff Certified Court Interpreter in the California State Court.

David Unger was born in Guatemala, grew up in Florida, and is now associated with the City University of New York and serves as U.S. co-ordinator for the Guadalajara International Book Fair. He is a published poet, and the translator and editor of Nicanor Parra's *Antipoems: New and Selected*. Taibo's uproarious story, like his detective novels well known to U.S. readers, shows the author's strong social concerns but does so "with straight-forward humor and earthy dialogue."

Nick Caistor, a producer in the BBC World Service and translator of novels by Argentine, Nicaraguan, and Uruguayan authors, was born in Lancashire, England. He edited *The Faber Book of Contemporary Latin American Short Stories* (1989) from which Puga's "The Trip" was taken, as well as a book of short stories, *Columbus' Egg* (Serpent's Tail, 1992). The

242

challenge of translating "The Trip", he says, lay in maintaining the ambiguity and suspense, so that only at the very end is it clear just what kind of trip this is – not the drugs trips so popular in much Mexican writing of *La Onda* in the 1960s and 70s.

Allison B. Peery is an architect with a master's degree in Counseling Psychology, and a long-time student of Latin American literature. He lives in San Antonio, Texas. He describes "Puzzles" (original title "*Lo Que No se Comprende*") as characteristic of Arredondo, with its "authoritative female perspective and haunting sensuality."

Naomi Lindstrom is professor of Spanish and Portuguese at the University of Texas (Austin) and Director of Publications for the Institute of Latin American Studies. Her most recent books are a study of Borges' short fiction, and *Twentieth Century Spanish-American Fiction*, appearing in 1994. Lara Zavala is remarkably successful, she says, in writing "Little Sister" from the point of view of the chronically overshadowed younger sibling. Conversely, we have Marta Cerda writing about puberty and the search for sexual initiation from a lower-class, male perspective typical of Mexican *machismo*.

Tim Richards is an associate professor of Spanish at the University of Missouri, Kansas City, where he teaches Latin American literature and history. His research focusses on Mexican and Central American narrative, and he has translated short fiction from Nicaragua and Mexico. He recognizes a strain of "conflict, ambiguity, and obsession" in Ramos' stories and points out that while "Doctor's Prescription" was written a dozen years ago, it deals with the currently fashionable topic of repressed memory, using a unique and ironic second-person narrative voice.

Irene Matthews is a graduate of University College in London, with a doctorate in comparative literature from University of California (Davis), and has written widely on gender, race, and war. She has published studies on Gabriela Mistral and Rigoberta Menchú and translated Nellie Campobello and Elena

Poniatowska, among others. She presently teaches at Northern Arizona University, including a course on Mexican women writers. Poniatowska's story in this volume she finds "wonderfully representative of one of the author's most significant recurrent themes: the urban married woman caught up in the manic tension between banal domesticity and romantic dreams."

**Adriana Valadés** is the daughter of Edmundo Valadés and serves as cultural attaché with the Embassy of Mexico in Bonn.

✳

**Juan Antonio Ascencio** (León 1937), co-editor, has conducted writing workshops for the past 15 years and is a member of the editorial board of the magazine *El Cuento* since 1984. His biography of Juan Rulfo will appear in 1995.